A WOMAN'S VOICES©

THE SECOND NOVEL
of the
SECRET BUTTERFLY SERIES™

A NOVEL BY

Rosemary Lightfoot Ness-Bitner

This book is dedicated to the need for love.

Hello, dear listeners and readers, I'm Melanie Monarch. In THE BUTTERFLY YOU LOVE© novella, nymphomaniac Marty was deciding whether to go to David's. In the first chapter of a WOMAN'S VOICES© her decision is revealed. We find Marty with David in his barn.

My dear friend, Poon, was fluttering south on her migration. She happened to put down to rest in David's barn. There she heard, in vivid detail, how Marty committed her perfect murder. Poon heard Marty's thoughts while relating her experience to David. Marty revealed to David her voices' clever step-by-step instructions which enabled her to impose her will on Carl's wife. Marty's voices understood that murder's origin, like love, begins in one's mind. With help from her voices guiding her, Marty executes the most ingenious, unorthodox murder in the history of murders. We Monarchs agreed that her behavior was beyond outrageous, and shockingly unladylike; but it succeeded! We still don't know why Marty felt obliged to share the details of her method with David. What right did he have to ask about it? What hold does he have over her? Perhaps we will learn a little more about their curious relationship.

After we butterflies placed the murder in the context of Marty's addiction state, we understood why the evening unfolded as it did. Marty cleverly used her addiction as a weapon! When we heard the final confession thoughts of Carl's wife, we realized this episode in Marty's life marked one of her most significant growth experiences, although a difficult one. We welcomed her freedom loving spirit into our butterfly hearts, as the Great Spirit does; and we love her. After all, no humans are perfect.

We butterfly spirits accept that humans have flaws. The way humans deal with their flaws determines whether they are welcome in the butterfly world of spirit freedom. Marty's treatment of Carl's wife, while ghastly, was necessary for the freedoms of Carl's spirit, his wife's, and Marty's. Butterflies do not judge the methods by which human spirits gain freedom. Butterfly love is not fickle or conditional like that. It is constant and enduring. Our love for Marty's spirit is undaunted and as strong as ever. Let's listen now, while Marty relates her unique murder experience to David.

SECRET BUTTERFLY SERIES™ CHARACTERS
INTRODUCED IN "A WOMAN'S VOICES©"
(MAJOR CHARACTERS ARE BOLDFACED)

Readers reference guide to where a character is introduced.

(CHARACTER, DESCRIPTION OF CHARACTER, AND
CHAPTER WHERE CHARACTER IS MENTIONED)

A WOMAN'S VOICES© (BOOK TWO)

**POON, MONARCH BUTTERFLY, SOULMATE OF TANG,
AWOMAN'S VOICES© (AWV), CH1**

**TANG, MALE MONARCH, SOULMATE OF POON, AWV,
CH2**

**GREAT SPIRIT, GREAT SPIRIT OF ALL LIVING THINGS,
AWV, CH1**

**U G G A, UNIVERSAL GLOBAL GROWTH ASSOCIATES,
FINANCIAL INSTITUTION FRONT FOR DAVID'S
RACKETEERING, MURDER AND BODY DISPOSAL
OPERATIONS**

**DOMINICK, BILLIONAIRE ENTREPRENEUR, FILM
PRODUCER, MARTY'S LOVER, FATHER OF JENNIFER,
AWV, CH2**

JENIFER (JEN), DAUGHTER OF DOMINICK, FOUNDER OF THE INFERNO PORN CLUBS, MARTY'S PROTÉGÉ AND LOVER, AWV, CH2

MISS HATRED, MARTY'S WICKED, CRUEL VOICE, AWV, CH2

AZTEC PRIEST AND AZTEC MURDER VICTIM, IMAGES IN MARTY'S THOUGHTS, AWV, CH5

GLORIA (MARTY'S), MARTY'S PSEUDONYM FOR HER VAGINA'S CLITORIS, AWV, CH5

FOUR J'S, BIG ED, FRED (MARTY'S FRED), BERTIE, BERTIE'S HUSBAND GEORGE, GWENDOLYN LEE, DOMINICK, SEDUCTION CONQUESTS OF MARTY, AWV, CH9

AMULET VISION, A HALLUCINATION SEEN BY CARL'S WIFE, AWV, CH10

CHAPTER ONE

Men have forgotten God. That's why all this has happened. (Aleksandr Solzhenitsyn: Acceptance speech for the Templeton Prize for Progress in Religion, Buckingham Palace, 1983)

She did not seduce, she ravaged. (George Meredith: Diana of the Crossways)

The ability to perceive or think differently is more important than the knowledge gained. & No one can really plomb one's own mind. (David Bohm, Quantum Mechanics Physicist, 1992)

LOOKING AND LISTENING

Poon saw the open barn door and the two people inside. She was determined to reach the barn and rest inside. Many in the kaleidoscope of Monarchs downed and rested behind her in the copse of trees. She glanced back and saw Tang put himself down. He was tucked under a pine bough where fast flying Swifts couldn't get him.

'Thank the spirits,' Poon thought, *'Tang is safe. Making love with him was so wonderful in our past lives. I want him in my next life. Oh, Spirit, please let me have him again. He is the most magnificent Monarch. Uniting with him again and again is the reason I live. Without him, I would die.'*

The downed Monarchs attached themselves to branches, away from approaching danger. Chasing Poon were the dreaded barn swallows with their flashing blue wings. They darted and dived at her from above, appearing suddenly out of the brilliant blue sky, attacking the slower butterflies. Poon, along with a thousand courageous Monarchs, fluttered onward. Her back muscles ached. The swallows were decimating the advancing kaleidoscope. They darted into the butterflies, snatched them in their beaks, downed them into their crops during flight; then spiraled skyward; twisting, then turning and taking aim at another Monarch. The butterflies were vulnerable. They fluttered in the air between the pines and the barn and rose bushes that bordered the barnyard.

But the butterflies were smart. They knew the swifts and swallows dared not risk hitting the buildings or getting their wings entangled in the rose canes. The Monarchs sought the safety of the buildings and the roses. Poon saw a human man and woman by some hay bales, set back a few feet from the barn door. A pair of woman's baby blue shorts lay on the ground near the humans. Poon's feelers detected an uncommon scent. It was natural for Monarchs, but rare for humans. It signaled freedom, love, independence, and determination. Poon fluttered closer to the barn. The scent became stronger. The scent sensation was coming from a sex pheromone. But Poon led her kaleidoscope! The scent could not be coming from another butterfly! Poon directed her feelers, trying to pinpoint the scent source. Her scent receptors were thousands of times more sensitive than any human's. Soon, Poon located the scent. It surprised her. It was emanating from the naked woman below! The woman sat upon hay bales with her lower legs opened widely. Poon fluttered into the barn. *'I'll be safe here,'* Poon told herself. *'And I'll learn more about this curious human woman.'*

She scanned the barnyard to check for danger. A gaggle of well-fed white European geese were clucking in a pond. There was no threat from them; they couldn't fly. A covey of guinea fowl was pecking the ground. They were safely penned within a wire enclosure. A wallow pit for pigs was on the far side of a fenced run that abutted a small side door to the barn. A flock of seven white sheep grazed away from the barn. Three goats played King of the Hill on a small mound of earth, old tires, and boards. One black sheep, oddly, stood apart from the other sheep. It wasn't grazing. It stood looking looked through the opened barn door, watching the humans inside.

Poon focused on the humans. The dark-haired woman's legs were splayed over hay bales. The man wore a green leisure suit and cowboy boots. His dark hair was slightly graying. Poon attached herself to the frame of the barn's large entrance door. The woman's pheromone signal was very strong. '*I have never encountered a human woman before. Her scent tells me that, somehow, she carries a butterfly's spirit within her. She loves intimacy and freedom; is supremely self-confident; and knows where she wants from life. The image of a Monarch is on her upper thighs. Is she a human version of me? Perhaps we are, in some ways, the same? I think I love her. She is very much like me!*'

Poon was in a perfect location to hear the humans below. Humans fascinated her. She desperately wanted to become one in her next life. She wondered whether one of the eggs she carried might grow into a human. She didn't understand such things. She believed it had to do with the Spirits. Her friends said it happens after a butterfly dies and after a human also dies. That's when the butterfly and the human exchange spirit souls and get their new lives. The Great Spirit of All Living Things has been exchanging spirits this way for many thousands of years, said her friends. And butterflies, like Poon, and humans, like those below her, have all had many previous lives.

None of her butterfly friends could explain how this mysterious process happened. But they all assured her that, after she mated above the southern Mexican jungle, she would die. Then the Great Spirit would exchange her spirit with a human's spirit.

She would get a human life and a human woman would get a butterfly life. Today, Poon was very excited about her chance encounter with the humans in the barn. By studying their movements and listening carefully, she believed she might gain valuable insights into the secret ways of humans.

The woman lay propped on hay bales, in the mating position. Her spread lower legs exposed her anatomy to the man sitting in front of her. Poon struggled to comprehend. *'Is the human woman a living spirit goddess of some sort? Can she tame strong winds and quiet angry storms? Do men worship her? Do they seek to mate with her? Could she ward off the damnable swifts and barn swallows that decimate our ranks? I hope so. Are my prayers for a good spirit to protect our kaleidoscope about to be realized? Perhaps this human woman can safeguard our flight? She must have extraordinary powers,'* thought Poon. *'The human man seems captivated by her. He rarely takes his eyes off her sex.'*

Poon hoped the woman possessed the spirit of a Monarch and the power of a human goddess. *'Whatever she says to the man must be worth understanding.'* Poon inched down the door frame, drawing closer. Her senses tingled with keen interest. *'I must hear what the goddess says!'*

The woman's upper human legs propped up her body. She rested her head atop her shoulders. *'She seems relaxed and self-assured. Her nakedness confirms her authority and confidence. That affirms my hopes. A goddess is naturally uninhibited and confident. Casual sex would be her normal, carefree, goddess way of having pleasure.*

'The goddess smiles often. She speaks casually of love and blood, as if she naturally blends those two life forces. She laughs a chortled laugh from time to time while throwing her head back, sometimes looking up at the barn ceiling, as if her mind recalls something that happened yesterday. Sometimes she looks at the man, as if reassuring herself that he pays attention to her words.

'The man seems fixated on the woman's sex and her butterfly tattoo; but his eyes occasionally lift and look into her eyes. He does that to assure her that he's paying attention and empathizing with her. Her head comes forward at those times. She does that to let him know she appreciates him as a trusted friend. Their eyes meet then; and they smile to each other. The man rubs his front arms slowly back and forth over the woman's legs. He reassures her that she does good things; that her intimate secrets are safe with him. Perhaps these two humans are preparing to mate. I can't be sure. The man helps the goddess release her feelings by rubbing her legs. Perhaps that is his duty. Somehow, he helps her express herself freely.

'His fingertips move from close to her anatomical center to her knee joints; then back up to her center again. He seems to enjoy touching her. His finger touches are soft and caring. Perhaps they will mate soon? Perhaps he loves her butterfly pheromones? She smiles, arches her back, and often lifts up her breasts. She obviously enjoys his touches. He smiles when she speaks; and sometimes they spontaneously laugh together. I believe he adores the goddess woman. This foreplay ritual must be the human prelude to mating.

'The man called the goddess: Marty.' Poon's antennae quivered wildly. 'Could it be? The Great Spirit of All Living Things, U, once told me that a human woman named Marty was one of U's special Monarchs, and that Marty's spirit carried within her the kindred spirits of Cecilia and Sheila, two very beautiful human women with intensely passionate love lives. In their human lives these women all highly promiscuous; but each in their own special way. And each has extraordinary, special talents.

'Could this Marty woman really be one of the Great Spirit's special human women? Perhaps she is! She is breathtakingly lovely! I yearn to flutter down to her and kiss her everywhere; and especially taste her sex, like I would taste a flower with my proboscis. That *would let Marty know that I understand her feelings. But I know my place. I must listen and learn all I can about these humans.*

'Perhaps I'll never meet Sheila because the Spirit told me that Sheila and Marty live different lives in different life cycle rhythms; but hopefully one of the eggs that I carry will meet Sheila some day; or possibly, its spirit will become Sheila's spirit if my egg's spirit enters a human. I can only do my part in the Spirit's grand scheme of life. And I must keep my wits about me. I have a vital function to perform. I need to find Tang and mate with him. That is my requirement. I need to fulfill it in this phase of my life cycle. I must stay focused on mating. Making love! Yes! I know that is my most important task in my present life. But here I am! So close to Goddess Marty, a real, live kindred spirit, human woman. Marty is stunning; adorable. I instantly feel love for her. After all, my own spirit has often entered Marty's past human bodies.'

David was the man caressing Marty's legs. Marty told him about the emotional issues that had burdened her since her childhood. She faulted her mother, Susan, for not loving her. Marty had deep seated feelings and passions. They were rooted in abandonment; and they explained why she exploited many men. Poon empathized with Marty.

'We Goddesses should only know love and happiness,' thought Poon. *'We are all so adorable and sexy. Men should cherish us and love us; and treat us with respect and understanding, no matter how our feelings sometimes make us do crazy things. We are special souls. Males need to understand that.'*

Poon's heart overflowed with amorous feelings. She had high hopes for the gorgeous human woman. She prayed to the Spirit that Marty would know great happiness, love, and joy, all the days of her life.

Poon learned that Marty loved Bob. Marty told David that she intended to take Bob for her husband. And she became jealous whenever another woman looked at Bob. Marty was concerned that Bob secretly loved another woman. Her name was Barbara. Marty mentioned that Barbara had a regal look, and a seductively glowing, caramel skin tone.

Marty tried to replicate Barbara's skin tone by sunning herself. Unfortunately, that resulted in frequent sunburns. Marty was frustrated and envious because her skin tone could not match Barbara's creamy golden tan. But Marty's envy was deeper than skin tone. She was also jealous of Barbara's subtle sexuality. Barbara and Bob had worked together in their own department, until David shut it down. He then assigned Barbara to Administration and Bob to Sales. Now they were separated and working on different floors. But Marty still felt uneasy about Barbara. Her intuition convinced her that Bob considered Barbara more desirable than she. Marty believed that her intimacy with Bob made him forget Barbara.

Marty was ruthless. She hated stress, and left nothing to chance. Under no circumstances did she want to chance losing Bob to rival Barbara. She believed getting rid of Barbara would relieve her mind of a great deal of stress. Thus, she intended to murder Barbara as a precautionary measure. She preferred relaxing and making love to concerning herself about Barbara. Making love relaxed Marty; but murdering relaxed her even more. She believed killing Barbara to ease her tensions was justified. But David did not want Barbara murdered because of her value to the company. He counseled Marty to delay Barbara's murder for the time being.

Hearing Marty and David talk so nonchalantly about murder disturbed Poon. Butterflies didn't kill other butterflies. The relationship between Marty and David perplexed Poon. It was enigmatic. They shared a type of love; but it wasn't a romantic or sexual love. It seemed David loved power and control over Marty and the others in his business empire. Murder was how he enforced his will.

Marty was harder for Poon to understand. She also murdered; but for different reasons than David's. She loved committing murder to experience a rare type of euphoric high. David paid Marty handsomely for her murders. But when Poon read Marty's mind, she learned that Marty loved doing murders so much that she would gladly do them, even if David didn't pay her. Poon couldn't understand how murders made Marty desire to make love, but they did. David and Marty's relationship seemed to have a hidden complication that went beyond committing murders together. Poon suspected Marty was wary of David, yet she had no reservations about exposing her sex to him in a very cavalier manner. Marty suggested that she and David should mate; and she offered him many opportunities to mate. *'David seems interested in having sex with Marty, yet he refrains from doing so. I've never known a male butterfly to refuse mating overtures from a female butterfly. Perhaps David's spirit is somehow different from butterflies' spirits.'*

Marty stated she was a nymphomaniac. She stated that making love was her natural outlet for happiness. No matter how often she made love, she was never satisfied. She always wanted more. Poon's antennae quivered again. Marty began speaking about Barbara. There was rivalry and friction between the two goddesses. Poon wanted to understand human emotions. She didn't want to miss a single word. She inched closer.

"I'd feel much better if she was out of the way, David. She's a nothing. Please let me kill her. Why won't you let me?" Marty voiced her frustration.

Poon trembled from the shock of Marty's words. How could such a beautiful, voluptuous, sexual goddess also be a coldly calculating murderess? Poon wished it wasn't true. Poon wanted her image of beautiful Marty to be that of a woman who lived her life only to love, the same way she did; like a beautiful Monarch butterfly should.

"And how would you propose to kill her, exactly," asked David. His eyes challenged Marty's, asking for a reasonable method to murder Barbara, doubting she would come up with anything.

"Like we've murdered all the others, in the same room, in the same way" Marty's tone was insincere and flippant.

"We?' David's eyebrows lifted and his head cocked to one side. His eyes held Marty's. A delicate thread of co-dependence and co-conspiracy joined them. David provided and arranged everything; the location setting; Marty's accessories and music; the implements of murder; the cleanup of evidence and body disposals; and Marty's secret orgy and lavish bonus rewards. David's *'we'* protested his own criminal involvement, He reminded Marty that she performed the actual executions. But both actors knew that David was expressing a distinction with little difference.

Poon was crestfallen. By her own words Marty had freely admitted that she was a murderess. The human goddess voiced no misgivings; and her body language showed no contrition or remorse about killing other humans. Instead, Marty smiled and massaged her female vagina when she mentioned murder, as if she had fond memories of past heinous deeds. Rather than flutter away to escape her thoughts about such horrible matters, curious Poon inched closer. Perhaps, the butterfly hoped, Marty's soul could somehow be redeemed. *'Perhaps,'* thought Poon, *'if only I, a lowly butterfly, could help Marty discover true love, this beautiful human woman would reform herself and change her ways. If only Tang, my childhood friend and soul mate, were here to witness this with me, he'd help me understand how to help Marty.'*

"Listen to you," David chuckled his rebuff to Marty's request. He opposed killing Barbara. *"There you go again, not thinking something through. You'd never even get her on the execution table.*

She's not that way, sexually. I thought you knew that." He spoke to Marty as if she were a naive child.

"Yeah, you're right. Give me some time. I'll come up with something else." Marty pouted; her lips puckered like a child's whose lollypop was taken away.

"No Marty, we are not killing Barbara. I'm not going to let you kill a valuable staff member. Your reasoning isn't sound. You're lashing out because of your insecurities. It's pure female emotion without logic; and why? You and Bob have been lovers for a year now. You're engaged to marry him. He isn't even interested in Barbara. Why would you murder a good employee? Susan needs her. And, if anything happened to Susan, I'd need her. So, stop thinking that way." David shook his head to dismiss Marty's nonsense notion.

"How many times have I told you that you need to think like an executive? You have a brilliant future here at U G G A. I'd rather you think of becoming your mother's replacement and having Barbara work for you. Wouldn't that give you greater pleasure than killing her? Imagine yourself as Barbara's boss. You could make Barbara work her skinny ass off. You'd have her doing whatever you ordered her to do; no matter how menial or painstaking. Meanwhile you get to go home with the man of her dreams every night. While she stays to work and lock up the offices, you're making love with Bob." David's eyebrows rose. His faint, sinister smile appeared. It told Marty to wise up.

Poon understood that these people ran a major financial institution. She listened in amazement as David kissed Marty's upper thighs, close to her butterfly tattoo. He told her how much her conquests pleased him.

"Okay, David. I know you're right." Marty sounded contrite and sheepish.

"Marty, Marty, Marty, I've told you: I'm very, very proud of you. You've learned that evil is absolutely necessary to succeed in

business. You've learned how to be evil and feel no remorse over it. You've done everything I've asked. I admire the way you overcame the moral hang-ups that hold others back. U G G A is at its pinnacle of achievement. With Dad dead, our company has finally emerged like a butterfly from those years Dad kept it tightly wrapped in a cocoon. We are devouring innocent fools like a caterpillar eats milkweed leaves. We've endured those insufferable years, Marty; but now the company is like you. It's emerged from chrysalis. It's free and glorious. I'm going to do our company proud, Marty. I'm going to honor you." David's lips pulled back, with his determined frown and nodding head.

"You're going to honor me, David? You'd honor a naughty girl like me? I'm beyond flattered. You're not joking, are you? The thought of you honoring me blows me away! What do you have in mind?" Marty's eyes widened with excitement. With one hand she stimulated her vagina in a circular motion. She hoped David wanted sex with her.

"I'm going to adopt the Monarch butterfly as our new corporate logo," David beamed, ignoring her hand gesture. *"That will recognize you as U G G A's exemplary model employee and let all employees know I wholeheartedly approve of the methods you use to achieve your outstanding results. Our logo will idolize you as our corporate standard bearer. The new logo means freedom and happiness. People project onto logos their wishes for themselves; but you and I will know the true meaning of our new logo. Its message is: Results matter! Here at U G G A, we respect results. And we honor those who get results. Marty, your methods produce fantastic results! I am extremely proud of you."*

"Oh, David!" Marty giggled like a school girl who was just given a new puppy. Her joyful heart beamed through her adoring eyes and delighted smile. *"That's a wonderful honor. You are such a thoughtful, wonderful man. I will never forget this, and I*

will never disappoint you. Is there anything you'd like of me, David? I'd love to express my appreciation. I'll be happy to do anything you ask, David, anything." Marty hinted, more strongly now, that she wanted to have sex with him.

David skirted the question. He preferred to speak in generalities. He had often professed that he and Marty were kindred souls. They had overcome their need for God's ridiculous rules and religion's storybook obstacles to human pleasure. He told her they had reached humanity's highest level of self-actualization. They had become masters of deceit and cynicism.

"Marty, we are kindred souls, aren't we? We don't need God or his ten commandments or all his silly mitzvahs, do we? Machiavelli's Medici didn't have anything over us, did they? We've discovered the ultimate pleasure, haven't we? And we love that feeling, don't we?" David was, of course, referring to the murders they committed together.

"Oh yes, David. We do, we do. There's no other feeling that gets me anywhere close to It." replied Marty.

And they had. This bad boy and bad girl duo had swept God from their lives like a dusty cobweb-laced relic. Corruption was their idol. They had sanitized their minds of integrity and of all things good or wholesome. Taking the lives of other humans was their ultimate thrill.

"Now, tell me. I want to know all about Carl and his pesky wife. How did you meet Carl, and how did things progress to where you wanted to kill her?"

"Sure, David. The affair started simply enough. Carl saw some of my porn films, called my service, and we met. Our sex was fantastic; so, we decided to meet on a regular basis."

"His wife? She didn't care?"

"Oh yeah, she cared. I disrupted her lifestyle. She cared lots."

"Lifestyle? How?"

"We're talking master-slave relationship, David. She wore bully pants. She had Carl bring home his paycheck; that's when his real work started. He has allergies to trees and grass. But she didn't care. She had him doing yard work and mowing grass. He makes plenty, so they could easily afford a lawn and garden service; but she preferred to torture him. She bought silly nick-knacks and porcelain figurines with his money. Their walls were covered with ridiculous overpriced junk. He couldn't stand the stuff. It's presence in their home insulted him. Also, she was a clothes horse; always buying new rags and throwing away rags that were only a year old. She was all about her image; but she had no substance. Total narcissist. Not much for brains, either. I didn't know what he saw in her.

"She made lists of handyman things for him to do instead of hiring handymen and painters and repair men. She kept score. Carl had to earn points in her book before she'd even have sex with him. She set a very high bar for her romps. That's what throttled me. She was never much to look at. While Carl slaved at chores, she went to her country club and her political meetings. She even took limos to her functions; anything for appearances sake. It was a one-sided marriage; all for her, nothing for Carl. She learned bully tactics 101 from her mother. That woman bullied her father, made a slave out of him. He died from drinking alcohol and smoking two packs a day. Carl's wife was killing Carl the same way; learned behavior, daughter from mother."

"So, you got into the picture."

"You bet, I did. I assessed the situation. I'm a take charge type. Carl needed pest control. That was me. I showed him how to divert his pay stream into a credit account for me. We started small and steadily increased it. I began starving his pest."

"After a while, she figured it out, right?"

"Right. He started ignoring her, and spent his slave time with me instead. Chores weren't getting done; and her money was getting

choked off. She got onto me and started trying to interfere with my time with Carl. She harassed him at home. She had us tailed. She made calls to him while we were at a restaurant. The bitch even threw red paint all over my car; childish prank stuff.

"That's when I started playing head games with her. I loved toying with her tiny mind. I did simple things, like calling her home phone and hanging up when she answered; or asking her if Carl was with her, when I already knew he was on his way to see me. I began driving her out of her mind, crazy. She was such a jerk. Her paint on my car tantrum backfired. Carl bought me a new Beamer convertible to make up for what she did. That's when Carl started seeing me on weekends, and that's when we started going up to the lake. The pest caught on to us. She figured out which cabin I owned. I didn't think she'd drive all the way up there to harass us. She became a headstrong, relentless little bully. Have you ever tried to get rid of ants, David? She was like those tiny sugar ants that get into a house. You can poison them. You can step on them. You can seal off their entry holes; but they keep getting inside. Finally, I'd had enough. I wanted to be rid of her."

"I know lots about ants." David had a wicked sneer in his smile; and deep intrigue in his eyes. He remembered his interactions with ants, beginning when he was a child. He stepped on them; tore their legs off, burned them with a magnifying glass; blew them up with firecrackers; poured gasoline on them and lit them. He even had interactions with secretly hidden ant colonies to this day. *"I know she bothered you for a long time. I've waited patiently to hear this. Tell me how you gained the upper hand. Make me feel what you felt while you destroyed her. Describe everything to the minutest detail. I want to place my mind right beside yours. And tell me what you did with her body. Victims' bodies are a very important detail that many murderers overlook. I want to pretend that we've murdered her together, like I was there beside you while you killed her; like I've always been right beside you; helping, while you murdered all the others."* Voyeur David continued rubbing Marty's legs. He was stimulating her body; putting her at ease; relaxing her mind with his caresses.

"I've never explained to you how I view my relationships or how I go about my seductions, have I David?" Marty took a long exhale and shook her head slowly with her most impish, devilish smile before she began.

"No, you beautiful, delightful, immoral whore, you never have. But you will now, won't you?" David's eyes gleamed. Murder fascinated him. He loved watching the expressions on victims' faces while they were being murdered.

Poon observed: *'Marty's tattoos on her uppermost inner thighs form Monarch butterfly wings, like my own. Marty even refers to her anatomy as her magnificent butterfly. I hope my next life will be like Marty's love life; but without the murders. I can't imagine hurting anyone. I know human lives and the life cycles of butterflies are spiritually related and the Spirit has made them interchangeable, somehow. The Great Spirit told me that. I think humans who hurt other humans do horrible misdeeds. That would be like a butterfly hurting another butterfly. That, to me, seems unthinkable.'*

'I must flutter on from here. I will only copulate one glorious time with flight leader Tang. We will mate high above the southern jungles of Mexico. I will feel Tang's shaft depositing his semen into my egg sac that one wondrous, fateful time. But here below me, my spirit soul-mate, Marty, has already copulated thousands of times! Marty bore no children, yet she continues to live! She fornicates for the sheer joy of it. She proudly states she is an unrepentant nymphomaniac.' Poon spread her wings widely. Despite knowing Marty was a serial murderess, Poon was envious of the promiscuous, uninhibited woman below. *'How wonderful it must be to make love so many times,'* thought Poon. She crawled even lower on the door frame to better eavesdrop on Marty's vignette.

"First, David, understand my mindset," Marty's eyebrows rose as she began. *"I tell myself I embody triumph over pretense, pomposity, and fake moral goodness. Women with phony moral convictions disgust me. Also, consider my butterfly tattoo. It represents the wings of the most beautiful butterfly, the Monarch. It attracts every man who sees it and sweeps away his inhibitions. When I spread my legs, his attention fixates upon my Little Miss Eager Beaver. My opened legs have a hypnotic effect. Eyes are drawn to me like they are to the opened wings of the Monarch. My legs signal 'Come inside me. Discover unimaginable pleasures.' My tattoo idea originated as a response to bullying. My best friend, Maria, was bullied. The tattoo, and my lady parts between its wings became Carl's refuge from his wife's bullying. My vagina became Carl's true home. It's where he's most comfortable and relaxed. My lady bits are where Carl comes for his love. And, David, my tattoo also attracts some women."* Marty's face now changed to an inquiring smile, asking David whether he believed what she just told him. She fluttered her eyelashes as if to confirm those implications.

"So, somehow, his wife saw your tattoo? Am I guessing correctly? Was she drawn to it, too?" David's face signaled that he thought he understood.

"Oh, yes, she certainly was. I'll come to that. But first, David, you need to understand my mindset; then we'll get into hers. My mindset, my feelings, all started with her husband. Carl had become my regular customer two years earlier. Whenever he was with me, I could believe I was a female reincarnation of Mephistopheles, Goethe's Satan. Carl obeys my every request. He traded his income and moral soul for uninhibited sex with me, many months ago. He's extremely strong and he has great endurance. He craves sex with me in every position imaginable. We make love for hours, basically for entire weekends. We are like two sex crazed minks."

"But why do you believe you're a feminine Mephistopheles?" David's interest tended more towards the psychological than the physical aspects of Marty's seduction story.

"Because I have helpers, David. None of them have a smidgeon of consciousness or guilt when I do something evil. My helpers are my inner voices. They speak to me; and I trust what they tell me to do. Together, my voices and I are deliciously sinful; and we can be very wicked. There's Miss Promiscuity, my mistress of seduction, Miss Shameless, my mistress of confidence and freedom from worry or guilt, and Miss Iniquity, my mistress of cold calculation and ruthlessness. I occasionally hear other voices too; but those three are my closest companions. They influence my thoughts and behaviors."

"Why do you need to feel like a human she-devil?" asked David. *"How does that help you?"*

"Because, David, when I'm having an affair with a woman's husband, I must believe that what I'm doing is good and right. I must believe that, what most people regard as evil, is actually good. I know I'm helping the man discover his freedom. Try to understand that. I can't allow my mind to feel guilt. That would dull my edge and ruin everything. Sex and seduction happen in the brain's limbic zone. That's where a man's hormonal cocktail releases. And that's where I impart my emotions to my lovers, from my first targeted kiss, through our mutual orgasms; and followed by my praises and assurances, afterwards. My lovers' limbic minds must believe that I unconditionally love them. My own belief that I am expert about what I do, enables me to create that love belief in my lovers' minds. I convince myself that what I do is sanctified by my glorious evil forces. Those forces actively block my lovers' love away from their wives and girlfriends and repose those affections within me. My devil-self is completely uninhibited. When I assume my evil persona, my feelings become honest and real. I have no

doubts about what I'm doing. I do not second guess myself. That's why I'm so successful."

Miss Promiscuity and Miss Shameless spoke to Marty. Poon's feelers could detect Marty's inner voices. *'That's good. It's okay to tell David how you feel; but be careful. Do not reveal that you've been seeing shrinks since you were a child at WEX School. He may think you have mental health issues. And you really don't, not anymore. Remember, Mrs. O'Dell says you are now perfectly normal.'*

Poon listened, now highly intrigued, as Marty described to David how she and Carl were inside her cabin making love on the night when Carl's wife drove up.

"What were your thoughts when you first realized you had an unwelcome visitor?" David probed.

"When I first heard a car crunching over the cabin's gravel driveway, I instinctively knew it had to be her. That night, my cabin was the only one that was occupied on the far side of the lake. Carl and I were far from civilization. No one from the lake community had reason to drive on that desolate road at that time of night. I lay in bed, suddenly awakened by the crunching gravel. My mind raced. Fear gripped my heart. I felt it pounding in my chest, like it might burst through my ribs. I thought she might have brought a gun. I thought: 'Why is she doing this?' Carl was with me in my cabin. We deserved our privacy. All I wanted to do was make love with Carl and take his money. 'Why can't she leave us alone? Why doesn't she find herself another life and latch onto another meal ticket? Why does she even care about Carl and me?' I asked myself: 'Why must this be happening, now?' I always knew I'd need to confront her some day. I'd even thought through different scenarios about what things I'd say to make her go away; but now all of my planned comments suddenly became a scrambled mess. She was here. Now. I needed to deal with her. Now. I felt hot blood rush into my head. I had a momentary panic.

"Then I got angry. My inner voice of Miss Iniquity reminded me that I was like my caterpillar cousins and Carl was like my milkweed. I was steadily devouring him and his marriage; making good money by happily eating away at his marriage. I could not allow her to put a stop to what I was doing! I could not let her take Carl away from me! That could not happen! He was mine! Besides, he was my best and truest lover. Whenever he and I were having our intimacy; making sweet love together, the entire world just fell away from us. And the world left us alone, swimming in our love. This night, my body and his body were doing incredibly well together. We were loving and feeling each other; enjoying each other; cooing and laughing, being the way lovers should be. He was holding and kissing me freely, unhurried. He was frequently performing cunnilingus and fucking me beautifully, completely unconcerned about his wife. We were having a wonderful time. We were very happy. We intended to go on loving and enjoying our intimacy for many hours; even days. 'No!' I thought: 'I will fight her.' I began seething inside. I could not let her have him. She could not take him away from me.

"I became crazed. I could not accept that I might have to live in a world where I couldn't call Carl; and that I couldn't have him in bed with me when I needed to be loved; when I needed to be held and when I needed to feel his penis inside me. I began to imagine what it would be like to not have Carl's hands touching me everywhere, to not make love like we do in all those positions we enjoy, not to feel so alive from the loving ways he uses his fabulous penis inside me. If she took him back with her, I knew I might never enjoy those splendid times again. I knew I'd simply go crazy, out of my mind, if she did that.

"Unless you could become a highly sexualized woman, David, you can't appreciate how important it is for a woman like me to have a man like Carl in my life. What I'm trying to say is: Most men believe they're good at lovemaking. They tell themselves that. But

they aren't. They just aren't. Most men simply don't know what they are doing with a woman. That's why Carl is one man in a million. I knew what we had together and I wasn't about to give that up. Carl understands my feelings when he loves me. He even takes a little pill so he can stay firm for hours, even after he comes a second or third time. For example, when I assume the missionary position, unlike most men, Carl puts his big hands under my tush. He squeezes and massages me while holding me that way. And, after he enters me, he thinks of my pleasure, putting me first; not himself, like most other men. His huge hands lift me up, pull my body tightly against his; securing my vagina firmly over the entire length of his penis; then he slowly rocks me; sliding me up and down over his magnificent, incredibly hard cock. That motion feels so lovingly intimate and erotic. I become a little girl play doll in his big hands. I cling to him, wrapping my arms and legs around him, while he lovingly glides his marvelous penis softly over my clitoris. His cock and my clitoris discover this incredible closeness; like they were created for each other's pleasure. My mind swoons. I meet his loving thrusts with my own; and I press my clitoris against the magnificent cock that's rubbing it. I want to feel the intimate contact of Carl's beautiful cock over the entire length of my clitoris. I need that feeling and Carl understands this. He squeezes my ass harder; tighter. He pulls me even closer, crushing my body and my vagina against him; our flesh becoming a divine unity. I feel my build. My mind lifts away from my body. My orgasm happens there, in my mind. A signal tells me that this is good; wonderful; special. I am loved by this man. Carl loves me. This elation is happening because his love for me is real; unbounded. I release. I gush explode. I flow. Carl's cock presses harder against my throbbing clitoris. His cock knows my body. It has this perfect sense of my feelings and what I need. I love how I feel. I love fucking Carl. I tell myself I am blessed beyond words. This feeling lasts. Minutes pass while I came back to Earth. I am transformed now. A woman loved.

"Some women claim they experience better sex with a dildo than with a man, but they haven't met Carl. He's like having a huge, strong, life-sized dildo. No dildo can lift a woman up by her ass like that, and coax her into long, sweet orgasms after orgasms, like Carl does with his marvelous cock. Dildos don't have semen fountains either. They can't give a woman that sensation of surrendered hot capitulation; acknowledgement that the woman has captured the spirit soul of her male partner.

"Some women claim that all men are alike. Those women are so wrong, David. No other man recharges his sex fountain as quickly as Carl, either. He's like that Yellowstone geyser, Old Faithful. It recharges and shoots hot semen every hour or so. How many women have a man that can do that? I have mine. I have Carl. Having him is batter than having precious jewels.

"Carl's patience and attention to the details of feelings are what makes him so different from other men, David. Many men can cause me to have an orgasm. After I pop, most men assume I'm done, so they assume that they're also done. I believe they think I'm like a little boy's toy cannon that just popped off. They don't understand that I feel like we are just getting started. They have no idea that my female libido desires longer intimacy and multiple orgasms; that I often desire to make love many times during an evening; or that I love to fuck all night. They just leave me lying there, wanting more; wondering why they stopped, wondering if I did something that turned them off; while they get a beer and watch football.

"But that's not Carl. He has a loving tenderness sense. It's about loving me; pleasing me; ensuring that, more than anything or anyone else in the world, including his wife, I feel loved and pleased. I am Carl's goddess. He puts me into a personal heaven, like I'm on cloud nine; above the world and away from all my cares. When he makes me feel ethereal like that, I can orgasm steadily for several minutes. He's that wonderful. I just flow and flow while my mind goes into *this sublime special place where I know I'm with a man who truly loves making love with me. He loves helping me feel relaxed, uninhibited; and free and uncaring while I continue flowing. No other man makes me feel as wonderfully loved as Carl does.*

"Slowly and softly, Carl continues gliding my Miss Muffy's clitoris over his penis, until I feel myself responding and getting into the mood to come. That's how much Carl understands how to make love with me. He's in tune with my body. He alternates the speed of his thrusts. He knows how to bring me to a rapid heat; then slow his strokes and gently massage my clitoris with his cock; letting my libido know that my eroticism is special and he wants me to thoroughly enjoy every minute of our lovemaking. Then he preps me for orgasm. He'll lightly tap his cock against my clitoris while gliding over it with endearing, gentle upward thrusts. He times those friendly little love taps perfectly, bringing me right there, to the very edge of having an orgasm. My clitoris is being teased and tickled, like it's a school girl and his cock is her ardent admirer. His cock loves her; can't stay away from her; can't ever get enough of her.

"I'm filled with this joyous feeling. Carl loves me! Carl adores me! Carl loves to play with me! I tingle inside while his cock lays with my clitoris. I laugh. I love this. I'm being a very naughty girl. I'm fucking another woman's husband. I'm taking him away from her. He's loving this. I'm loving this, too. We are being bad together; and it's such fun! I hug him tightly. I whisper into his ear that I love him. I remind him that we're being immoral. And he tells me that he knows we are being immoral; and he's perfectly fine with that. I kiss him. My mouth finds him. His lips are warm and anxious for mine. Our tongues kiss and play. We squeeze and laugh together. I tell him his wife might not approve of this. And then I squeeze him harder and kiss him again. He tells me that he doesn't care what his wife approves of. And he tells me he loves me and my happiness is all that matters.

"*I appreciate that he cares more about me and my happiness than he does about his wife. He says some very graphic things. He tells me that he loves having his tongue inside my hot, slippery wet vagina. And I tell him that I love it when he does that. I know by how tenderly he holds me that he senses my body is getting ready to come. He watches my face with his loving brown eyes. He watches my expression relax and then turn joyous. I am coming. He's smiling. I'm smiling. We know what we have together is beautiful. We laugh together. We kiss repeatedly, with our faces close. He begins coming with me. His semen feels hot and wonderful. Like life is entering me. I imagine we are creating a new world, even though I'm on the pill. We giggle and talk dirty to each other while we are coming. He calls me his glorious, adorable, immoral whore. I call him my wonderful stud horse. While I orgasm, he baits me; teases me; asks me how I'm feeling; asks whether my feelings went where I wanted them to go. Then he melts my heart. He always tells me that he loves me; no matter my mood; whether it's wild and crazy, or soft and cuddly. He professes that he totally loves me; that he would die for me; that he will always try to please me. Carl and I can make love an entire weekend like that. The two of us, together, easily become obsessed with each other. We only stop making love long enough to rest and eat. We both enjoy our sex that much. That's why I couldn't imagine losing him.*"

"*You love Carl, don't you?*"

"*Yes, David, I do. And I knew I had to do something about his pesky wife if I wanted to keep him as a lover. I heard her car getting closer. I quickly tried to imagine some schemes in my frazzled mind. My brain started to kick in and think. I instinctively knew I could not allow Carl to see his wife. I needed to keep him inside the cabin. And I needed to keep her outside. I had to keep them apart. A woman can never tell, for sure, about a married man. Married men have secrets. A married man can suddenly present unexpected issues.*

"There had to be something; some 'it' factor that I didn't under-stand; some unfathomable reason why Carl ever took up with her in the first place. I couldn't risk that she'd use her magical married woman's 'it' factor, whatever that invisible 'it' thing was. I couldn't comprehend what it was that his wife had going for her; but I knew I was up against it. But, damn it! My backbone stiffened. I said to myself that I didn't give a damn what her 'it' factor was. I was not going to let her take my beautiful loving Carl away from me. He's mine, because he's like me. His soul is like my soul. He's about love making and fun and freedom. Just because he was stupid enough to marry her, doesn't make him like her. He's not at all like her. He doesn't even like her. He likes me! He likes to laugh with me; have fun with me; make love with me. And the two of us like to tell the world to just go fuck itself; leave us alone to make love. He likes to wrap his big arms around me; not her. And he likes me wrapping my arms around him; not her arms. We enjoy our private world of love. And have our deliciously, endlessly beautiful sex. We obsess over our lovemaking; and she is not going to stop what we do. It's too beautiful!

"I schemed. I thought about going down to the driveway and meeting her as she got out of her car. I thought I'd slap her, pull her hair, spin her around by her hair and throw her to the ground; make her hit me and scratch me; and if she wouldn't do that, I'd hit and scratch myself, even draw blood. Then I'd run to the cabin and cry to Carl about how mean she was. Maybe then he'd get pissed at her and tell her to go away and leave us alone. But then, I came to my senses. I couldn't let myself get scratched. I'd need time to heal. I might even become scarred. That could hurt my film schedule. My porn sales could possibly suffer. So, I ruled out having a cat fight with her. I thought a while longer. I thought of another idea. I thought I'd conk her on the head with a rock; knock her out; then put her back in her car; push her car into the lake. That would drown her.

"But then I realized that idea wouldn't work. The lake bed declines very gradually by the cabin. The water is too shallow to hide a car. I'd end up with a botched murder attempt; then I'd go to jail and lose Carl for sure. However, the idea of murdering her had a very strong appeal. That part of my thinking seemed important. At least I had a goal; like you always say, David. 'Everyone should have goals.' I held on to my goal. I kept it in mind. I realized I'd need to think and plan and wait for my opportunity to murder her. I knew I needed to do my thinking and planning on the fly, so to speak. I knew I needed to be alert for my opportunity.

"I was so totally sick of her, David. She was inconsiderate and rude to drive to the cabin at night with her high beams on. I think she believed she'd surprise us; maybe catch us in the act; make us feel guilty. She could have at least waited until morning; and then politely knocked on the cabin door. Then we might have had an adult discussion about things. But, no! Not this bitch! She had to be a jerk. She had to interrupt our beautiful sex. Some women have no consideration for the needs of other women. I find that sad. While a woman is having sex, she deserves to have privacy and to be respected. Sex is a very personal thing. No one should ever feel that they have a right to interfere, especially not a husband's wife. That's asking for an ugly scene. I can't understand why anyone would want an ugly scene. I couldn't understand what was wrong with her mind. She had no class; no sense of decency, David. I couldn't imagine how anyone could become so self-centered.

"I thought: If there's some way to get rid of her for good, that would be the best solution for Carl and me; and probably for her, too. That would end this insane tug of war she's having with me. I would get Carl and his fabulous cock; and she'd be out of her misery. At first, I could not see how I might pull off an impromptu murder; although I relished that thought.

"I realized I needed to get a grip. I needed to assess each of our strengths and weaknesses. It occurred to me that she must have anxieties about confronting me, just as I had anxieties about confronting her. I quickly tallied my advantages. She had to be exhausted. She was likely dehydrated from her long drive. But I was well rested. She was out of her element; the frazzled wife in a strange place. I was in my element; the confident seductress in my familiar love nest. I had rights to the cabin. She was, by law, a trespasser lawbreaker. She had gone for months without sex. Likely she believed she was an inadequate failure. She would likely act out of frustration. Probably, she had no self confidence. I, on the other hand, had just made love. I felt accomplished and supremely confident in my sexuality; a superior femme; highly successful prostitute and porn star. I could project confidence. While her spirits likely crawled beneath a dung pile, mine soared. I was on top of the world! She had no career, little money, and a collapsing marriage. I had everything: money, fame, career success, and her husband! I realized I could be poised and commanding. I grasped our reality. I could take control of the situation; and her! I understood our tiff over Carl was a game. And it should be played like a game. She had her advantages. I had mine. She was visitor. I was home. She had a marriage license. I had love. And, I had my welcoming, playful, vagina that Carl loved visiting with his tongue and his cock.

"I took a few deep breaths. That slowed my racing heartbeat. I told myself to stay calm and in control; and to keep my wits about me. Many women would have run away and hidden behind the cabin while the wife made a scene and dragged her husband back home. But I decided not to let myself be bullied. I decided to stand my ground. My calmer mindset summoned my courage. I vowed to not flee; but to fight.

"A perverse thought crossed my mind. Could she want me to kill her and put her out of her misery? It was not inconceivable. She

was a highly emotional woman. Carl had often commented that she couldn't think straight. Possibly, she had a twisted motive for coming to my cabin. That thought and my recollections made me feel better. The thought of killing her began taking shape. I reminded myself why Carl and I came to the cabin. We came to make love because Carl wanted me, not her. Her marriage did not confer upon her the right to interfere with our love making; no right, whatsoever. I kept that in mind. That bolstered my confidence. I knew I had every right to put an end to her nonsense.

"Long before that fateful night, I became convinced that destroying her disgusting marriage was a deliciously wonderful, glorious project. Freeing Carl from her became my goal. I was making great progress. And I was proud on my efforts. I was demolishing her finances. My home calls to Carl were ripping her guts out. I was getting to her. She was becoming frazzled. Her emotions were driving her crazy. My uninhibited wantonness was inflicting unbearable stresses on her life and marriage. Her efforts to keep us apart were failing. I was succeeding. I was methodically taking Carl away from her. I felt smug about that. I had no empathy for her; only contempt. I despised her.

My inner gut knew our confrontation moment would happen someday. Now it was here. It was time. I felt a sudden surge of courage; a summoning of will, similar to what soldiers must feel before they engage in battle. My psyche and willpower toughened. I refused to fear her. I reminded myself that I had every right to be my uninhibited, immoral self; and to be proud and shameless of what I was doing."

"So, how did you translate your feelings of courage into taking control of her?" David's eyes held Marty in awe.

"It was a process, David. Consider a hapless fly that lands upon a spider's web. Like a fly, Carl's wife had alighted on my turf.

From the moment I saw her, I began thinking of her as my victim. I dismissed all thoughts that she could be a threat to me. I decided I first needed to crush her spirit. I had to make her understand that she wasn't going to interrupt my love making by causing a scene. I thought of myself as her nemesis; her spider. I would first place a controlling thread over her, my victim fly, to immobilize her."

CHAPTER TWO

Stung by the splendor of a sudden thought (Robert Browning: A Death in the Desert)
Playing for love? Play for keeps. (Rosemary Ness-Bitner, author)

PREDATORY THOUGHTS

Marty's love nest was a modified A frame, lakeside cabin. Its glass front widow wall faced the lake. Remote controlled drapes could, by the push of a button, close over the soaring, cathedral-like front windows, ensuring complete privacy. A massive double-fronted oak door opened the living room to the cabin's spacious redwood deck, which wrapped around the cabin's four sides. A side door from the main floor's master bedroom also opened onto the deck. The cabin's interior had cream-colored walls that rose twelve feet before they gave way to the triangular frame that defined the structure. Huge, roughhewn log beams created an open ceiling effect and braced the structure from its interior. The ceiling roof had two large skylights with electronically operated shades.

Marty's décor set a man's mood. A massive stone fireplace accented the cabin's master bedroom. Each of the bedroom's four walls hosted an antlered elk head. The mantle above the fireplace displayed life-sized bronze statues of two Lynx who stood guard over the bedroom's California king-sized bed. The bedroom was ideal for seducing a man who craved solitude, masculine dominance, and sex. Adjoining the bedroom, in the cabin's open living area, were two masculine leather sofas, a matching pair of massive, overstuffed leather chairs, a kitchen and wet bar. Picture books of mountain peaks and cocktail coasters rested on a roughhewn Bristlecone Pine coffee table.

This evening one of the chairs was draped in Carl and Marty's clothing. Her black silk panties lay on the bedroom floor, beside the bed. After their walk about town, Marty and Carl were naturally eager to make love. Their garments waited to be closeted in the morning, after the lovers enjoyed their night together.

The cabin stimulated Marty. It was a rugged outdoorsy contrast to the prints of pastoral scenes that decorated her city bungalow. Here, Marty felt free to accent her love making with her inner wildness. Here, she felt immersed in raw frontier times, before civilization imposed its spirit-crushing, ridiculous rules.

A Clark's Jay perched in the high pines by the cabin. He carefully studied the scene below and observed the couple's arrival. He watched them leave their car and enter the cabin. The man had his hand on the woman's hip and his arm wrapped around her waist. He held her close to him. The Jay surmised these two were up to something; and once they entered the cabin, they'd stay inside. The woman laughed and giggled softly as they walked. She frequently kissed the man's cheek; holding her kisses long, like she was suggesting they make love. After the two lovers went inside, the Jay waited a few moments. He assured himself he was right about the humans staying inside before he lit down upon the deck's railing and examined the deck's floor, hoping the humans had dropped a morsel for him. No such luck. Their minds were on intimacy, not food.

Yesterday, the humans had left him a piece of strudel from the village bakery. Today, the human had left him nothing. Then, from the far side of the lake, the Jay heard a screaming sound. He recognized the sound and immediately understood its significance. A cougar had ambushed an unsuspecting deer. The Jay flew toward the sound. He settled himself in the pines above the cougar's kill and waited. The bird understood that cougars always left a large part of the carcass behind. Back, inside the cabin, Carl and Marty had entered the bedroom when they heard the cougar make its kill.

Marty put her arms around Carl's neck. Her eager lips found his. They were inviting; warm. She kissed him and teased the back of his neck with her fingers. *"Survival of the fittest, my love. That sounded like a female cougar killing a deer,"* she whispered, while pressing her body close to Carl's. *"That's what I love about the wild animals. They have no pretenses. They don't second guess themselves. They have no shame or guilt about living. They live natural lives and do what is natural. And they accept that about each other."*

"Too bad for the deer," Carl mumbled, drawing a breath from their kiss, before finding Marty's lips again.

"Don't feel sorry for the deer. But feel joyful for the cougar," Marty instructed. *"The meek do not inherit the Earth. That's bull shit. The meek get eaten, and rightly so. They exist to be eaten. That's why I root for the predators. They are special, and beautiful; and, they're smarter than the meek."* She placed her hand on Carl's pants, felt his stiffening cock, and stroked it.

"You love the predators because you are one, yourself, aren't you, Gorgeous." Carl smiled into her eyes, kissed her again and squeezed her closer to him, placing his hand on her breast.

That was her signal. She squeezed his cock. *"Yes, my love. I am. I am hungry for your body. Tonight, you will be my deer; and I will devour you. I believe I will begin with your marvelous cock."* Her eyes promised adventure. She stroked and pressed her hand hard against his cock. Embracing, kissing, they moved next to the bed.

Marty and her prey removed their clothes. They had drawn the cabin's skylight shades open, creating windows to the stars in the heavens. A vase of artificial poppy flowers sat on the nightstand beside the bed. They were Marty's. She left them there because she frequently used the cabin. She liked to look at them while making love. Poppies signified her whimsical, carefree mood about morality. The flowers helped bring out her happiness mood. Freedom, love of nature, of sunshine, and resilience against adversity was the poppy's essence, and hers. Stars twinkled above and light from the full moon streamed into the bedroom. Its moonbeam had moved from the wooden floor onto the bed. Now it shined on Marty's body and graced her voluptuous figure with shining luminescence. Clouds briefly crossed the moon's face and played their seductive shadows over Marty's relaxed, predator body. Her oiled, cream-white skin glowed in the starry moonlight. Her smile allured; her eyes captivated. Her enchanting, ethereal, lustrous, silky hair begged to be touched; then tented over her prey's head while her lips devoured him. Her pinkish-red nipple buds and lips assumed a darker, cinnamon-crimsoned hue, signaling that her butterfly body art lived. It was even more alluring and sensual in the starry moonlit night than it was in daylight. Carl's infatuation for Marty and her enchanting vagina burst containment. He had to express his adoration:

'Un tattoo, Mi amour, Mi Deise, Mia esprit libre! (Your tattoo, my love, my goddess, my free spirit!) '*There is an aura of tantalizing mystery and wonder about it, like it has a life and will of its own; as do you. As your lover, I am naturally drawn to it; wanting to enter it and surrender my soul to it; and to you.'*

In this moment, in this place, Marty became a most salaciously skillful sexual predator. Tonight, Carl was her willing victim. She gently pushed her prey down, directing his fall onto the bed. She smiled: *'You know you are about to be devoured, don't you?'* Then she joined him on the bed. He lay naked, surrendered; eagerly anticipating being sexually ravaged by his fantasy dream girl, here ensconced in her wonderfully uninhibited world. Carl idolized Marty's firm body. He adored her immoral soul. Everything about her infatuated him; her smiles, her spunky playfulness; her carefree attitude about life and sin; her willingness to take risks; especially her passion for love making. Carl cared about Marty's life. Her dual careers of business sales and pornography fascinated him. He had never, in all his other dalliances, encountered a woman as brim-filled with life as Marty. Since they became lovers, she had become precious to him. He adored her. He doted on her every wish and whim. He worshipped her and obsessed over her. She had become his goddess. And he deeply loved her.

The dark eyes of the silent elk and lynx glistened in the moonlight. Their heads were believably lifelike. Marty's soul resonated with the evening's mystical allure. She imagined that she was being watched by living elk and lynx; imagined that they wished they, too, could romp freely with her this night. The wildness of her thoughts charged her libido; animating her to a euphoric sense of animal-like procreative bliss.

Marty sought to make passionate, uninhibited love. This night she would become Pagan Nymph Goddess of the forest's darkness. Carl's wife, meanwhile, was driving on the highway, fifteen miles from the cabin, nurturing a decidedly different, hostile mood. Unsuspecting Marty was thrilled. She believed she and Carl would be together for the entire weekend. No business calls to make; no porn scenes to shoot; no Premium Members to entertain; just her and Carl, his fabulous, superbly toned body, and his wonderful, highly educated penis. All of him! All hers! She had planned this romantic get-away over a month ago. Tonight, her thoughts were dreamy and serene. Everything was perfect. Tomorrow they would go to the upper lake where they would make love and take another set of pictures in the sunlight. He would not mention his wretched wife and the misery she caused him. They would make love by the lake; hear the breezes rustling in the pines; perhaps see butterflies again. Tonight, their first night of three, Marty's mood was filled with thoughts of romance and delightful erotic pleasure. She thought of making love; the many positions she would assume to feel Carl's penis so many wonderful ways. Life for these days and nights would be as it should be: perfect!

She was already naked when she pushed Carl onto the bed; free; about to make shameless, uninhibited love, safely secluded in her wilderness hideaway. Carl's fingers and tongue followed his touchings and kisses. She loved his touches. Electricity surged through her muscles and skin. Predictably, Carl was performing his magic. Her vagina became lubricated. She felt heated there. She was anxious for coitus. Her breath heaved. She kissed her lover's neck. The animal heads maintained their reluctant silence, empathetic witnesses to Marty's moans, chortles, and pleasured squeals. These stoic sentinels knew his lips had located her nipple buds. She became as one among them; animals that had once known her same sexual freedoms. Now she became a naked animal herself; fully engrossed in her delightful love making. Her imagination knew that the silent observant heads understood her need. She knew they looked upon her and favored her pleasure-takings with their adoration and blessing. Here, in Marty's imaginary pagan world, morality became whatever pleased her. Pleasure was her highest morality; her only duty was to herself. This night, Carl's magnificent, lovely cock especially craved her licks and kisses. It had waited ten long days since it last visited her. It led his soul to her butterfly tattoo; touched her vaginal lips, coaxed her to spread her legs widely and offer it their inner heated lips. It rubbed against her slippery inner lips while Carl kissed her mouth; and while her fingernails dug into his back; and while she begged his cock to enter. And then it had entered her. It felt at home; welcomed; safe; loved. It knew her vagina well; filled and stretched her; stimulated her countless thousands of nerve ten-dril endings; lifted her passion mood to breathtaking, exhilarat-ing heights; caressed and stroked her clitoris beautifully, lovingly; pleased her in the uniquely sensuously felt ways that only it could.

Marty felt Carl confirming his adoration by placing his hands on her breasts. His fingers skillfully massaged her nipples. He was confirming that he cherished these precious moments with his deity. He had this way about him. He made her feel deliciously sensuous. All her senses were heightened, aroused; highly stim-ulated; and honestly appreciated by this particular lover; this one man who, more than any of her other lovers, understood her infinite desire for erotic sexuality. He was again proving that his love for her was absolute. He lived to please her. Everything was perfect. Their lovemaking was going splendidly; her pent-up pleasure needs were being reached and satisfied. Poon's antennae quivered when she heard Marty extoll her sexuality:

'Oh Carl, I've waited so long for this. Too long, darling. Please, please, Carl; fuck me better than my porn partners fuck me. Fuck me all night long tonight, like only you can do. I want to come so many times with you. I need you, Carl.'

Marty was on the cusp of exploding with her evening's first joyous orgasm, when she first heard the car. Her nemesis! She had driven all the way up here to the lake. At night! The woman had to be insane. Poon edged even closer and pointed her antennae directly at Marty, eager to hear the profligate sex goddess explain how she destroyed the intrusive interloper.

"Did she pull her car right up to the cabin?" David asked.

"Yes, she did. She was crass and inconsiderate, David. The woman was an asshole. She didn't have a subtle bone in her body. I heard her tires crunching the gravel stones all the way up my drive-way. My cabin was the only one this far away across the lake from its civilized side. It's quiet and dark at my place: no shops, bars, boat

ramps or people. I like it that way. No one who drove that far around the lake could possibly be lost. I knew it had to be her. I finished my thoughts and paused my lovemaking. I recovered my composure and found my courage. Then, I touched my hand over Carl's hair. I told him to relax and stay put; and to let me handle everything. I plucked a white poppy flower from its vase, got out of bed, slipped a sheer nightgown over my shoulders, and walked out onto my deck. It was a beautiful moonlit evening. The sky was filled with twinkling stars. The Milky Way's white band looked like a celestial river that journeyed forever into infinity. The white birch trees that line my long driveway reflected a bluish tint of moonlight off their bark. There was a light evening breeze and the lake was calm. The moonlight laid a silvery-blue path before me on the lake's placid surface. It was so undisturbed it seemed one could walk on it."

"Birch trees, moonlight. Bluish tint?" David shook his head, not understanding.

"Yes, well, I hadn't taken my contacts out yet. I do that right before I go to sleep. I wore lenses that matched the blue pleated skirt that I wore earlier, while Carl and I walked around Lake Village looking at art galleries. He bought me a beautiful Navaho sand painting. It has two wolves about to eat a sheep. He said it made him think about how the two of us were devouring his marriage. We laughed over that imagery. He wanted to present it to me as our symbolic predator piece. It even has a spirit line that allows the sheep's spirit to leave life and enter eternity after its body dies. Anyway, as soon as we got to the cabin Carl began kissing and hugging me. We had foreplay and love making late that afternoon, before we even got into bed for the evening."

"I didn't know you used contacts." David interrupted like that whenever he needed to process a hitherto unknown detail.

"I often do, David. I don't need them to see, though. These were tinted accessories to compliment my dress, that's all. Bertie, my porn

coach, took my idea to a whole new level. She said my eyes are the windows to my soul; and their color should match the erotic moods that I create with my film scenes and outfits. She believed my fans look into my eyes as much as they watch the intimate explicit artistry. She wanted my fans to love the way my mind works; to love my uninhibited immorality. That's why she worked so hard with me to coordinate my eye shades, my outfits, and my script lines. She believed if my fans loved who I was as a person; especially as a profligate sinner, they would be far more loyal to me than if they only obsessed over my vagina while I fornicated.

"Bertie believed erotic romance occurs inside the mind; and my eyes enable me to enter the minds of my fans and helps them empathize with my natural need to make love. That's why, according to Bertie, fans fall in love with me and buy so many of my films. She had me get contacts in green, red, fuchsia, purple, and aqua marine to match my different nightgowns, scarves, bras, and panty shades that I use in my films. She had me wearing red tints and long black eyelashes and nails in one of my naughty orgy scenes. I played a she-devil in that one. It was a huge success. It got me tons of new members and film downloads. My porn ranking shot up to ninth after that. That film convinced her to match my eyes, lashes, nails, and makeup for every scene. You remember Bertie, don't you?"

"Of course. How could I ever forget? The way you did her and her husband was breathtaking. It was your best performance ever."

"I had you turned you on that night, didn't I? Come on, admit it, David. Remember how you kissed my neck and shoulders, and held me close, that entire time? I certainly do. I tingled with excitement. It was so different and wonderful. Remember how hard you became? I was certain you wanted me. Why didn't we?"

"Well, you had to do the assistants; and I had to finish things."

"I know; but I really wanted to. They could have waited. Do you feel that way now? I hope you do. We don't have the assistants here."

"I know we don't. I think I'm getting there; but first, I want to hear how you did your perfect murder."

"Okay," Marty smiled her hopeful, suggestive offer. *"Well, there I stood on the deck, waiting for Carl's wife. I heard lake waves gently lapping onto the beach. Sometimes Moose pass close by my cabin. They wade into the lake and graze moss-weeds from the bottom. Tonight, there were no moose. The lake was placid. I heard the low-pitched hum of crickets and the croaking from an occasional frog. It was a perfect evening for romance. She had me unsettled at first. I knew she intended to ruin everything. 'Such a glorious romantic evening,' I thought in the moments before she got out of her car; 'and here comes this wretched bitch, driving with her high beams on, pretending like she's the Lake Police; thinking she's got the right to interrupt me and spoil my weekend.' My mood was jarred from cuddly romantic sex to frenzied uncertainty; and now to abrasive unpleasantness. I felt myself getting angry."*

"She was totally unexpected, wasn't she?"

"No, not totally, David. I knew I'd be living a moment something like this one, sooner or later. That time had finally come. And here she was. She got out of her car, slammed her door closed; then stomped up the flagstone walkway toward the cabin. I could see that there was no graciousness or tenderness about her. Just by the anger in her face and the way she walked, I could see that understanding and empathy were alien concepts to her. She was brim-filled with a hostile, menacing attitude. I saw, by the determined way she planted her boots and set her jaw forward, that she was convinced her behavior was righteous. Her lips were clenched tightly together. The veneer of moral high ground was written all over her face. She had no doubt that she was an aggrieved woman. I stood in my nightgown on the deck above her, poised and composed, observing her antics, and sizing her up. She was intently set upon what she intended to do. She wore ugly rage feelings on her face. She was madder than a riled-up

hornet. Her goal was to make a scene and retrieve her husband; and possibly inflict bodily harm on me in the process. I imagined that her face had 'bitch' written all over it.

"I wanted to sidestep her game. I thought it wise to avoid a physical slug fest or the ugly scene of two women brawling in the dirt. I cautioned myself to not get drawn into a cat fight. I did not want her twisting facts and calling Lake Police; making a false report about me. I'm not stupid. I do prostitution. I need to avoid getting a rap sheet.

"But confrontations do not intimidate me, David. I've had runins with my Swim coach at WEX school; and, with other upset wives and girlfriends before this night with Carl's wife. My experiences with outrageous bitch-like behavior told me I needed to stay confident and unafraid. She was, after all, just another bully. I knew that putting an end to her behavior would require that I shatter her illusions and make her see how wrong headed her attitude was. It would require my firmness and patience. I told myself that I needed to keep my wits about me; that I needed to be creative and clever. I decided to meet my nemesis, face to face. I was not about to let her get into my cabin or see her husband.

"Visualize the setting, David. The cabin deck is ten feet above ground level. It juts out from the steep mountainside and gives a wide, sweeping view of the lake. Now, visualize this skinny unkempt woman, about five feet two inches tall, standing directly below me. Are you seeing this?"

"Yes, I think so," David's eyes squinted, taking his mind to the lake.

"Good. Well, I took the offensive right away. I knew she could not possibly have expected what I did. I used one of my poppy flowers as a prop. I wanted to send her a subliminal signal that I was unashamedly committed to being an immoral whore; that I would be spending the entire weekend with her husband; and that I didn't give

a damn about her trumped up sense of indignation. I held the stem of the flower upside down and placed its petal flower head directly in front of my vagina's tasty lady lips. Then I rubbed the poppy flower slowly up and down over my darling, fuck crazed vagina. I was certain she would notice. And she did! She stopped below the cabin deck and scowled; her jaw was clenched tight. Then she glared her squinting, beady eyes straight up at me. Her eyes were adapting to the softer moonlight. I stood directly above her, nonchalantly teasing my lady lips and her mind with my vagina and my poppy flower. All I was wearing was my opened sheer nightgown, shoulder-draped over my naked body."

"Did she say hello? Did she say anything? Did she ask where her husband was? Who spoke first?" asked David?

"No. I didn't give her a chance to say anything. I decided not to wait for that. I wasn't about to let her take the initiative. I noticed her eyes had caught my poppy's rubbings and touchings. My ploy was working. I was stimulating my own lady lips and I was taunting and teasing her sex starved eyes. I took the initiative right away. Before she could even open her mouth, I had confronted her by doing the unexpected. I made a brazen move to demonstrate my fearlessness and assert my dominance. It was somewhat risky, but I decided that I needed to boldly challenge her prudish sensibilities; put her in her place, so to speak; let her know that I was not about to be bullied. I wanted to communicate, through my body language, that she was not going to have her way with me, or her husband; that I was very proud of my wantonness; and that my vagina was adored by her husband. She needed to see that I was uninhibited and unashamed; that I was unapologetic and not about to change my licentious behaviors; and that I was willing to give her a nasty fight. By standing up to her, I believed she'd back down, like bullies typically do. I wanted her to gulp and choke from shock while she stood there, looking up at me. Before she could even get a word out.*

I showed her that I was completely immoral and proudly shameless about the erotic things I did with my downstairs lady parts. I also communicated that I was a mean wildcat.”

“Well, what did you do next? Tell me.” David salivated, wanting to hear how this test for dominance played out.

“I widened my stance. I watched her eyes while I slowly pulled my poppy flower away. Then I suggestively rubbed my hand in a circular motion over the crown of my vagina, as if to say: ‘Surprise! Look what I’ve got! Look at Little Miss Muffy! She’s been shamelessly fucking your husband! Can you appreciate what a craven whore I am? Can you understand how proud I am of my immoral whoring? Do you get it now, Bitch? Do you understand that I’m not afraid of you? See? I don’t care that you are finally facing the vagina that is wrecking your marriage!’

“When I used my body language like I did, an amazing thing happened. Carl’s wife stopped moving forward. She simply stood frozen; immobilized, like she was cemented in her tracks. Absolutely, David, she became paralyzed. Her jaw gaped open. Her boot stomping tactic and angry face deserted her. She gasped for breath. For the first time, she beheld her full view of my lady parts and butterfly tattoo. Now, David, you know from my performances, that my tattoo rivets viewers’ eyes to my vagina and keeps their focus on it. Well, Carl’s wife was no exception. She instantly surmised that I was completely carefree and immoral; and that I wasn’t about to apologize or retreat from what I was doing with her husband.

“I could only imagine what went through her mind. She was probably thinking; ‘What sort of woman would tattoo herself with that kind of tattoo, right next to her vagina like that?’ My tattoo signaled to her that I was either a sex addict, a professional call girl, or both. She had already seen me use the poppy flower to mock her sensibilities. And now, by fully revealing my penis ravishing lady bits to her, I was further mocking her; telling her that she couldn’t shame

me. My reveal move made a bold declaration that I was proud to be an immoral whore; and that I had contempt for her. I looked down at her. I smiled smugly while I canted my pelvis forward slowly, flaunting my sexuality even more. I was telescoping my vagina right into her face; invading her sense of decorum by flaunting myself; making sure my beaver shot commanded her full attention. It was the same move I make for the full screen views we shoot in my porn films. My body language dared her to deal with me. My silent message was, 'This is the honey pot, with her flaming lips and butterfly wings that has taken your husband from you, 'Bitch!' And, there's nothing you can do about it.'

"Did you say anything when you did that? What did she say?"

"Oh, I didn't say a word. I didn't need to. She was spellbound. There was this weird moment that passed between us. I expected her to say or do something, but she did absolutely nothing; said nothing. She became paralyzed, like her neck had broken and left her head planted back on her shoulders. She simply didn't move. I don't think she could. The shock of confrontation was too much for her. She'd never encountered a woman like me. That's when I realized I had turned the tables on her. She was like that infamous ship Titanic, that struck the iceberg. She couldn't go forward. It was like she knew she was doomed. She lost all her focus and direction. She continued standing there, like she had become a frozen statue, gazing up at my sex."

"She just stared at you?"

"Yes, David. She just stood there, her legs spread to give her balance; her head resting back on her shoulders, staring up at my vagina. This went on for the longest time. It was weird and unnatural, but it also told me something. A normal woman who had some self-confidence would have hurled an insult at me, or thrown something at me. But she didn't do that. Her fixation on my sex signaled a transition in her mindset. I instinctively knew it was the beginning of something. Unwittingly, she was handing me my opening. It took

her way too long to get past her initial shock of my taunt. A brief glance would have been understandable; but her stare was unnaturally long. I knew something else was happening. It was like there was this surrender of her power. There was an element of wonder by the way her beady eyes studied my lady parts. Her startled look had disappeared. It was replaced by more of a focused stare. Her gaping jaw closed back up. I think her conscious self tried to conceal her interest; but her eyes remained fixated; intensely riveted to my vagina. They didn't blink. Her face assumed an unnatural, awestruck look; like she had arrived before the presence of her god. I did not expect this reaction from her.

"Carl never told me that his wife had sexual tendencies towards women; probably because he never suspected it. I don't think she ever revealed it to him or talked to him about it. I don't believe Carl understood the extent and power of her inner lesbian cravings, as I suddenly did. I intuited something profound had happened in that brain of hers. Her body's demeanor also changed. Her anger and hostility seemed to melt away. I noticed her facial muscles relaxed. Her lips pursed outward ever so slightly. They became like a child's, desiring a lollypop. I have seen that look come over a woman's face several times before."

"You have? Where?"

"At private sex clubs, where I get bookings to perform live pornography on stage. Often a woman who loves lesbian oral sex will take a seat near the stage. Typically, she'll be wearing a loose-fitting skirt and no panties; or panties that don't cling very tightly, so she can move them aside. I'll be on stage, seated on a low bench, facing my audience. I usually begin my routines by seductively massaging my vagina and fingering myself; stretching out my lady lips. I study my audience carefully while I do this. When a woman with lesbian tendencies sees me turning myself on like I do; often enough, she'll open her legs and reveal herself; then she'll start mirroring my

stimulations with her own. Her face will relax, just like Carl's wife had relaxed her face. Her facial lips will raise up and form a slight smile. That's her subconscious way of telling me that she wants to have oral sex with me. When I motion with my finger for her to come join me, she'll come. Those women almost always join me. We'll kiss and hug and touch to get a feel for each other; and before very long, she'll be doing lip massages, mouth suctions, kiss pops, licks, and tongue vibrations on my lady lips. You'd be amazed at how erotic some women are, David.

"As good as a man?"

"Depends. Many women are more into stimulating than many men. They understand a woman's body better and they take their time. For them, it's more of a pleasure excursion than an encounter. Most who come onstage with me love all aspects of cunnilingus. They take foreplay very seriously. Ultimately, they bury their faces in my vagina and their tongues lovingly stroke my clitoris. Many also work my vagina with their finger stimulations to amplify the pleasuring from their tongues. Naturally, I reciprocate their passions. Often, we'll orgasm into each other's mouths, on stage. We achieve that magical bond of human connectiveness. My audiences love watching girl love."

"I never knew you did women?"

"Sure, you did, David. You watched me do two in the chamber before we killed them."

"But I thought that was just about getting rid of them. I never thought you liked that."

"That's because you have male dominance complex. Most men think like you; but that not how it is."

"How it is?"

"With lots of women, it's wonderful. I love doing women."

"Lots?"

"Yeah, lots. It's just suppressed, below the surface of social pleasantries, that's all."

"Suppressed?"

"Yes. Suppressed."

"By who? Since when?"

"By men." Marty lifted her head. Her eyes held David's. Her smirk told him she thought him disingenuous. *"Since you pecker waging T men took over."*

"T men? Took over? Took over what? Stop with the riddles." David's pursed lips told Marty it was time to come clean.

"Testosterone driven male hierarchical religions. Power, David. Wealth and power. Before the T men, the people worshipped prostitutes like they worshipped the sun's return from winter solstice. They revered life. They worshipped and adored the beginning of life, the Earth's natural cycles of greening up in springtime. And they worshipped the female womb because they understood that life begins there. They knew that, without the womb, life ceases. So, they worshipped, revered, and adored the female vagina. It was a time when mankind worshipped what seemed natural to worship. Going back five thousand plus years, thereabouts, you power and control crazed T men banned ritual prostitution worship; replaced it with your imaginary god, that long white bearded guy, on his sky throne; who throws thunder and lightning at us and tells us all the things we can't do."

"How come I've never read about this?" David's canted head and raised jaw signaled he was sparring for a confrontation.

"Come on, David! Don't act disingenuous." Marty wasn't having it. *"The male religions wrote our histories. You know that. Anything that contradicts those histories got trashed and burned millenniums ago or it got buried beneath the Vatican in some hidden corner library. That's how come."*

"*So, you are about wealth and power, yourself, then. Aren't you?*"

"*Duh; same as you, David. We're no different that way, are we?*" Marty's eyes held David's in the silent contest of power that often played out between them. It was the same unspoken battle that countless other opposite sex pairs had engaged in over the past several hundred thousand years. Neither broke off their quiet purposeful gaze; both blinked only as nature required.

"*And your sex; other women like you, I mean, do they feel this way?*" David finally said something. He was intrigued with this other dimension of Marty's world. He had never known it existed.

"*Some do. I'm not alone. More and more, others are coming to this view. Porn stars are the leading edge of the natural return to prostitution worship. People need to believe in something that gives them hope; something that's real. The female vagina is real. It's not an abstract concept. And it's making inroads into the male-based religions. There are female rabbis and priests now. Our female Vaginas are coming for you boys, David.*"

David snorted a laugh. He wanted to break out of this uncomfortable conversation and get back to Marty's perfect murder. "*And you intuitively knew that this woman, this Carl's wife woman, wanted to have oral sex with you, too; like the women you do in those sex clubs?*"

"*Yes David, definitely. I knew what I was seeing. I've seen that same look in the faces of other women, many times.*"

"*I didn't know you did live porn. How did you get into that?*"

"*Through Dominick and his daughter, Jenifer. Dom produced those ten full length porn films. I starred in them. I became friends with Jen after her mom divorced Dom. Jen started the Inferno Clubs. I love her. I'm like her mentor for all things erotic. I also perform live porn for her clubs.*"

"*Did you make money on the films you did for Dom?*"

"Yeah. I got my standard $2000 hourly rate plus 2 ½ percent of the gross. They are projecting to gross over a billion dollars."

"So, you'll make 25 million?"

"Actually more, David. The sell through is huge; and I get a 3 percent royalty on the Premium Bikini line; so, another 10 million."

"You're almost doing what I do! I had no idea there was that much money in porn."

"There is at the top, David."

"So, you're committed to it?"

"Yes, of course I am. I love fucking. Where else could I make that kind of money while I'm enjoying myself?"

"But you'll stay with the Firm?"

"You know how much I love doing the murders. I can't get those feelings anywhere else. And, I assume you'll be good to me from now on. You will, won't you?" Marty smiled her coquettish smile and rubbed her vagina, obviously displaying her desire to get intimate with David.

"Of course, I'll be good to you. You know I love you, and how your mind works. No morals. No guilt. No qualms about murdering. You are special. Where else could I find a gorgeous woman with a mind like yours?"

"All good, David. Would you like a special treat with a special woman? This seems like a good time. Let's stop playing games and come together, completely. You want to, don't you? Don't deny it."

"I'm not denying it. I dream about it. I know it will be special. And I'm not playing games with you, okay?" David's blood pressure rose along with his voice. He didn't like it when his control was challenged. *"But get back. Get back to where we were, okay? You were saying that Carl's wife gave you that same 'limbic look' that you get from lesbians when you do live porn? So, at this point your still operating on a hunch. Get to the part where you murdered her. How did you kill her? Did you stab her?"*

"Let's not get ahead of ourselves, okay, David? Relax." Marty leveled her gaze. It was her story to tell and she was in control. *"Let me take you through it. A story means so much more when you don't jump ahead. Didn't your rabbis tell you that?"*

"Yeah, they did. They said a lot of things." David shrugged his shoulders, signaling that he wasn't challenging Marty's control.

"Okay, then. Just listen. Whether Carl's wife consciously knew it or not, her involuntary limbic zone had switched on; and she was sending me her subconscious emotive signal through her facial muscles and her mouth. Sexual attraction cannot be faked. I am highly attuned to that signal. No matter how hard a person tries to disguise it, I can detect it. Her head stayed rested back on her shoulders, and her eyes stayed riveted on my vagina. That confirmed her signal. I looked closely at her eyes. They were love thirsty eyes, David. I was certain of it." Marty nodded to David, communicating confidence in her assertion.

"You could read her face and her eyes?"

"Oh yes, David; most definitely. The desire look is unmistakable. I have a strong intuition about these things, and I trust it. Her parched sex-thirsty eyes were beholding my lovely pink valley; imagining it would become her fantasy oasis. My playful Miss Muffy did more than intrigue her. It tantalized and tempted her. I was certain of it. She imagined it might provide her fulfillment; yet, it was beyond her psychological grasp. She was not a liberated woman. She had been trained since childhood to be subservient and submissive. Sex out of wedlock was taboo for her. Her thinking was conditioned to believe that oral sex with another woman was unthinkable and ungodly. She'd been brainwashed to believe that cunnilingus would cast her into hell; or worse. Now, as an adult, girl-girl sex was beyond the boundaries of her psychological comfort zone. She believed that any sort of non-monogamous relationship with anyone other than

her husband was forbidden behavior. She knew it existed; but only in a different, distant world, far from her world. She understood this unreachable world had different rules from her world; and her upbringing had conditioned her to believe she had no right to enter my world. It was forbidden to her. She believed she'd be cast into hell if she even dared to experiment in my world.

"But her eyes told me she wished to ignore all her cautions; cast away the shackles that bound her to her rules-based world; and join me in my world. She wanted to embrace me, kiss me, and love me. But those same eyes told me she was terribly conflicted. My world was dark, morally murky, and off limits. Mine was a bad girl's world that she was not allowed to enter. Her eyes revealed there were unseen forces holding her captive in her mental jail; intimidating her and blocking her from coming forward; preventing her from even being honest with herself. These demons held her true feelings captive with their invisible bars and chains. They played on her innermost fears; threatened to throw her into damnation if she dared to break free. She was conditioned to summarily reject a woman like me."

"But you had no way of knowing if you were reading her correctly, right?" David couldn't help but ask his question. He craved certainty in all his endeavors.

"Yes, that's somewhat true, David. But once my mind engaged hers, I had to depend upon my sense of her and not allow myself to waiver or second guess myself. I had to go with the flow of what I sensed, kind of like two forces engaged in battle need to trust their sense of conditions as the fight progresses. My sensory read was coming through strongly, though; and I trusted it. I sensed that Carl's wife was psychologically trapped in her mental prison. I saw a frustrated soul peering out from unblinking prison-window eyes.

"And, those eyes beheld her soul's destroyer; my welcoming, iniquitous gateway to sin. Did they ever! Her eyes saw her salvation. I knew what I was observing. My mind heard her tortured soul silently

cry out; seeking to savor my forbidden, reprehensible destroyer of morals. Her eyes betrayed her soul. They pleaded; begged her mind for permission to slake her limbic desires, like a thirsting body cries out for water:

'Would my righteous soul dare permit me? Might I quench my blistering, searing, lust thirst? Could I permit myself to savor this immoral whore's, forbidden place?'

"Her eyes were windows into her tortured soul. For a long, lingering moment, they basked in the countenance of my profligate ungodliness. Her thoughts asked herself:

'How can I approach this immoral woman and partake of her cavalier intimacy, when my soul needs to heed its learned proprieties? How might my soul honestly approach the whore's soul? How can I communicate my desires to her? How can I enter her vagina with my adoring kisses, and still play the impossibly ridiculous role that I have traveled here to play?'

"I watched her mind asking itself:

'Can I dare risk my eternal damnation by savoring this adulteress's sweet sins?'

"Then I watched her eyes answer her:

'I must resist her. I cannot chance the wrath of my soul's jailers. I must be strong. I must resist her; but I do so much want her!'

"I paid close attention to her conundrum. Shock, uncertainty, and desire all conspired to keep her standing there, frozen in place. I knew I was witnessing her psyche's pivotal moment. She had stared into my vagina far too long. It was an unnatural, prurient stare; not the repulsed stare from a husband-loving housewife. It told me she couldn't possibly be a loving wife and homemaker. Those was only her pretense roles. I pegged her for a phony person; living a phony life; an abused, self-tortured woman repressing her natural lesbian tendency. She was horribly conflicted; forcing herself to live her sham housewife role every single day; pathetic. I deduced she was raised

and trained for her role; kicked, shoved, pushed, and locked into her dull, confining space, like a hapless prisoner of war; and hating it, and every single day of her wretched life; and hating herself for not leaving it, too. But I told myself that that was her lot in life. And not my problem. That she didn't have the guts to change her life was not my problem either.

"My insights told me to be bold and unorthodox. A normal well-adjusted woman would have never stood still for what I was about to do; but I was confident that there was nothing normal or well-adjusted about her. My gut instincts told me she masked serious psychological issues that could be used against her. I reasoned if I could pry open the hidden closets of her mind's limbic zone, then I could coax her dark skeletons out. I could then use her secret demons to destroy her. I told myself I would do both of us a huge favor by getting rid of her; sending her on to her next life. I reminded myself that I hated her, too. That was my best reason to be rid of her. Was I being too calloused to think that way? I considered that thought for a second; and dismissed it. Maybe I should have only hated what her pedigreed world had made of her, and left it at that; maybe spare her life by convincing myself that her wretched life was separate from her contorted soul. But then I told myself that, thinking this way, I might always have a difficulty, bringing myself to murder her; and that this night was the perfect time to kill her. Remote. No witnesses, assuming Carl stayed put inside the cabin. No phone calls from her to Carl or him to her. He's been with me this entire time. Still, one can never be too careful. No tire tracks on my pebbled driveway. Just her and her car. Nothing that detective could use to link her to me. I only needed to make sure her cell phone would not, somehow, link her to me. And I did so much want to murder her. All I needed to do was figure out a way to get rid of her, her phone, and her car; and not leave finger prints or my DNA on her, her phone, or the car. Challenging? I thought so. But I also thought: 'If I'm clever enough

and careful to not to leave any physical evidence, it's doable!' Then I saw her differently. She, in her flesh and blood body, represented both my problem and the solution to my problem: her. I just needed to work my problem: getting rid of her.

"Finally, her gaze lifted, slowly. Her eyes met mine. Their entire continence changed as they traveled that short distance from my vagina to my eyes. Her imprisoned soul had recaptured her mind. Their forced, angry look returned. It told me that her forces of moral rigidity understood how to control her; and they controlled her very well.

'You're a whore!'

"Her pained voice blurted out her damning words. Now, her eyes no longer gazed in dreamlust. Now, they were embittered and squinting, comporting their agreement with her words. My gut told me I was seeing a brave, but ridiculously pretentious act. Obviously, her imprisoned soul now controlled her tongue. It was hard not to laugh and mock her pretense, but I didn't laugh. I decided to play this game through to its conclusion. I believed I would win."

"Win what, exactly? At this point, were you thinking you would win her husband?" David was intrigued by the psychology of the interaction between Marty and Carl's wife. He wanted to meticulously deconstruct every minute detail of it.

"No David. I had won her husband away from her long before this. I had already been fucking Carl for over a year. You can tell when he started having sex with me from our sales reports. I was going far beyond taking Carl away from her. I intended to take her life away from her. I wanted to completely rid myself of a pest. I viewed her life as no more significant than a lowly insect beetle's life. I wanted to step on that life and crush it, rub my shoe clean of it and be rid of it, forever. And I believed I could."

"You mean you believed, at this early juncture, that you could successfully murder her?"

"*Yes, I did. I had not yet figured out how I would do it, but I believed I could do it. Having that confidence in myself was all I really needed, David. The rest was all details. I knew I needed to maintain my conviction in my belief and my determination to carry it off; otherwise, I'd lose the upper hand. Then, I'd never accomplish my murder. I couldn't let her ridiculous insult affect me. I was not about to cry and say:*

'Oh, my goodness, I'm terribly sorry. It never occurred to me that I am an immoral whore. Thank you for telling me. I didn't realize that I was intentionally committing sinful adultery with your husband all these past evenings and weekends this last year. My goodness! Oh, shame on me! What a terribly naughty girl I've been. I'm so sorry. I promise you that I will never fuck your husband or suck his cock again. Please take him back. Thank you so much for telling me what I am. I'll go to church right away and confess. Speaking of church, may I bring you a cup of coffee and a donut? We can sit down and chat about today's liturgical lesson.'

"Can you see how I needed to side-step the initial verbal arrow that she directed at me and turn her focus inward, right away? Taking that initiative was key. And I took it. Her whole charade was not about me, David. It was about her mental issues. I was not about to allow her mental health issues make this confrontation about me.

"Her outrageous behavior needed to be nipped in the bud. She had interrupted our beautiful lovemaking. That forced, quivering voice of disgust she used when she called me a whore contradicted her bravado. It confirmed my gut instinct and everything Carl told me about her. I saw right through her pretentious voice and into her soul. She rarely performed wifely duties. Carl told me that she hated heterosexual sex. He said a man's penis actually terrified her. I surmised that was true by the way her voice inflected. She sounded like a tremulous child, pretending to be brave. Hers was a jittery little girl's voice, shocked to discover that some women love sex. And here

she was, confronted by a real woman who was totally uninhibited and unapologetic about making love. Even more horrifying: I was more than a sensuous woman. I was a living, breathing nympho-maniac; the incomprehensible opposite of her persona." Marty laid her head back upon her shoulders. She invitingly smiled her deep breath while subtly twisting her torso, suggesting to David that this incomprehensible woman wanted him to interrupt her and make love with her.

"Didn't her husband come out; try to referee this brewing cat fight and keep you two apart?" It was so like David to dodge an invitation with a question.

"Nope," Marty shook her head. *"Actually, at that point, David, I sensed there wasn't going to be any cat fight. It was going to be more like an adult tigress tearing the head off of a cowardly rabbit kind of fight. Carl, the bitch's husband, was way too smart to get involved. He obeyed my earlier instructions. He stayed inside. That told me he was confident that I could handle her. It also told me that he had no feelings left for her and that he couldn't stomach making love with her anymore. By not coming out he was also intimating to me that he wanted me to get rid of her. He just wanted to not know or see the details. He knew both of us very well. He knew I was the fighter and that I would prevail. I was sure he had every confidence I could deal with her without his help. But he had no idea that I had previous thoughts about murdering her. I never told him that."*

"Never told him that? Never even gave him a hint of that? He had no advanced clue? Not even during your liaisons over the prior year, that you wanted to murder her?"

"No. And I didn't. Up until that night my only thoughts were to take his love and his money from her. I had never formed the actual intent to kill her before that night. If she had not tried to barge in on our love making at my cabin, the thought would have never entered my head. Intending to carry out her murder; taking

deliberate premeditated steps to do that had not, before this night, even occurred to me."

"So, she enraged you? That's what triggered your intent?"

"Yes. I seethed inside. After I got over my initial panic, I wanted to wring her fucking neck. How dare she interrupt us, making love in my cabin? I wasn't going to have it. I was not going to allow this bitch to intrude into my life ever again."

"So, you never saw the situation as you intruding into her life?"

"Not even, David. My business is whoring. Hers is being a docile, mousy housewife. They are separate and mutually exclusive roles. I take her husband and their money. She accepts the situation until he and I end it. That's it. Whore's needs trump wife's needs. Wife suffers silently. That's the wife's role in this. There's no intrusion on my part. There's only the reality of my business. She's a wife. She needs to stay out of my way."

"So, you had no respect for her? No feelings? Nothing?"

"Absolutely none. I have a hard edge about what I do, David. I lose all empathy for the wife. 'Carl,' I thought to myself, 'what could you have possibly been thinking when you married this pathetic excuse for a woman? Surely you could have done better.'

"You should have seen her, David. She was a disgusting pile of skin and bones. There was nothing soft or inviting about her. She looked like bad smells stuck on top of toothpick legs. I couldn't imagine any man wanting anything to do with her. But here she was outside our cabin. 'How did I get so lucky?' I cynically asked myself. She called Carl's name and ordered him to come out. But Carl never made a sound or any effort to interrupt us."

"How did you feel when he didn't come out?" David chuckled.

"Oh, that made me supremely confident, David. I knew Carl's mind. He wanted to leave her to me and stay out of this. He had mentally divorced her over a year ago. That was the unspoken dynamic here. He completely loves me; only me. I'm the woman for

him; the way I am; my porn; everything. He's totally into me. He didn't want anything to do with her; not anymore. Their marriage was finished, except for the formalities. That was well established; but they kept putting off getting the divorce. She knew it was over; but here she was putting on this ridiculous act, pretending not to know what Carl and I had been doing for over a year. That's what made me furious over her audacity to interrupt us. She knew she was being an annoyance. I hate annoyances while I'm making love.

"She interrupted our wonderful intimacy when she drove up. She ruined my beautiful mood. I couldn't simply ignore her and leave her outside our cabin yowling like a sick cat. I knew that doing nothing would not stop her. She wasn't about to go away. I knew that much about her.

"I own the cabin. That made her presence my problem, not Carl's. I needed to deal with her. I left him lying on the bed with my music playing. I love making love to music, especially religious music. I believe making love is a sacred experience. That particular evening, we were listening to a continuous playing loop of the Latin movements from the Mass of Saint Cecilia. The recording I had was created by a magnificent orchestra inside a magnificent cathedral. The structure captured the acoustics beautifully. The soprano's trilling high notes in the Sanctus portion, followed by her joyous cascading vocal descent sent resonating harmonic chills through my entire body. It made me feel so beautifully sensuous. Hearing that portion of the mass had just lifted my spirits. I was feeling my orgasm beginning to build. I had convinced myself that my immoral whoring was divinely inspired. I love feeling that way when I make love."

"But you asked me how I felt about my interaction with her when I knew Carl wasn't coming out to save her. Well, David, I was highly pleased with Carl. By staying inside, he was proving that his loyalty was to me. He didn't come out and say: 'Oh, you poor dear. Let me take you home. I can explain everything;' or any sort of mush

nonsense like that. And, of course, my own reaction was that I was furious with her. She was way out of line coming to the lake; interrupting me. She interfered with my mood and some wonderfully sweet love making." I was mad enough to hit her, but I kept my cool. I told myself: 'Bide your time and remember not to leave any DNA evidence.' But, damn it! I wanted to hit her so badly that I thought about indirect ways to hit her, like by using a baseball bat or something. But that evidence issue stayed in my mind.

"How did she look?"

"Wretched, just like Carl described her. She was an unkempt, skinny, pathetic mouse of a woman. When I first saw her my initial impression was: 'She is disgusting! She's a human barf bag!'"

"How did you feel about yourself after you sized her up?"

"Well, I felt grateful that I didn't look like her. I remember thinking to myself that she would never grace the cover of any porn magazines or do a centerfold layout with its breasts and vagina reveals, or get paid to endorse any products. I felt like the two of us were from worlds apart. Beyond that, I felt contempt for her. I despised her and her phony world, so much so that if I could have thrust a stake through her heart and twisted it, I would have. As she stood there looking up at me, I began feeling this inner hatred. My mind began dehumanizing her. It boiled up from deep inside me. My soul wrestled to separate itself from her psychologically tortured existence. I didn't want her mental problems affecting me. I wanted separation from her. I couldn't stand being near her. With every breath I took into my lungs, and every heartbeat that moved oxygen into my brain, that recurring thought of getting myself away from her resounded from my subconscious. It was a thought so dominant that I almost screamed it out into the quiet night. I wanted to shout: 'GO AWAY, BITCH!' so loudly that every creature around the lake would hear me.

"'I must rid my life of this damnable human pest.' That was my thought. 'Yes! That's what I must do! If I'm ever to have peace of

mind while Carl is my lover, I must get rid of her!' "She had no consideration, no dignity, no femininity, and no poise, no anything. She was a despicable vile wretch. She was of no possible use to me. Her gauche manners were unforgivable. She was disrespectful of my privacy. She was just obnoxious and rude. I began thinking she had no right to exist.

"Imagine how I felt, David! That woman had the audacity to interrupt me while I was beginning a beautiful, memorable orgasm. I was making love. Carl's penis was slowly rubbing my clitoris, doing it perfectly with me. I was listening to a night owl hooting and the breezes in the pines and the lake's gentle waves lapping on the shore. My concentration was working wonderfully. I was right on the verge of coming. I felt relaxed and loved; and I was just beginning to release. I felt like I was poised at the top of a beautiful waterfall, about to let myself go. I was incredibly ready. My second release of that evening was only precious seconds away. I knew I was about to have one of my sweetest, most loving orgasms, ever. I was dreamily thinking how wonderful my long continuous release was going to feel, like I feel when I'm in my perfect mood; like I was that night. That's when I heard her car crunching over the driveway pebbles. That ruined my concentration. I tensed up. That bitch ruined everything. What she did was unforgivable." Marty closed her eyes and shook her head to erase the bad image of Carl's wife.

"Marty, did it ever occur to you to just find another steady lover to satisfy your sex needs?"

"Oh David, no! You don't understand my nymphomania. I've told you before, I already have… many other lovers, but Carl is special. Whenever I see a man eating with a fork, I think I see Carl eating with a fork; and then I'm suddenly remembering all the great sex we have. My mind will suddenly flash to where I'm holding Carl's cock in my hands. It's only a few inches from my lips and I'm about to suck it and I start salivating and becoming all wet inside. It's

like that when I see a pair of men's shoes in a window. I ask myself whether they'd look good on Carl; and then I think about all the great sex we'll have. I'll suddenly see him standing naked before me; and our lips are about to touch; and I imagine I have his marvelous cock in my hand and I'll be rubbing it against my pink outer lady lips, about to guide it inside me while we're standing there, just the two of us in our private world. The smallest little incidental things like that will set me off. It's automatic with me. It's how my mind works, David. It's one of the mental aspects of my addiction.

"I'll imagine I'm in one of our past moments; and I'm climbing onto Carl while he stands so strongly, holding me; and I'm wrapping my legs around him; and his splendid cock is inside me while we're making love standing up. I often mentally relive those feelings of his penis inside me, as if it was happening in the here and now; wherever I am, whatever I'm doing. Sometimes I even imagine that I've become Carl's penis and that I'm inserting it into my own cock-crazed vagina. That takes my mind far away from everything; and I can't come back to reality until I imagine having an orgasm; or until I use a vibrator or my fingers and give myself a real orgasm. I don't expect you to understand, David; but it's like that with almost everything I see, every day. It's the mental effect from my nymphomania. It's like being a heroin addict who can't stop obsessing about getting more drugs. I can't stop thinking about the great sex I have with Carl. That's because he knows how to use his marvelous cock; and he can feel my feelings. He loves enabling me to totally let go and enjoy sex. He's my special love cat."

"So, you're really hooked on this married guy, aren't you? I mean, you seem to be in love with him. Are you in love with him?"

"Yes, in a way; but no, David. You don't understand my nymphomania at all. I'm totally in love with Bob."

"Well, then why are you so fixated on this Carl fellow?"

"David, you'd need to be a woman nympho to understand. It's a

need I have. I can't help it."

"Well, what is it? I don't get it."

"It's about my orgasms, David. It's the orgasms Carl gives me and the euphoric feelings I have while I'm having them. It's all about those wonderfully special orgasms. I live to have them. I love having them and I love having them often. It's my sex addiction, my nymphomania. Some people need a drug hit or a smoke or a drink. Most people can understand those addictions; but if I told someone that I sometimes absolutely must have sex with Carl, most people would think I'm some kind of nut case. But I'm not a nut. I'm perfectly normal. But, I'm a normal nymphomaniac, that's the difference. Maybe there are normal drug addicts and normal alcoholics, I don't know. But my shrink tells me I'm a normal nymphomaniac; a normal nympho who loves a certain cock at certain times, like a druggie loves a certain kind and quality of drug. No man or woman gives me long, sweet, loving orgasms like Carl does. No one else gets me there like he does. No other man holds me lovingly during my orgasm's nirvana state while I scream and claw or purr and kiss and hug, depending on my moods; no one does that like Carl. He's the only man I've ever known that understands me and my body the way he does and patiently gives me what I need all the way through my orgasms, until I'm finished. If I were a heroin addict you could understand that I'd crave the best heroin on the street, right?"

"Yes, I could understand that."

"Well, then you could understand if someone was in a room with that heroin addict, trying to hold her away from her supply of the world's best heroin on the other side of the room, she'd go crazy. She'd even want to kill that person, right?"

"Yes, I can see that. So, you are telling me that your addiction to this Carl and his cock is so strong it made you want to kill his wife?"

"Oh, yes, David. That night it did. Yes, and hell yes. When she drove up and I thought there was a chance she'd take him away from me, I nearly lost my mind. Until I gathered my wits and started thinking, I was frantic. Fear of losing those long sweet releases in the arms of the one man who loves my body like he does and understands how badly I need those heavenly releases sent me right into a mental tailspin. It was worse than the fear of losing my life."

"That bad, honest?"

"Oh David, yes, my fear was palpable. Carl and I have this thing about sex. It's like we both live for those special times when we can be together. I don't know how else to explain this, but it's like we live so our sex organs can spend quality time together. We exist to enable our organs' addictions to each other. It's an intense ecstasy we create together; and we're in love while we create it. I know that sounds crazy, but it's true. Carl and I have talked about it. We have a co-addiction to sex with each other."

"But I thought Bob and you were really getting along."

"Well, yes, we are, David, we really are. I love Bob. Bob brings me into a place that no other man can bring me. He makes me feel loved for who I am as a person that belongs in the world, as part of the world; and as his partner, because he wants only good things for me and for us. He's a lot like my dad was that way. I love him because I can love myself much more when I'm with him than when I'm with any other man, even Carl. With the others I love myself because I love the whore I am and I love my own sexuality; but with Bob, I love myself because I love being alive and being part of life. I can't help it if all this seems complicated, David; but being a nympho is complicated. I'm not like most other women. I can't help it. I'm different, and I can't fight it. I don't want to fight it like I once did. I accept it. I'm okay with who I am. But you need to understand, I'm extremely sensitive to my feelings about sex and love making. And

the feelings I have for Bob and for Carl are very different feelings, honest."

"But you don't obsess over Bob, do you? I mean you wouldn't kill another woman over him like you would over Carl, would you?"

"No, I don't obsess over Bob, not now; because Barbara is staying away from him. But you know I want to kill her. I know she wants him; and I know he is her friend; and they enjoy talking together. And you know I don't like it." Marty pouted her little girl who can't have her way pout. "Bob is mine, David, and I don't want her anywhere around him."

"What if she quits or we fire her? Wouldn't that be easier than killing her?"

"No, that might be worse. Then she'd feel free to call him, meet him places. Outside of the Firm she'd have more freedom than in the Firm."

"Maybe she'll lose interest; or maybe he'll lose interest."

"That's not going to happen, David. They have this intellectual bond. It's strong. It's not going to go away."

"Well, I don't want you to kill her."

"I am going to kill her, David. I'm not putting up with her. You want my sales and the murders. She's what I want. I need to kill her."

"Okay, you can kill her, but not just yet, okay? I'll tell you when. I need to keep things the way they are for now, okay?"

"Okay, for now." Marty pouted again; but this time there was a twinkle in her eyes. She had hope. For the first time, David had agreed to let her kill Barbara. He just hadn't told her when.

"All right, then what is the attraction for Carl about? Can you explain that?"

"All right. Carl fills an addiction need for me. It's like how some people need a certain drug to keep them alive; well, I need Carl to keep my nymphomania satisfied. The relationship is that important.

It was so important I murdered his wife so she wouldn't interfere with it. If Bob was there sexually, the way Carl is, I suppose I could let Carl go, I don't know. I might want to keep Carl anyway. That way I'd have both of them. Bob doesn't have Carl's high level of sexuality yet. He's getting closer every time we make love, but he's not quite there. Bob and I orgasm well together, but I don't feel that same rocket ride up, or those sweet drifts into long-sustained orbits; or have my delightfully long, slow, dead silent to the world, reentry orgasms with Bob; like I always have with Carl. It's almost impossible for other men to get to Carl's sexual level. It's much harder for them to reach his level of sexual mastery than it is for them to get their Boy Scout badges or their corporate promotions. Carl has accomplished something miraculous. When his cock is inside me, I feel like I'm riding a massive Saturn Five rocket, way, way up into orbit. It's the biggest rocket ever made, and it keeps taking me up higher, forever. And I can ride it far away from Earth, way out into deep space, while I'm orgasming beautifully and continuously while I'm riding it; and then I'm orbiting Earth on it, touching all the stars in the universe. Carl is the greatest of lovers. He makes a woman feel the true meaning of the words those NASA astronaut's use when they say: 'GO FOR THROTTLE UP!'

"Bob is my best friend and my ultimate destiny lover. We go to shows, hike, ride horses, shoot clays, play tennis and golf together, all that sort of stuff. Bob's working hard learning his skills to become a great lover, while Carl is my perfectly finished partner. If Carl's sexuality could be in my NFL of sex, he'd be my league's most valuable player, year after year. He's fantastic at sex. But, like I said, I do not love Carl. I only love having sex with him. He doesn't make me feel like I'm part of the world and enjoying everything about the whole world, like the ways Bob does. Carl just makes me feel like I want to make love and continue making love, forever; until the end of time."

"*I had no idea your sex drive caused you to obsess this way. I now understand why Carl's wife drove you crazy. Her mere existence threatened to keep you from your addiction, didn't it?*"

"*Yes. I was terrified of losing the most wonderful cock and lover I've ever known.*"

"*So, there you were looking down at your mortal enemy. How were you feeling?*"

"*By then I had calmed down and collected my wits. My mind was calculating. It understood it was 'game on' in a mortal contest. I had already determined she deserved to die for interrupting my orgasm. I realize I sound harsh and capricious about her life, but I'm very sensitive about my orgasms. Her interruption infuriated me. Ending her life was the appropriate remedy for her transgression. If I didn't put an end to her nonsense that night, she'd likely repeat her same idiotic behavior. She was 'inscius pestis,' an ignorant pest. I wanted to be rid of her. I decided to make her pay with her life. I was confident that I would kill her that night; but I didn't yet know how.*"

"*You had said she first stood below you, looking up at you. Do you think your butterfly tattoo startled her, made her freeze?*" David's face was filled with curiosity.

"*Oh yes, seeing me displaying myself like that shocked her motionless. I was using my vagina to flaunt my iniquity, brazenly touching my lady lips; taunting her while smiling shamelessly down at her. When I knew I had captured her fascination, I decided to inflame her desires. I rubbed the poppy flower over my vagina; brought its petals up to my lips and kissed them. Then I mouthed a kiss to her. I intuited that would send her imagination soaring to prurient, forbidden places. I was confident that she could not have anticipated my seductive defiance of her persona and her morals. When she realized that I was inviting her to explore my pink valley; not merely confronting her, her lips trembled. That told me she was not the angered bully she pretended to be; not a real fighter; rather,*" *an uncertain soul with misdirected intentions. She had arrived expecting that I'd run away from her and hide. She believed she'd berate and bully Carl until he became sheepish and apologetic. She had imagined that she'd yank him out of the cabin, shove him into her car and scream at him during their entire drive home. She had never considered that I would boldly confront her assumptions. But I did. I faced her with my naked truth.*

"Her presumed scenario was not happening. Instead, the music of the Credo sounded softly in the background. It made her pause briefly, and consider that, by intruding, she might be the one who was behaving badly; intruding upon something beautiful. I stood on the deck, defiant and proud, while she walked toward the steps leading up to it. My music flowed melodiously from the opened cabin door. It seemed to pacify her. Her walk became less martial and more like that of a child being lulled along a fairy tale's fantasy path. She was hearing the haunting refrain: 'God from God, Light from Light, One Substance with the Father, begotten not Made.' She could just as well have been a neolithic pagan Druid, listening to the Credo's resonating notes being struck upon Stonehenge's blue worship stones. A countenance of wonderment came over her face. I witnessed the transformational effect of the music on her psyche. The savage heart within her had paused from its mission; deliberated whether it might allow itself to be seduced and tamed. My music combined with my vagina's taunting invitation had opened a tiny wedge in her preconceived beliefs. Awe and sexuality can have that effect on a person's limbic zone, David. Through her sliver of indecision, I witnessed her calculation. She considered that, possibly, I might have been placed before her by a higher being to confront her hidebound assumptions.

"Fear passed across her face. Suddenly, she was unsure of herself! Her limbic mind was considering the possibility of grasping my ass, savoring the juices of my inviting pink lips, and plunging her tongue deeply into my inviting pink canyon. Yes, I read her mind.

She fantasized about having oral sex with me. But she was conditioned to be afraid of that emotional need raging inside her. It conflicted her. My music suggested to her emotive mind that I was placed before her as a divine presence from some spiritual source; freely and shamelessly presenting her with my offer of immoral love. She didn't know how to process what her senses were signaling. My music was connecting her, Carl, and me, the three of us, together; telepathically. It was the harmonic bridge over which all our thoughts flowed simultaneously. My insight guided the initial formulation of my plan. I realized her suppressed limbic desire was a fatal weakness that I might exploit. I could use it to victimize her. If I succeeded, I could be rid of her. Showing off my sex, taunting her; teasing and tempting her by offering her imagination erotic possibilities would be my formula for undoing her. I would first establish my psychological dominance over her. That would prove to be a brilliant tactic.

"Please continue. Describe what happened between you two. Your mind fascinates me, Marty," said David.

"Sure, David, gladly; next I opened my sheer nightgown so she could see my naked body. Carl had slathered me in oils. My skin glistened in the moonlight. I knew I looked magnificent. My nakedness confirmed what I'm certain she imagined and feared; that I was a predatory shameless whore, with a stunningly beautiful face, packaged in a voluptuous, gorgeous, oil sheened body. Seeing her dumbfounded stare made me feel deliciously wicked. She saw I was far more desirable than she. Our eyes met. They glimpsed each other's' souls. I loved this unspoken moment. I sensed that she began fearing my powers. Her posture shifted slightly; from confident and confrontational to wary. Her one foot moved back a step; steadying her; slightly retreating; a clear signal that my strategy was working.

"I seized the initiative. I first needed to make it clear that I had my hooks deeply into her husband; and that I was never letting him go. My music looped to the Sanctus. I read her mind as she heard:

'Hosanna in the Highest, blessed is he who comes in the name of the Lord, and God of power and might.' My cathedral captured harmonics swept emotive chills through her body. Her conscious mind didn't know how to process my cascading signals. Her doubts about her mission and the wisdom of coming to my cabin, compounded. A sense of awe swept over her body. I saw it happen. She suddenly comprehended that she was in a precarious situation. She realized I was a determined iniquitous woman, unashamed and uncompromising about my wanton sexuality. Obviously, I was supremely confident in my seductive powers. Also, I brazenly flaunted my promiscuity. She saw I could not be buffaloed.

"Her eyes returned to my vagina. This time they gravitated there naturally, like they wanted to escape her reality, enter my valley, and live inside. They rested there and remained fixated. The image of my eyes had retained their place in her mind. She couldn't dismiss the image. It haunted her. She saw my butterfly tattoo; continued visualizing my eyes peering out from behind it. She stared at my invitation to have sex. It originated from my eyes behind my butterfly wings; sending its summons into her eyes. The duality of this image invited and challenged her soul to forsake all its beliefs and enter me. Her eyes next expressed fear. The image of my eyes behind my butterfly had challenged her beliefs; dared her to challenge me; dared her to intrude further into my life. Her conundrum showed on her face. Should she capitulate; abandon her ingrained beliefs and surrender her face to my vaginal lips; or should she physically attack and destroy the iniquitous whore standing defiant before her? Respect for my personage cautioned her. I felt it enter her soul and her heart at that very moment. Empathy for me, and the salacious unapologetic whore that I am, presented itself upon her face for the first time. That empathetic weakness would prove her downfall. I knew I held her mind in my own.

"Her limbic region's natural desires had made its first intrusion upon her willful thoughts. That revealed her emotional make up. In *poker, card players would call what her eyes betrayed a blink. I saw that blink. Beneath her bitter façade, this wretch needed someone to love her. Her emotional self desperately wanted to make love with me; but her conscious mind could not yet accept it. It was through that tiny crack in her composure, that I saw my pathway to her destruction.*

"I considered that I might anger the spirits if I believed too much in my own powers. But I returned to my thought that the small opening in her mind was revealed for a reason. The spirits awakened inside me. They encouraged my iniquities and offered their help. 'Could this really be happening?' I asked myself whether my mind could actually see into hers. 'Can I look inside her mind and go into it with my own thoughts, and discover her deepest, most well-kept secrets? Will my spirits reveal to me the ways to use those secrets to destroy her?' A warmth surge flooded my senses. I was blessed by a wonderfully evil essence deep within me. My confidence grew, knowing my wicked forces would guide me."

"You're saying this was your pivotal moment?" David's eyebrows rose.

"Yes, one of them. You see, David, once I knew my vagina captivated her and that her limbic zone had come to life, I realized I could control her mind. I knew I'd need to use a measured approach so she wouldn't suspect anything. I needed to abstractly visualize the hypnosis process to manage my own thoughts, while I simultaneously invaded hers."

"You needed to perform mental gymnastics to do this, didn't you?" David was sympathetic to Marty's challenge. He knew perfect murders were rare.

"Yes, but I was determined to work the problem. I used a mental trick to keep my mind focused and in control of my own thoughts. I imagined that her mind was a swimming pool filled with clear water's conscious thoughts, memories, and sound reasoning. I

knew that I needed to gain control of that uncontaminated mental space. I intended to gradually, imperceptivity, displace her pool of clear water's conscious thoughts with thoughts of wanton lust and debauchery. Black ink-colored water represented my suggestions and manipulations. I intended that the black ink water would pollute the clear water, giving me control of her mind. I imagined I'd do this by partitioning her mind's pool into tiny segments of one or two percent of the pool; then I'd go about stealthily, imperceptibly, replacing her mind's clear water's conscious thoughts within each segment with my black, ink sin water.

"Slowly, but surely, I would lead my wickedness through her mind's limbic passageways and remove rational reasoning from its most vulnerable compartments. Then, as her resistance to my black ink sin water retreated, I would make progressively greater inroads into her clear-thinking mind. My evil would advance like weeds choking a garden. My wickedness would initially seep into her mind, barely noticed. As my invasive process advanced, I expected that I'd make bigger and faster strides. Eventually, I'd displace ten, twenty, thirty percent increments of her mind's good, clear water with my sinful, inky darkness. Then, I'd race through her mind with purposeful, contaminating evil. I'd seized control of her entire mind. After her evil infested limbic zone had achieved dominance of her mind, and after I established my vagina as the essential, must-have object of her limbic desires, I'd then reveal my instructions to her."

"You are deliciously evil, Marty. I greatly respect your talents." David smacked his lips as if he were about to sit down to a feast.

"Thank you, David. It's quite simple to understand. It's like what happens to a person's mind that watches pornography. The more porn that's watched, the more addictive it becomes; until finally, thoughts of sex and love-making entirely crowd out the mind's other thoughts. It's escapism from reality and stress. And David, if you'd care to pause for a while, if there's anything you'd like me to give

you; anything at all, I'm more than willing. I'm eager to please you. I want you to know that."

"I appreciate that, Marty. You are extremely tempting; but, please, let's continue. This is incredibly fascinating to me. There's nothing I'd rather do than hear how you destroyed Carl's wife."

"As you wish, master. As I was explaining, I decided to destroy her and her ignorant fantasy world in a subtle, methodical way. I next pulled my opened nightgown away to one side of me. I turned my body to give her an unobstructed view of my hips. I wanted her to imagine how my hips often held and rocked her husband's cock. I wanted her to notice my perfect up-lilted breast mounds with my beautiful, protruding pink nipple buds. I believed when she saw my nipples, her impulse would be to kiss and suck them. I wanted her to imagine her tongue caressing my nipples. And I wanted her to feel dmoralized about her own sagging boobs."

"Marty, this is fabulous. Is this when you became confident that you could read her thoughts?"

"Yes, I believed I could read her like a book. I observed her closely. I believed I could visualize her thoughts racing wildly through her mind. As the Sanctus repeated on its continuous loop, I visualized her imaginings. Carl and I were standing in a naked embrace. Her mind was present in mine. I knew what she was thinking. She visualized Carl and me embracing each other in our arms; kissing lovingly. She saw his hands clutch my back and pull me close against him. She gaped as she imagined observing him fondling my breasts. She gawked, while she visualized his fingers pinch my nipples. She watched longingly while his hand glided across my stomach; then reached down lower, and lower still, until it touched my sex. Her breath quickened and her chest heaved when she imagined Carl putting his fingers inside me while the palm of his hand stimulated my vagina around its crown. Her imagination heard my squeals of naughty delight as her husband's lips found my inviting nipple buds.

*She heard more squeals and giggles as Carl kissed and bit my nip-
ples; softly, adoringly. She wished hers were the lips that were kissing my nipples. Her mind next heard my lust moans for Carl's cock
while I pressed my breasts into his mouth, encouraging his tongue to
play over my nipples; bite them, tease, and tug them.*

"Her imagination heard me whispering to Carl that I wanted
him to love me all night long, as I ran my fingers through his hair
and over his muscular shoulders. Then her mind opened in wonder
as I pressed my vagina against his thigh and took his erect cock into
my hands. She visualized me lead him onto my bed; watched my
mouth kiss, suck, and lick his shaft while I stroked his cock with my
fingers. She imagined seeing Carl kiss my stomach, as a prelude to
the joys he would soon give me. She wished that she was the one
kissing my stomach. And she wished that she, not her husband, was
about to explore my vagina with her tongue. Yes, David. I could
read her mind. It tumbled through endless chasms of her imaginings; racing fast."

Carl's hapless wife, meanwhile, stood before Marty. Her mouth
was agape with her thinking:

'I never expected her to look like this. Prostitutes are supposed
to walk dark streets, do their quicky sex tricks in cars, or work in
their tiny crib rooms out of seedy, hourly room-rate houses. But this
woman is a different kind of whore. She's an officer of a major company. They must sanction what she does. Sexually, she is more of a
wife to Carl than I am. She gets to do all the fun things and go to the
fun places with him and I get stuck with the bills and the drudgery.

'My God, please help me! What has Carl gotten us into with
this immoral whore? She's so casual and shameless about what she's
doing! She acts like I'm the one who is out of place. Her skin! It's
creamy soft; nearly translucent. There's not a single blemish on her
body. She's beautiful; actually, she's stunningly gorgeous. And the
way her breasts stand up, proudly and pronounced, make them*

delicious looking. And her nipples and her beautiful nipple buds! Now, I see. Carl loves to squeeze her breasts with both his hands. He kisses her luscious nipples like a baby seeks its mother's milk.

'And her vagina with its tattoo! It's stunning; beautiful! It makes my mouth water. It's plumped up, too. They were having sex when I drove up. I interrupted them. That's why Carl is not coming out. He's too embarrassed. Heaven, help me! Forget Carl. I feel captivated by her vagina! I can't take my eyes off it. It's inviting. I'd love to kiss it. I'm sure she does women. After all, she is a whore. I wonder whether she knows what I'm thinking? It's hard to not give her a signal. If she discovers I want her, I'll lose all control. I'll never get Carl back.

'God, give me strength! It's hard to not let her know how I really feel. I'm tired; but I could forget my weariness if I could only kiss her. That would be heavenly. But I can't let her know what I'm thinking. I must get Carl back. I need him to pay our bills. They mount higher and higher. He sends our money to her! Damn, she is remarkably beautiful. It's hard to blame Carl for this situation. I want her, too. But I must be brave. She cannot know my real feelings.'

"She imagined Carl moving his head lower and lower until his tongue found my vagina," Marty continued. "She was awestruck by her own dreams of cunnilingus. That drew her limbic mind into our world; mine, and Carl's. She desired to join the two of us. She imagined her naked body, not Carl's, lay next to me; and her tongue, not her husband's, kissed my vagina's outer lips. She imagined seeing Carl tease my vagina's crown and inner lips with his fingers. She imagined it was her tongue, not Carl's, that discovered my clitoris, found it eager and welcoming, and licked me there; and that her hands lifted my tush, holding my vagina closely to her mouth, not Carl's hands. She dreamily wished that I yearned for her tongue touches instead of Carl's.

"I watched eroticism sweep over her entire being. Her resolve to confront me was melting. Her mind was torturing itself. She wanted

to kiss my vagina; discover my clitoris; slather it with her tongue; and release her pent-up desires. I could read her thoughts as they turned carnal. She wanted to plant her face between my legs. She imagined her tongue gliding over my clitoris; vibrating against its sides and touch teasing its base."

"Were you trying to dash her hopes at this point? How dark were her thoughts?"

"It was too soon to crush her hopes, David; that had to wait. I imagined her limbic zone was ten percent invaded by my dark forces; but on her conscious level, she knew the possibility of losing her marriage was real. She was already aware that she could not simply order me to stop my immoral liaison with her husband. She swallowed hard a couple times. It was an awkward moment for her. Her Adam's apple moved noticeably. She literally choked on the sexual things she imagined I did with her husband. I noticed her hand trembled. "

"A tremor? She had a disease?"

"No, she was only losing her composure. Her nerves gave her away. She was distraught and frightened. Her conscious mind wanted to run from my reality. It wanted escape to another world. But her limbic forces held her feet in place. They made her stay. By staying, she signaled that she was sex deprived; and captivated by her fantastical thought that she might, somehow, become my lover.

"She imagined tasting my valley's juices, like Carl does when he tickles the base of my clitoris with his tongue tip. She visualized holding me tenderly, while I writhed from her finger stimulation. She fantasized hearing my moans of ecstasy when my orgasms began. She dreamed of sharing my inner tingles with me, while my hands guide Carl's huge throbbing cock into my welcoming vagina.

"Can one woman know another woman's feelings like that?"

"Oh yes, David. Absolutely. We are much more emotive than men. When a sister feels strong emotions, we're right there, feeling

them along with her. Our limbic zones are extremely sensitive. When we're aroused, our feelings release like unstoppable Tsunami waves. When her jaw dropped, I knew she had opened the gates of her limbic zone. She unwittingly welcomed my Trojan Horse to pass through her protective façade. My sexuality was her faux gift. And now it was inside her mind. I could unleash my invasion. She was tired from her long drive. Her eyelids were heavy. She needed sleep. Her defenses were compromised. I felt emboldened to accelerate my stimulations; stress her sensibilities, and make her resistance crumble. I summoned my most shameless, iniquitous powers. I willed my wanton promiscuity to enter her mind and run wild inside it. I intended to ravage her sensibilities, purge them from her consciousness. And replace them with my forces of immoral lust and desire. Then, I would destroy her.

"Appreciate what she saw, David. The flames from the cabin's fireplace silhouetted me through the partially opened door. I widened my stance a little further. I signaled that I was proud, unapologetic, and shameless about ruining her marriage. I messaged that I was brazen; thoroughly immoral. I would not compromise. I would not retreat from my illicit behaviors."

Seeing Marty's wider stance and shadows of the cabin's fireplace flames licking at her vagina, Carl's wife had thoughts of her own:

'What a delicious peach! I'm certain she's even juicier than a peach. She's flaunting. Is that an invite to kiss her? How else should I take her signal? Should I? Dare I? Should I throw away all hope of retrieving Carl; just go to her; stand before her and drop to my knees; kiss her lady lips? That would be so out of my character, and against everything I represent. But it would shock her.

'No, I cannot. I must restrain myself. She represents everything my upbringing instructed me to avoid. My parents and my priests all warned me that women like her are evil. I must not give in. But she

is beautiful. And so naturally casual about her immorality! I want her. Maybe I could touch my tongue to her vaginal lips, just to see how I'll feel. No, I can't do that! What am I thinking? I MUST resist her. I must stay strong.'

"I wanted her limbic zone to identify with my own," continued Marty to David. "I played a mind game with her. I wanted her to imagine that she, too, could become an immoral whore. My darkness was invading all the reaches of her mind. Her limbic thoughts were capitulating. My opened, shapely legs were silhouetted on the cabin's wall. The flickering, fireplace flames made dark shadows that leaped and lapped at my tantalizing vagina. She envisioned the flames to be reaching, lusting tongues. They licked upward, kissing my wanton cock-obsessed vagina from below. The dark shadows and dancing flames made my vaginal lips appear to be on fire. In the glowing shadowy twilight darkness, my flaming lips tempted her tongue to quench her hot desire. She imagined herself reclined beneath me. Her tongue gained her nirvana, the inner lips of my lust-seething valley. In her voyeur's mind, it explored, tasted, and savored every facet of my insatiable wantonness. It treasured all its touches that pleasured me.

"I gave her a huge, widemouthed smile, acknowledging those first words she had uttered from her awestruck expression. Her face was filled with wonderment, like an innocent child's who believed she had discovered the Easter Bunny.

'Why, yes, of course I am a whore. Did you expect to come here and meet an ingénue?'

"I chuckled, confidently. I knew the best answer to her truth was to acknowledge it; and not show shame in it, but pride."

"Did she answer you?" David's smile was wide. His eyebrows lifted. Marty's story intrigued his predatory nature.

"No, David, she was too intimidated. She was speechless. I decided to establish control over her, like a spider does when it wraps *silken threads around the fly tangled in its web. I talked to her in a lowered confidential voice, like I was sharing a closely held, girl-to-girl secret. I needed her to understand that I was an unapologetic, no nonsense, businesswoman. My dark forces next made a deliberate verbal push against the clear conscious portion of her mind.*

'But,' I said, 'I'm not some cheap, two-bit whore. I'm a very high-class, expensive whore. I'm also shameless. And I'll be your worst nightmare if you don't behave yourself.'

"At that point, her conscious mind fought back. She summoned her resistance and started marching up the steps, like a true trooper.

'Get out of my way,' she ordered, as she tried to brush past me and enter the cabin through its door. Her conscious mind was making a mighty try to forcibly resist me. It pushed back hard against my dark invasion forces; but I didn't take this response seriously. I saw her effort as more of a gesture than an actual challenge. She needed to prove to herself that she could resist her temptation, even if it was only to perform this symbolic feint.

"I put my hands on her shoulders and gave her a gentle push backward. That startled her. I raised my voice, implying a threat.

'You need to understand a few things,' I said. 'You can see, can't you, that I'm the women, that whore, your husband loves to be with, not you? See my skin? It's soft and lovely.'

"I rubbed my hand over my cheek and neck and sides. I wanted her to imagine her husband's hand stimulating my erogenous zones. I lifted my breast and smiled to her; then I lowered my hand to my stomach; and finally, brought it to rest over my vagina."

"Didn't she push you back or swing at you?"

"No David. She was too startled and dissembled. She looked frightened. I read fear in her eyes. And I noticed that her lower lip also trembled. I knew my dark invasion forces were now ensconced in her mind. They had their beachhead from which they could *attack her innocence. Her failure to attack me, or even utter a single word in response, signaled her gaping vulnerability. She was wide open to my advancing evil forces. I sensed she had no fight in her. When a fly gives up fighting, it no longer lifts its wings. That's when the spider puts tightening wraps around the fly. I smiled and looked deeply into her eyes. My eyes told her that I knew she could not win. Her attempt to bully me had fallen flat. Instead, I had broken her resolve and made her question her very womanhood. My dark forces were rapidly overwhelming her resistance. It was time to tighten my control over her."*

Meanwhile, Carl's wife had her own thoughts:

'I'm glad she stopped me. I'm glad she's taking control of me. I'd rather sit here and stare into her beautiful vagina, letting my imagination explore the depths of her sinful wonders, than go into the cabin and have a shouting match with Carl. I can shout at Carl when he comes home; but for now, I just want to hear this gorgeous whore talk to me while I contemplate her lovely vagina. I wonder, does she have any idea how much I want to make love with her? What would she do if I pulled her vagina against my face? No, stop! You must stop thinking that way. You must not think evil thoughts.'

Marty continued describing her seduction to David:

"Your husband loves touching his hands over my entire body,' I said to her. 'He touches me everywhere; and he caresses me like this.' I slowly rubbed my hands over my vagina while I spoke: 'I'm the woman who gets massages from a personal masseuse, paid for by your husband. That keeps me feeling good about myself, and keeps my skin looking soft and beautiful. I'm the woman he takes on out-of-town trips to theater shows and fine dining. He buys furs and fine dresses for me. He buys exotic lingerie and expensive perfumes for me. He also pays for my hairdresser, my manicurist, and my pedicurist.'

"As I spoke, I felt my dark forces pushing her resistance forces back further, invading an additional ten percent of her innocence. I studied her expressions. Her facial muscles had slackened. That was her dead giveaway. She beheld me in wonder. Her resistance had badly faltered. It was mortally weakened. She was succumbing.

"I continued to pressure her." Marty recalled the words that the voice of Miss Iniquity spoke to her at this point:

'Why waste your time toying with this wretched bitch? She doesn't belong here interfering with us. She's rude. She doesn't know her place. She has no respect for others, or even for herself. How can it be that people as disgusting as her are even allowed to exist?'

"Slowly, inexorably, David, I felt my resentment give way to a feeling of vicious darkness and visceral hatred. I lost all human feelings and empathy for her. This fresh evil birthed in my soul. It awakened within me, stealthily entered my mind, and took possession of me. I welcomed it. I needed its strength to absolve my conscience for what I was about to do to her.

'We will murder her, together.' Marty remembered how the voices of Misses Hatred and Iniquity assured her of success:

'We will destroy this impertinent intruder,' declared Miss Iniquity.

'We will do it perfectly. You will leave no trace of your murderous deed; and you will feel no guilt about it,' affirmed Miss Hatred. Hearing Miss Hatred's voice gave Marty a boost of confidence. The voice reassured her that she was not crazy. Getting rid of Carl's wife was not only doable; it was likely; and the murder would be a successful one. Miss Hatred never equivocated; never wavered; was always supremely confident; always selectively focused her beam of wrath upon one person; never broadcasted it like a shotgun's scattering pellets. Miss Hatred's voice was not the same as Marty's other voices which arose out of her head, and which often

gave her conflicting advice. Miss Hatred's voice was deadly serious. It came from within Marty's bones.

"David, that woman had no inkling about how evil I could be; or that I was capable of murder. I decided to first complete my dark invasion of her mind; then control and direct it; and finally use her own demented mind to blot out her life. I rinsed my thoughts clean of her, much like an Aztec priest would wash his hands clean, to absolve himself of personal responsibility before he murdered his victim in the name of his gods. I despised her; but I could not let that emotion interfere. I had to lay the blame for this on abstract, mysterious forces. I needed to be measured as I went about this; and I needed to stay in control. If a murder isn't cold blooded and calculated there are greater chances of mistakes. I needed to first advance my dark invasion methodically. I continued my taunts, studying her expressions as I spoke:"

'When we go to the opera or the theater,' I said, 'or to fine restaurants, Carl always makes sure everything is first-class. He always holds my chair and seats me comfortably. He always opens my car door and he always drives the car to the door for me. He just bought me a new BMW convertible to honor me and celebrate our second year together. Does that surprise you?'

"She just stood there, duly informed that her stunt of throwing paint on my old car had backfired."

'He's a wonderful gentleman. He appreciates being with a beautiful, profligate whore. Now do you understand your husband?'

Meanwhile, Carl's wife was thinking:

'I believe she hates me. She wants me to go away. I wonder if she'd change her hatred and her mind if I summoned the courage to kneel and kiss her vagina? Would that shock her? Would that change her hatred to love? But I can't do that. That would be so wrong. Daddy and Mommy would be so displeased with me. I'd fail my

upbringing. I'd give in to my urges. They told me never to do that. I cannot fail them. I must be strong. I must be stronger than she is!'

"She didn't answer my last question," Marty continued with David. *"She didn't have to. I took a measure of her face. It told me I was shredding her world into ribbons. She was reeling inside. My truths clawed at her guts."*

'Get out of my way!'

"Her voice was choked and pained now. Her outburst was laughable. She knew she was in trouble. She tried to step around me. I gauged my dark forces now controlled twenty percent of her struggling mind."

'I'm not getting out of your way,' I said. 'I'm not going anywhere and you're not going inside. I own this cabin and you're not welcome here.'

"She needed that factual reality check, David. People often assume that whores have no rights; that we live in dark shadows, like we're cockroaches or something; but we're just normal well-adjusted people with the same rights as righteous moralizing types. My community covenants said I had the right to invite guests, and I had the right to privacy. I wasn't about to let her invade my privacy or brush away my rights. Her husband and I were consenting adults. We had every right to enjoy each other as we pleased."

"Did she understand that? Did she know you had rights? What did you do when she tried to get around you?" David's eyes flashed curious.

"I doubt if she had any concept of contracts or legalities, David. Her tiny mind stripped its gears. There I was, telling her to her face that I had every right to be in my cabin, fucking her husband; and, there was absolutely nothing she could do about it. You should have seen the expression on her face, David. Ha! I loved it. I gave her tiny mind mental whiplash. I thought my brief explanation gained my dark forces another ten percent control of her mushy mind. I stepped

directly in front of her. That let her know I intended to guard our pri-vacy. My raised chin implied I'd hit her if she persisted. She stopped and stood there, frozen. She felt helpless and stymied. I think that's when she realized she was dumber than a tree stump. I looked her up and down with scorn to make her feel even more worthless; but I talked to her to keep her engaged. My tone conveyed that I knew she was incredibly stupid:

'Just look at yourself,' I said. 'You wear polyester jackets and torn dungarees. You wear your hair like you're a forgotten war orphan. It's no wonder Carl can't stand you!'"

Carl's wife's mind spoke its silent thoughts again:

'Oh, she's humiliating me now, like I'm not worthy of her. If she only knew how easily I could fall in love with her; maybe then she'd accept me? But I must resist her. I must continue to be strong. But, oh my God, I notice I'm salivating. I want to kiss her vagina so badly. I wonder, can she notice how horny I feel?'

CHAPTER THREE

Boys will be boys, and even that wouldn't matter if we could pre-vent girls from being girls (Sir Anthony Hope Hopkins: The Daily Dialogs)

TAUNTING AND TEMPTING

Then Miss Shameless whispered to Marty:

'Taunt her some more,' she said. 'Shove your sex appeal in her face. She won't be able to withstand the humiliation. She'll crack.'

"I listened to my instincts, David. I put my hands under my breasts and cupped them higher, proudly lifting them a little. 'Take a good look at my perfectly smooth breasts,' I said. 'Your husband loves holding them. He loves pinching and sucking my picture-perfect nipples, too. He sends chills through my entire body while he plays foreplay games with my nipples. You wouldn't know about nipple foreplay techniques, would you? He told me he hates the sight of your sagging boobs. That's true, isn't it? Admit it. I know it's true. He's told me everything about you.'

"She didn't answer me. She was shocked. I figured my evil darkness was now up to forty percent control of her mind. Her resistance was in shambles. I sensed I could go faster."

'That threw her way off balance,' Miss Shameless coached Marty. 'You have the initiative. Now, mock her righteous indignation. Walk all over her sensibilities. Humiliate her.'

"My instincts were working, David. Her mind was reeling and off-balance, so I continued my taunts: 'While I'm sitting on Carl's lap, making love with my back to him, he wraps his arms around me and holds my breasts. He loves squeezing my nipples.' For effect, I pinched my buds and stretched them outward an inch. 'He's special that way. He loves giving me pleasure! How do you feel knowing he'd rather give pleasure to a whore than to you?'

"Did she answer you?" asked David.

"No, she wasn't answering my questions. She just stood there. She was numbed by her new reality."

'I squeal when he pinches my nipples,' I continued, 'I can tell he loves hearing me experiencing erotic delight, because his cock gets even harder. Sometimes that alone gives me an orgasm. When I sit on Carl's lap, facing him while we make love, he always sucks my nipples. He loves sucking them. They fascinate him. He kisses them and plays his tongue over them while he squeezes my breasts. I tingle with desire when he gets my nipples hard like that. While he kisses my neck and French kisses me, he tells me I have beauty queen breasts and flawless, button nipples. He tells me he's in love with my tits. He doesn't compliment your breasts, does he?'

Carl's wife thought without answering:

'Yes, damn you. You have gorgeous breasts. I'd love to suckle you. I'd love to kiss your whoring vagina and crawl into your bed. I'm falling in love with you, but don't you understand me? I can't let that happen. I just can't!'

"Without speaking she raised her palms to her eyes and covered her face, as if in prayer. She shook her head hoping her dismay would disappear."

'Push her until you get a reaction,' coached Miss Shameless to Marty that fateful day.

"When she looked out from her palms, I slow twerked my hips and tugged again on my nipples. That drew a new picture for her.

Carl's penis was inside me, thrusting rhymically with my twerks. He was straining himself to give me all the love he has, to please me in his most ultimate, intimate way, while also stimulating my buds. The image of two impassioned lovers, fornicating animal-like, finally got her fighting mad. She tried pushing back. She had to sense that I now controlled more than fifty percent of her thoughts. She raised her hand to hit me as she prepared to speak; but I knew she was bluffing. I was three inches taller and much better muscled than her. I didn't flinch. She didn't really want to hit me. She slowly dropped her hand. Her jaw went slack again. She stared in dazed wonder at my vagina. Her thoughts became frantic:

'I desperately want to kiss her vagina; but I must not give in to temptation. I must despise her and her vagina for what has happened to my marriage and my life!'

"Her face told me she didn't know whether to love me or hate me. A latent passion had awakened within her. It neutered her hateful vengeance. It was causing her feelings to commit treason against her sensibly ordered world. Confusion swirled wildly through her mind."

Carl's wife's mind protested with one silent feeble thought:

'Please stop. You're torturing me. You're killing me by behaving this way. Can't you see I could love you more than Carl loves you; but I can't let my love show itself? I can't, Marty. I just can't. I want you. I want my tongue to live inside your glorious sex pot. I want to be with you, holding you in my embrace, while you're fucking someone every day. I adore you, you glorious magnificent whore. I wish I could prove that to you, but I don't know how to do that. Please stop taunting me! I'm conflicted! Can't you see I'm about to have a breakdown and start crying? I can't let that happen. I just can't! I must keep up my brave front.'

"She never did hit you, did she?" David's eyes twinkled, lifting his smile. Clearly, Marty's behaviors and sales methods pleased him. His top employee's calloused immorality made him prideful.

He respected her devious character trait. He nurtured and praised it, doing everything he could to enhance and strengthen it. She was, albeit female, David's ideal conceptual protégé. Her treatment of others was like his own core behavioral drivers. Marty was a user. She understood how to use others; knew that was the key to success. And, with every passing day, David could see how she was sharpening her skill sets. Hurting others in a remorseless, sinister sort of way; objectively, unfeelingly observing her victims' anguished pains; sensing their desperate feelings of hopelessness: these were the macabre sorts of pleasures that David had, since his childhood, relished and nourished himself. And now, at last, he had Marty with him. Finally, another kindred soul, whose blood coursed thoughts like his own, had joined with him, building his firm; another, much like him in so many ways, who sought the same psychic pleasures as his own, working alongside him, making every working day a delightful happenstance.

Now, hearing Marty's exploits; savoring her absence of remorse; her formulations and refinements of her intents; listening to her recount her methodical destruction of Carl's wife; appreciating how she sharpened her annihilation focus throughout the entire process; and recognizing how Marty's destruction of this foolish woman resulted in yet another salesman's capitulation to Marty's demands for more sales, thrilled David to no end. He understood that all of Marty's efforts ultimately inured to his personal benefit. One might think that David would open the floodgates of gratitude to his protégé; rejoice with her over her successful crime; even become intimate with her and share Firm ownership with her. But that was not fated to be. There was an inner kernel in David's soul that cautioned him to hold back; never give more than necessary; never gild a lily, as he termed it. That would not be David.

"Nope," Marty answered David as Miss Shameless refreshed her memory:

'Can you recall that moment?' Miss Shameless whispered: *'Her stare signaled she lusted after you; otherwise, she would have hit you. Possibly she was praying for you. Can you remember? I think she imagined herself making love with you!'*

'You're disgusting. I want my husband,' Carl's wife said meekly. She didn't sound like she meant it. *'I'm warning you,'* she spoke with her uncertain, already defeated voice, *'if you don't stand aside, I'll—'* she said, then stopped speaking for a loss of words. The air escaped from her voice.

Miss iniquity caught the wife's uncertainty: *'I believed her spirit fled the fight.'* She whispered to Marty.

"*I interrupted her right away,*" Marty recalled to David. "*I wasn't about to give an inch in this confrontation, so I called her bluff. 'You'll what?' I asked, 'Will you hit me? Don't try that, sweetie. I'll slap you back. You don't want that.'*

"*She moved back a half step. She knew she didn't want to hit me and she especially didn't want me to hit her, either. She decided to submit to my dominance.*

'She does not want to hit you. SHE is falling in love with YOU. The limbic portion of her mind doesn't care about Carl. He is just her meal ticket. This evidences that her limbic mind has wrested control from her conscious mind!' Miss Iniquity's voice correctly assessed the situation.

"*Slowly, smiling my friendly invitation to her, I suggestively rubbed my vagina, using my first two fingers to partially open and pleasure myself. I was playing a subtle game with her mind. Her trained rigid mind was now in full retreat. Her limbic commands had overtaken her hostility. Her facial muscles had slackened. Staring dreamily at my parted lady lips, she whetted her lips; her breathing quickened.*

"*Temptation happened between us. A harmonic resonance was taking place between our bodies. We were crystal goblets, struck by a tuning fork, singing identical notes. Rhythms of lust flowed freely between our body cells. We heard our desires urging us onward. I felt a silent elegance about that moment. I absorbed her wistful feelings, all the while knowing I was going to shatter her fantasy crystal world. She sucked her cheeks in, to gather up her saliva and swallow. Her facial expressions cried out from her imprisoned soul. She badly wanted to have sex with me. That was obvious now. She would gladly depart from her intended goal if she could have an illicit liaison with me. I knew my dark forces had pushed her reasoning ability into retreat."*

Carl's wife's mind sensed a similar change in Marty:

'She must know I love her and I want her. I think she understands my conflict. Oh, goodness, what can I do? I can't give in to her; and even if I did, I'm not sure she'd want me. She might be happier if I simply went away and died or something. Maybe that's what I'll have to do to resolve my conflict and let her know how I truly, deeply love her. I admire her for being a whore and not letting herself get trapped into a world that doesn't understand her, like I've let myself get trapped. She's everything I'd love to be, but I can't be like her. I just can't. I must be strong. I must be!' The incredible power of neurosis was deeply ingrained in Carl's wife's psyche. It was a hurdle too high. She could not overcome it. It held her back. She was like a harnessed animal, unable to take what Marty offered; unable to take what she wanted.

"I controlled our sexual signaling. That was hard because I am extremely promiscuous; but by keeping my focus, I managed it. While her limbic system was taking control of her mind, I forced my own limbic system into submission. My business mind reminded me I needed to get rid of her. Carl gives me money and sales. She doesn't.

"If I allowed her to join us; enter the cabin for a threesome, I realized that Carl might possibly want both me and his marriage. I couldn't risk him backsliding into some idiotic notion about

reclaiming their trashed love. I had worked too hard wrecking that love. I needed to keep his marriage off the table. I quickly dismissed my wayward fanciful thought of a possible threesome. My gambit was to continue teasing her hopes of having sex with me, while simultaneously reminding her sensible mind, what little remained of it, to reject it. By being brazen, I figured I could shock her back into her sensibilities whenever I needed to. While being licentious, I knew I could penetrate her refined propriety, partner with her limbic mind, and directly appeal to her prurient impulses. I continued with this back-and-forth strategy, alternatively appealing to her primal lusts, then taunting and belittling her to control them. It was similar to the methods that trainers use with circus animals. It's tried and true. It develops the desired behavior. I used my body language and words to alternate her rewards and punishments instead of carrots and prods."

"You played mind games with her, didn't you?" chuckled David.

"Yes, and what delicious mind games they were! I walked a very fine line between making her want me as a lover and making her feel revulsion over everything about me; and, ultimately, through transference, revulsion over her own life. And all the while I did this, I coaxed her lust up; way, way up, to higher and higher peaks.

'Look closely at my delicious love muffin,' I said. I casually grinned, smacking my lips, as I rubbed myself, overtly flaunting my sexuality. I shamed her. She saw my vagina was blushed with blood redness. It was slightly swollen from my recent intercourse with her husband. I imagined that her vulva was lifeless as a dead fish. My vagina was inviting, sensuous, freshly fucked, and semen filled. I shamelessly dribbled semen and smiled confidently into her eyes. I emphasized my shameless pride in my whoring. She needed to see that adulterous sexual relations are a matter-of-fact aspect of my life, and that I felt no shame about it.

'This is what you're up against. Take a really, good look!' I taunted her with a confident laugh. 'Your husband begs to kiss my tasty lips. Imagine taking a delicious, juicy peach into your own mouth. That taste is what your husband loves about me. Can you imagine what I taste like? Notice how I'm smoothly waxed. He loves me soft and smooth that way. He buries his face in me without the slightest hesitation. He begs, like a little boy, to slide his penis into me.'

At this same time, Carl's wife nodded while her thoughts swirled:

'Yes, you are a luscious whore. If you only knew how sweetly my tongue would treat your clit. If you knew how deeply I feel for you, you wouldn't tempt me. Please be as brazen as your talk. Take my head in your hands and pull my face into your sweetness. Then I could justify my surrender to you. I could tell myself that it was impossible to resist. But, don't you see? I can't be the aggressor. I can't be the one to start this. I must be strong for my upbringing and my family values. You're the professional here. You must dominate me! Please, help me. Please, take me. Take my head and pull my face into your luscious pink. I want your peach juice all over my face. I want to taste you. I want you so badly, I tremble for you. What more do you want? Tell me. I'll do anything.'

"She gave an almost imperceptible nod of her head as I continued chiding her," Marty related every detail of the ensuing events to David:

'See my soft inviting crown and my outer lips? I rub my upper thighs and lady lips with a mixture of baby oil, gardenia, and lavender oils, and drops of Chanel No. 5 and sandalwood every day. Carl adores my scent.'

"I spread my legs and tilted my pelvis upward to show her my Monarch butterfly tattoo with its wings flared open. Seeing how I appeared in the missionary position; she took a deep breath. I smiled *and let a tiny, teasing giggle escape. I held my sex open with my fingers, revealing the same signal that I give Carl.*

"She needed to present a brave front. She sharpened her voice in a last-ditch threatening way:

'I'm not going to stand here looking at your cunt; you sick whore,' she said. A slight tremble betrayed her. She couldn't hide the stresses she felt. 'Get out of my way, damn you. You disgust me.' My spread legs had provoked her a second time. Her reaction proved my taunts worked. My darkness was assuming full control of her. Her mind was almost completely mine.

"Again, she tried stepping around me. This time I pushed her back with one hand, while holding my other hand over my vagina. She didn't resist. She relaxed. I could tell she welcomed feeling my other hand resting upon her shoulder. My enslavement of her mind took a firm hold. Her ability to think clearly was lost. She could no longer think for herself. She sought guidance from me, like a confused child looks to its parent. She didn't know what to do. I told her:

'Now listen,' I said in a confidential tone, 'you're going to learn something.'

"I lowered my voice as if giving a tutorial to a child. She stared at my vagina, stunned, as if her head was struck by a brick. She knew she had a serious problem. She realized she would not be taking Carl home with her; but she had yet to comprehend her marriage was irreparably destroyed. My next step was to completely demoralize her."

"You played her like a fiddle, didn't you, Marty?" David leered. He had no respect for victims. He sensed he was getting close to the moment of the wife's destruction.

"Yes, David. I was more like a matador or a spider, both deceptively deadly. But playing her like a fiddle, marching her to oblivion, also describes what I did:

'I place a touch of oils mixed with gardenia and lilac on my vagina's inner lips,' I told her. I didn't mind sharing my seduction secrets, since I planned to murder her. 'My scent is like catnip. It drives Carl crazy with lust. He says he can never get enough of me. Has he ever spoken to you that way?'

"She shook her head slightly. She was stunned by that sharp contrast. Carl, never once, had ever spoken complimentary words about her sexuality."

'Would you like to know more about my incorrigible sex-crazed vagina?' I asked her. I refused to dignify her use of the word cunt.

"She froze and stared at my vagina, fearful of what I'd say next. I intuited that it was time to crush her self-esteem.

'Well, for starters, I really love sex. I absolutely adore the sensations I feel while having a man's cock inside me,' I said, mocking her diminished libido. 'I especially crave Carl's cock. He gets it. He loves my insatiable appetite for sex. I guess you could say we have a symbiotic relationship. And, did you know that he has a secret name for my vagina's clitoris? He does! He calls her Gloria! He's told me he wants to divorce you and marry me. Did you know that? Has he ever told you that? Imagine that! Even though he knows that I do lots of other men and make pornographic movies, he'd still rather be married to me than you. Isn't that amazing? How does that make you feel, now that you know that my whoring vagina means more to him than you and your marriage? My loving Gloria owns your Carl. Wait! Did I say your Carl? I meant my Carl.' I laughed my taunting in her face; giggled to inform her that her situation was ridiculous."

Carl's wife's mind had thoughts of its own at this time, thoughts that it could no longer contain:

'Yes, I understand that your vagina owns my husband. So, please stop taunting me. Can't you see? I know you love fucking. Your vagina owns me too, now. I love you, you incorrigible whore. Anything! Just stop this game. Tell me what you want from me! I'll

do anything you ask. But please, stop taunting me. I'm about to have a breakdown.'

"My revelation about Carl's infatuation with my vagina got her attention. It's amazing, David; hearing a man's innermost thoughts during pillow talk. She gasped. She knew she heard the truth. She knew Carl had confessed to me; his adoration of my vagina; of me and my immoral lifestyle; that he wanted that lifestyle for himself, all of it; accepting me and my other lovers; my pornography; all of it; all of me. She hung her head in shame. Her eyes welled up with tears.

'Please, stop. I've heard enough,' she whimpered. 'I don't want to hear any more about your whoring.'

"She spoke in a dignified manner as if she was an upper-class country club's pampered poodle. And she was, before I took Carl for my lover. But she couldn't recover the past. Not now that I made her face reality. It was too late to move the conversation back to an earlier, safe place. My darkness now controlled nearly all her mind. I sensed her defeat was near. I reminded myself that I couldn't allow myself to pity her. She started this confrontation. I needed to finish what I started. I needed to totally destroy her. I meant to take her life from her; rid myself of her. I sensed I could."

"Oh Marty," sighed David. "I know why I adore you like I do. You love being cruel, don't you? Is this when you plunged your knife into her?"

"Yes David, when the situation requires, I can be cruel and hurtful. Do you want to hear more? I'm coming to the best part. I hate to disappoint you, David, but I didn't use my knife. That's what made this murder perfect. I'd like you to hear all of it. Then you can grade me on how I did, okay?"

"Oh, yes, Marty. I want to know every little detail. I love this. I can even feel her pain. You know how I love seeing people in pain."

"Gladly, David," continued Marty.

"'Look,' I said to her, 'You're the one who drove up here. You wanted to see if your husband was having sex with another woman. Well, I'll show you!'

"I rubbed my vagina with a circular motion again, while smiling at her with a full, joyful smile. I laughed a little belly laugh, to taunt her more. I treated her like the imbecile she was. I imagined my darkness now controlled ninety percent of her mind.

"'Can you understand that I love making love for the sheer pleasure of it? I'm addicted to love making. Carl pays me because he knows I love to make love. That's important to him. He loves pleasing me, too. That makes our times together wonderful. He always wants more of me. He's addicted to me like I'm addicted to making love. It's a perfect arrangement. You'll never change it.'

"She stared, dumbfounded, at my vagina. I knew I commanded her full attention. I continued speaking slowly, tauntingly. I wanted my darkness to reach the one hundred percent invasion level. I wanted complete dominance of her mind.

"'Your husband lives to make intimate love with me. I know that makes your life a living hell; but honestly, I don't care, and I won't stop. He's addicted to me. So, get this straight. He's not coming back to you. Not ever! He's mine. He loves me.'"

Carl's wife's mind was in full retreat:

'I've lost everything. I know it. And you don't want me. I know you don't. I don't know what I can do to make you want me. I'm worth nothing. I know that. I know I've lost Carl. I can't stop feeling the pain of all this. I'm losing control of my mind. I must not give up. I must force myself to try to get Carl. He's my only hope; but I don't think he wants me. Maybe he'll pity me if I go to him. I'll wait for the right moment. I'll try again.

'I implore you. Stop this. Please, stop.' she cried. "She hurt inside. Her chest felt crushed.

"'I'm not ready to stop,' I said. 'You're not in charge here. You can't stop me. And you can't stop nature, just like you can't stop the moon from rising. Carl's semen will gush into me tonight; and all day tomorrow. But not into you.'"

'You're unbelievable.' she choked on her words. She was dumbfounded and beginning to understand her hopes of retrieving her marriage were lost.

'Yes, I am unbelievable, and I am incorrigible. You've hit on something! But understand how your husband feels. Then you'll believe me.'

"She clenched her teeth and stared at my vagina. She wanted me to go on, so I did:

'He told me he'd rather lose everything he has than lose my tasty, hot slippery vagina. He loves when I lie on my back and bring my legs up, over the top of me. Then he caresses the undersides of my thighs, and enters me while standing over me. We're incredibly intimate when his cock plunges deeply inside me like that.'

'Please, don't tell me any more.' she begged.

"That time she spoke to me as if I was someone she could relate to, woman to woman. But I wasn't about to stop.

'No, oh no! We need to keep going,' I said. 'Take a good look at my legs. They're not flabby, like yours. They're long, shapely, and beautifully toned because I work out. Carl loves it when I wrap my legs around him and pull him into me. My legs hold him tightly, helping him get really deep inside me. I love taking in all of him; having that special closeness. His cock plays my emotions like a fiddle. He sends my feelings soaring. Sometimes he makes me erupt like a volcano; other times he makes me purr like a happy kitten. His cock understands all the ways to stroke my vagina. He knows that. He loves being inside me, playing his tunes. He stays long. He never wants to leave.'

"She turned and tried to walk around me:

'I told you I don't want to hear any more,' she said. 'That's enough. I'm going into that cabin to see Carl. He needs me. I'll save him from you.'

"I had miscalculated. She still had some slight presence of mind. But I had patience:

'You're not going inside, Bitch,' I countered, realizing this was probably her last hurrah. 'We're spending tonight in the cabin together. Maybe we'll stay a few extra nights. I'm sure he'll be UP for that!' I let out a low, lusty giggle to torment her.

"She stopped and faced me. She wanted to hit me, but she knew she'd get the worst of it:

'Sit down and calm down.' I ordered her. 'Listen,' I said. 'You know nothing!'

"She sat down and glowered. I had reestablished my control over her. My thoughts raced. I frantically grabbed for these swirling wisps of thought tails. I needed instructions from somewhere; perhaps one of my voices. I needed to make sense of where I was; where we both were. I needed to stay in charge; and also appear confident, or all my hopes could be lost."

At this crucial time, Miss Iniquity rescued Marty with some quick advice:

'Her emotions are boiling now. She knows her marriage is on the rocks and she's looking to you for answers. She hates your guts; but at the same time, she very attracted to you, sexually. Her insides are roiled. She's not even sure who she is anymore. Keep her emotions churned. Tell her about your intimacy with her husband. That makes her feel diminished. Make her feel revulsion about her life, until she's sick inside. Continue taunting her, until she snaps. Then, she'll turn to you for a way out of her turmoil. She'll be putty in your hands then; and you'll be able to do anything you want with her.'

'When Carl enters me from behind, he kisses the back of my neck and licks my neck, behind my ears,' I continued, seductively.

CHAPTER FOUR

But never to a seductive lay let faith be given; nor deem that light which leads astray is light from heaven (William Wordsworth: To the Sons of Burns)

VOICES OF CONTROL

Marty ran with Miss Iniquity's advice. Miss Shameless voiced her approval:

'*That's it! Be explicit. Know no shame. Spare her not one detail. Remember to always be proud of yourself. Draw mental pictures of what you did with her husband. Make sure she never forgets. Burn indelible imprints into her brain. Steal her mind from her, like a cattle rustler steals a cow. Imagine that you are branding her brain with your lewd poison; and you are thereby establishing yourself as the owner of her mind. Deprive her of ownership. Take her mind from her. Be vivid with your descriptions. Make her visualize you doing things with her husband. Make her see how you live your intimate experiences with him.*'

Miss Iniquity confirmed what Marty heard from Miss Shameless:

'*I agree. Remember, she has a sexual thing for you. Bring her to where she wants to forsake her marriage and become your bitch; but this is key: take yourself away from her at that point. Leave her feeling empty and frustrated. You'll know when you've reached that moment. She'll feel a strong need. She'll want to turn away from the life she has and journey inside herself. There, she'll discover who she really is. Have her under your hypnosis by then. From that point on, she'll do whatever you tell her to do. Do you understand?'* Marty's inner voice of self-confidence answered Miss Iniquity: *'Yes, Iniquity, I can do this.'*

'You can. And you must; for yourself, not for us voices,' replied Miss Iniquity. *'You cannot hold back. You must go through with this. We've gone too far to stop. You need to get rid of her forever. Let's get on with this. Let's get rid of her so we can all get back to Carl. Think of his pheromones' tastes while you lick his balls and suck him. Think how hard he'll be while you stroke his cock and guide it into your vagina. Think how pleased he'll be when he learns you've gotten rid of his wife. We all want to enjoy that rewarding moment; but we must be rid of her first. Got it?'*

'Yes, I've got it.' Marty answered Miss Iniquity a second time. It was time to bedevil her enemy's mind:

'When Carl licks behind my ears like he does, he sends erotic chills from my brain all through my entire body and into my eager vagina; and I want him so much more.'

"I chortled as I taunted his wife:

'He lays his hands on my shoulders and gently massages me while he kisses my back and gently thrusts his cock deeper and deeper into my vagina; probing me; playing me like a fiddle; bringing us into sweet harmony. My clitoris swells. Gloria loves this. She knows we'll make love for a long time, and she'll orgasm repeatedly."

'Do tell.' Carl's wife tried to sound cynical. But I was not going to let her cynicism stop me. I wanted that ownership of her mind.

'Sure, gladly,' I replied; excited, happy to share with her: 'I have erotic sensations when Carl kisses me that way, with his penis deeply inside me. I go wild with desire while he does that. I twerk gently, until I feel his cock so deeply inside me that it nudges my cervix. I back hard against him, until I can feel his cock all the way inside

me, tightly; rubbing its head against my cervical opening; when he's tightly plugged into me. Then, he hugs me close to him. This is the closest intimacy I ever feel with any man. I feel Carl's chest press against my back as we move together in our slow, deliberate rhythm. I glide his hot, throbbing cock back and forth over my swollen clitoris. It taps my cervix. I feel like I'm opening my soul to life; life with Carl, your husband. It's a marvelous feeling. We make love like this, long and slow, until we explode into our orgasm frenzy. Erotic lust sensations run wildly through my vagina, like an untamed stampede. I feel warm fingers of lust traveling up my spine until they reach my mind and flood my consciousness with ecstasy. I feel marvelous, insatiable, incorrigibly wanton, and slippery hot. I become this unholy, sinful, unrepentant creation force of all things immoral; and I love my feeling. I savor and cherish it. We cling to each other and make love for hours like this. Does this help you understand how Carl and I feel about each other?'

"She sat there; her eyes focused on my stomach: 'Oh, you're not speaking, are you?' I said, 'It's too bad you don't know what it feels like to have sexual sensations like mine. Your husband's ejaculations are worth more than the world. I tease him. I tell him he has Cum DuMonde, or cum of the world! And he does! His cock explodes with these fabulous eruptions of semen. He has the most fabulous cock, ever! When Carl's red-hot semen flows over my clitoris, I convulsively spasm into this wild orgasmic frenzy. I scream for joy when he and I make love that way. I can't hold anything back. The hot semen gushing from his cock makes me quiver like pudding. He pulls me onto his cock afterwards. He holds us tightly together while we slowly come down from our sensational intimacy. He stays hard for most of this. How does he do it? How can he be so wonderful? Most lovers shrink and wilt, way before Carl does. He never hurries me. He's such a wonderful lover!'

'That's enough! Have you no shame?' She cried while holding back her sobs. 'Must you squeal about how much you love fucking like you're some barnyard pig? Don't you realize you're not the only woman who knows how to fuck? Congratulations! You're a very sick nymphomaniac! Am I supposed to clap?' She was dejected. She was fast losing all hope for her marriage. But the voyeur within her had turned its interest to me. Her eyes stayed riveted upon my vagina. Despite pleading that I stop, her body language and eye focus told me that she wanted to hear more.

At this moment, Miss Iniquity spoke to Marty again:

'She feels how we want her to feel. She knows you've killed her marriage. She's extremely vulnerable. She wants you to save her humanity. She has nowhere to turn. Continue your shameless onslaught until she surrenders her soul to yours.'

'There's much more to making love than simple sex,' I told her. I was burning scenes into her mind; making them permanent, like ranchers do when they burn their brands into a cow's hide. I wanted my mind to own her mind. Her mind was beginning to comply. It followed the pictures I drew. She was at the beginning stage of hypnosis. She had come under my spell. In her mind, I drew one explicit picture after another. Her mind believed it was lost in an erotic art gallery filled with explicit scenes of my vagina, Carl's cock, and our love making. It was an endless gallery with no exit door. It had endless rooms and paintings of me making love with her husband. We were in many romantic settings; and everywhere she looked were pictures of his penis and my vagina, copulating in every conceivable angle and position. I drew in exquisite detail the erotic sensations I felt when Carl licked my vagina from behind me; how wildly stimulating that was; how he made me feel like a shameless animal in heat; and then how he worked himself around until he was lying with his head under my vagina, licking me; causing my endless orgasm. This

imaginary picture gallery became her mental immersion place. Her mind drowned in images of my vagina, oozing out its flows of Carl's semen. These images didn't repulse her. She didn't try to leave. She chose to stay.

'Carl savors the juices from my orgasms while he licks my clitoris,' I continued. He makes me gush continuously. He never pulls away during oral sex. He stays with me, kissing my lady lips and licking my clitoris tenderly; and thirstily drinking my love while I pulse flow after flow into his mouth. When her man thirsts for her in that way, that's when a woman knows her man deeply loves her. Have you ever had orgasms like those? Oh, I forget, you're not saying anything.

'Well, that's too bad. You've never squealed for joy while you orgasmed, have you? Oh, that's right. You don't orgasm, do you? That's unfortunate. Never mind. You said I was sick, didn't you? Well, you just stay sitting there like a stump, while I continue. You'll see. I'm not sick. I'm Marty Wonderful.'

At this moment, Miss Promiscuity tugged playfully at Marty's ear:

'She's listening. She loves hearing this. She can't get enough.'

'I had another orgasm from Carl's licking, not long before you arrived! And that was after he shot a huge wad of semen cream way deeply inside me. Imagine that! He's amazing! Then, he'd gotten very hard again; and he was inside me again. He was about to help me release my third orgasm. It was going to be a long, sweet one; but then you had to come along and spoil everything. Carl is such a great lover. He always places my pleasure above his own! How many men love their woman so much that they'll lick her cream filled vagina to help her experience another orgasm? How many men will help their woman have three releases in one evening? I've had as many as six releases in one love making session with Carl.'

"I laughed at her. She started to stand up, but I pushed her back down. She was sitting on the porch steps. I stood in front of her. This time she allowed me to invade her space. She was almost ready to obey me:

'Your husband kissed my clitoris so sweetly, so delightfully. I squealed with my happiness. I felt so erotic. I came all over Carl's face while he squeezed my breasts and pinched my nipples.'

"I cupped my breasts again. She noticed that my nipples were still red from her husband's pinches:

'Carl was loving me so beautifully before you got here. I felt wonderful and free from inhibition. You should have seen my vagina engulf his penis. He shot a huge semen wad over my adorable Gloria a little while ago; right before he licked me again. See?'

"I let my nightgown fall to the deck and kicked it aside to emphasize my nakedness. I tilted my vagina upward, spread my legs apart wider and moved within inches of her face. I intentionally canted my vagina toward her face and held myself open so she could see inside me, beyond my pink inner lips. My music loop continued cycling. It had reached the 'Gloria' again. That seemed so appropriate for this setting. David. My timing was perfect. She stared awestruck into the deeper recesses of my vagina. I had entered her mind. I could read her thoughts. Her thoughts entered my pink channel; her imaginary heaven, from which she would never escape."

"I'm surprised she had any thoughts. Why did you do all this? Why didn't you just stab her, like you murdered the others?" David's eyes couldn't comprehend this woman's game.

"Because, David, this was my solo murder. You weren't there. I had no assistants. Besides, I was developing this idea as a new technique, okay? Please have some patience. This disheveled, frazzled woman sought communion with me and forgiveness for her miserable life. Feelings of unworthy disgrace and inadequacy were

overcoming her, like I intended. Shame for interrupting my joy had crept into her thoughts, as I planned. My plan was working. I wasn't about to get a knife and stab her. This way was so much better. You'll see. So, bear with me."

"Okay, sorry." David held a deep breath and exhaled. Sometimes in discussions such as this his attention span became challenged.

"Slowly, I allowed Carl's creamy white semen to ooze from me. My successful whoring seared its proof into her dirty Victorian mind. I moved my vagina within two inches of her face, intentionally placing it inside her personal space, forcing her mind to become flooded with this indelible image."

Carl's wife's thoughts flickered:

'I can't resist her any longer. I can't think of anything but her cunt. I should try to resist her; but it's so hard. She's telling me the truth. It's over for me and Carl. I have nothing left. I'll try to push her away one more time, but that's all I've got left in me.'

"She summoned all her crumbling will. Her last vestige of self-respect tried to resist. She pushed me back a foot away from her with her woefully feeble effort and a muffled sob. Then, her hand fell away, limp; almost as if her hand was apologizing for its transgression. I came right back and stood before her face again. She didn't push me back this time. Her spirit was crushed. I had crushed it. I felt very pleased with myself. My darkness now controlled one hundred percent of her mind. Her mental clarity was gone. It was drowning and flailing aimlessly. Her eyes no longer cast about. They fixated on my vagina in hopes it might save her. They didn't want to see or think about anything else. My vagina offered her an escape from her harsh, clashing reality. Her mind sought to lapse into a dreamy, peaceful, welcoming hypnosis. My adorably inviting, iniquitous fuck-happy vagina, became her hypnotic amulet; her ultimate passageway to freedom."

'Smell,' I now spoke in encouraging, caring, imploring voice tones. *'I told you how exotic I smell. Gloria's and your husband's*

pheromones are blended. Here, I'll come closer to you. Smell the sweet love making that just happened inside me. Smell how Carl's love and passions became joined with mine.'

"*She was hesitant, but she finally took a close, shallow breath. Her inhale contained an element of curiosity. My taunting had shocked her at first. But now she had a resigned determination to continue the hypnosis process. My truths were so painful she was willing to invest her hopes in my amulet vagina, wherever it might take her. She turned her head away, briefly, as if to deny her husband's semen was oozing from me. But then she returned her gaze deliberately. She directly faced her truth. She had opened her heart to me. She wanted to trust me; and hope that, through that trust, she could find peace of mind. She had, at this point, invested her trust in my vagina amulet. She had crossed into a darkened mental place, from which she'd never depart. I wrestled with my own self-doubts:*

'Do my dark forces rule her mind now? Might her mental clarity return? What could I do if it did? Was she slipping into a hypnotic trance? Could she be faking it? How could I be sure my dark forces were in control of her thoughts?'

"*You were just about to kill her, right?" asked David.*

"*Not just yet, David. Please be patient. There's a twist in this drama. Wait for it. I know you'll like it. Meanwhile, David, the Gloria continued sounding. Its beautiful strains filled the air. I love hearing it. It made this whole experience wondrous. My spirit lifted. My vagina felt it too. I tingled, remembering I had recently had Carl's penis inside me.*

"*Her passion for the Gloria resonated with my own. We shared the subliminal feeling of Eros. But within Eros, my feelings separated from hers. Mine submerged themselves into the demands of remorse-less sins, immersing themselves ever deeper, into a still darker, more remorselessly evil place. I lusted for her blood.*

"The cooler evening air brought our thoughts together. And it reminded me that I must finish my task. She may have wondered if I'd take her into my life and embrace her with my warmth. But there was no chance of that happening. All this while, a cold inner hatred within me patiently coiled and waited. I seethed with contempt. I strained to conceal my viciousness. In near madness, I kept my hatred in check. I continued the hypnosis process. I yearned to finish my deed; rid myself of this hapless pest, and return to love making. I wondered how much longer I needed to suffer this fool before I could hold Carl in my arms again, and experience another fantastic orgasm.

'Stay focused. Do not betray your plan. She's begun hypnosis now. Keep your vagina positioned directly in front of her face. Continue your taunts until your unashamed carnal lewdness makes her feel sexually worthless as a woman. Then you will be able to direct her will. Be patient. It's a process. Engage her. Draw more pictures for her mind.' advised Miss Iniquity.

"I took a deep breath. I knew I needed to be measured about my task. My desires needed to wait patiently until my enemy's end was in sight:

'Come closer; touch your nose to my vagina,' I encouraged her. 'She won't hurt you. Inhale her scents. She wants to get to know you. Look, she's welcoming you.'

"She reflexively pulled back her neck. She was such a timid coward:

'Carl's penis was caressing Gloria, just a short while ago. Can you understand why he wishes you were dead?' I confided to her. My comment mentioning her death didn't faze her. I thought it was timely. I figured it couldn't hurt my efforts if she were to start considering her death as a possibility.

"Next, I got very bold. I held my vagina widely open, with my hands, so she could see her husband's creamy white semen, pooled inside me. I said:

'I'm proud to be an unrepentant, beautiful, sensuous whore. I am a wanton, immoral, committed to my life of whoring, type of whore. That's why you'll never prevent me from doing the things that I do. You do not intimidate me. I will never apologize or make excuses for any of the things I do. I love doing the evil, sinful things that I do. They give me great pleasure. I've taken your husband from you. Nothing you can do will change that.'

'Why must you be nasty'? she bleated. 'How do you live with yourself?' she whimpered. But she kept her eyes fixated upon my vagina.

Now the wife's mind spoke its silent, brutal, truth to her inner self:

'Oh God, forgive me for my unclean thoughts. I do love her. I love how bold and unashamed and incorrigibly unrepentant she is. I want her more than anything in this world. I love her evil, her immorality, her pridefulness in her choice for her life. I respect her most for her unflinching pride. I love everything about her.'

'Because you interrupted something beautiful. You have no respect.' I whispered softly in my most intimate tone. I tried to comfort her and help prepare her to accept the inevitable."

'But do you love him; or is this only a sport for you? she asked.

'Yes, of course I love him; among others,'

'Does he know?'

'Know? About what?'

'Your others.'

'Yes, of course he does. I do not make pretenses. He also knows I star in pornographic films. He's come to my place often, and we've watched them together.'

"She gasped at this revelation: 'He's not repulsed by that?'

'By what?'

'By seeing you doing other men.'

'No, goodness no,' my belly laughed to her, 'not in the slightest. He loves watching me; holds me tighter while watching another man's cock tapping my outer vaginal lips, seeking permission to come inside; then, observing it gaining entrance. I dare say, seeing me performing porn thrills him. It's as if he's fortunate to have a relationship with a special sort of woman; a woman who does the sorts of things he loves seeing a woman doing. It makes him cherish me all the more. He's never complained when I've upped my prices.'

CHAPTER FIVE

See how love and murder will out. (William Congreve: The Double Dealer)

No mask like open truth to cover lies, as to go naked is the best disguise (William Congreve: The Double Dealer)

MURDERESS THOUGHTS

"Then her eyes pried themselves away from my vagina. She looked up. They settled into my face and carried an expression to my eyes that I will never forget. She knew I was truthful and determined; determined to continue my whoring and determined to possess her husband, not only for this weekend; but for always. And she understood that she could not stop me. She suddenly understood that she had lost her reason for living. Her baleful expression must have been similar to the one that victims had before they were sacrificed to the gods of the Aztecs. As if her eyes had betrayed her mind; revealed her thoughts of defeat to me, she quickly returned to her fascination stare, fixating her eyes once again on my vagina."

"*Is this where you put the knife into her,*" asked an anxious David, "*and how did you kill her without my help? Tell me.*" His impatience was palpable.

"*In time, David, I promise I'll tell you everything, in time,*" Marty said. "*You'll see. This murder was very different from all my others. Be patient. Allow me to tell it slowly like you said you wanted me to.*"

"*Okay.*" David's voice was sheepish, resigned.

"After the Aztec priest plunged his dagger into his victim's stomach," Marty continued, "the priest's hand reached up, into the man's chest cavity, above his liver, until it found his heart. Then, he tore away his victim's heart with his hand; lifted it out of his victim's chest and held it high, offering it to the sun. It was a beautiful Aztec religious moment. Well, Carl's wife gave me that same pleading look that the Aztec victim gave the priest, before the priest plunged his dagger into him. I saw her eyes tell me that she was entrusting her life into my hands and begging me to spare her life.

"When the Aztec priest rips his victim's heart away, the sacrificed man isn't dead yet; but he knows he soon will be. He first experiences the trauma of feeling his heart being ripped away. He then looks at the priest with eyes of shock and awe. It's a questioning, pleading look. His eyes ask why; and if, perhaps, there's faint hope that the priest will put his still-beating heart back inside him; but of course, the priest can't do that. He simply smiles while watching his victim's life expire; knowing that he's taking all his victim's power away from him.

"He smiles into his victim man's eyes. He engages the man's dying brain during those last recognition seconds of life. The dying mind dims. With vision memory of the priest's eyes, it accepts death as its fate, and fades into eternity. Those priests witnessed these serene moments often. It was their spiritual thrill to sacrifice lives to their gods.

"I was experiencing the same feeling that the Aztec priest felt. Carl's wife had stared spellbound into my vagina. She had watched her husband's life force ooze out of me. She, too, looked into my eyes with eyes that pleaded for mercy. She knew I'd taken her life from her. But, like those priests, I didn't see myself as the evil one. I was commanded by my gods, the gods of immoral lust and sensuality, to do their bidding, just as the Aztec priest was charged by his gods to take his victim's heart. I was the victor. I was enthralled by a *sublimely, righteous feeling. I was figuratively ripping her heart out. I'll always savor that feeling.*

"She covered her mouth and gasped while holding her stare on my vagina. It had become her hypnotizing amulet. The essence of her marriage and her life slowly dribbled from it. She beheld her conqueror. Proof of my consorting took her breath away. She trembled again. We were sharing our divine experience.

'Smile into her horrified eyes,' Miss Iniquity said to me: 'Enter your mind into hers; partner with her thoughts; feel and imagine the same things she does. Feel her mind racing? She sees you loving her husband. She imagines seeing him shooting his semen-life into you, giving you life, honoring you by sending his life into yours. Then, she sees those life fluids dribbling out from you. That represents her hope. It's her life, dying; spent; slipping away, inert, and useless. Look at her sunken chest! It's crushed. See how her breath heaves? She's devastated. Her reason for living is gone.'

"I felt divinely evil. I flexed my buttocks slowly, erotically. I tilted my pelvis upward, nearly touching her face. Sensuously, slowly, my hips and stomach undulated in a mock belly dance in front of her. I flaunted my insatiable craving for sex and my profligate, licentiously immoral, lusty whoring. I personified creation life! At that moment, the Credo began playing again.

"She imagined my wanton vagina, undulating in perfect rhythm with her husband's semen-gushing shaft. The Credo sounded its call! Her god knocked on her door; opened it. That allowed me to peer into her mind. She visualized me straddling her husband; bumping down hard and rapidly onto his cock, taking all of him inside me. Her mind pictured her husband's penis strokes sliding deeply, irretrievably, inside my vagina's slippery, velvety nirvana-like walls; reaching my deepest depths, pushing hungrily against my cervix. She saw my vagina effortlessly coax all life's semen from her husband's thrusting cock; channeling it into my fallopian tubes. She imagined

feeling the same joyful rapture that I felt. Then she imagined seeing me cradle and rock Carl's penis while I rolled, cat like, over onto my back; wrap my legs tightly around his body and continue holding him deeply inside me; continue draining every vestige of every semen droplet from him; receiving them into me; taking his life into mine.

"Miss Iniquity's voice came into my head again:

'*She's your victim now. She's captured like a helpless insect in a Venus fly trap. That's appropriate. She drowns in her own imagination. She feels nirvana by imagining that she is inside your vagina. Release more semen. Wash it over her imagination, engulf her with it. Drown her in it. Remove her resistance to death.*'

"*We shared that fateful moment. Our minds met as one. As the Sanctus played, acceptance came over her. Her mind was captured inside my sex; encapsulated there, never wishing to leave. It loved imprisonment there. She mentally savored my nectar. Her mind imagined it drank the semen inside me. My lust ingested her mind. On an unspoken primal level, her mind knew it was fated to die. It intuited it was to become a sacrificial offering to my rapacious whore-lust. These vivid imaginings seared themselves in her memory.*

"*I read her mind. It glimpsed peace, acceptance, and surrender. She felt happiness for her husband's erotic bliss. Her heart felt reality shock. Her old reality was torn away from her. She knew she could never take it back. I held it in my murderous hands; like the Aztec priest held his victim's heart; proudly high and away from her. I was victorious. A horrible sorrow swept over her conscience. It knew she must succumb. Grief, horror, and desire clawed simultaneously against the insides of her stomach.*

"*Her eyes rose, as if slowly lifting hope to the heavens, forcing her gaze upward from my amulet vagina to meet my eyes once more. Her pitiful, soulful look begged me to stop; spare her. But I was in her mind now. I tasted erotic, evil joy. My eyes studied hers. I saw her spirit dying. I watched her mind lose hope. She knew she could never reclaim her moral life. I took it. I could force her to accept everything that she had once resisted. I could be heartless and sadistic. I could infuse her thoughts with lurid desires and drive her insane. I asked myself: 'Should I?'*

Miss Iniquity replied:

'Of course, you should. Do it. Infest her mind with prurient immorality. Brand her with it. Sear her corruption in. Make it permanent. Enjoy doing it.'

"I called her: 'Sister.' 'Come on, Sister, we're almost there! We're purging all unaccepting thoughts from your mind. You'll love my evil. It will be good for you! Look!'

Her mind succumbed:

'Yes, do with me as you wish. I will obey you. I love you.'

"I took her husband's semen from my vagina and placed some onto my lips. Her husband's cream basked on my tongue. I savored it. I immersed her imagination in it. I pressed my tongue against the back of my front teeth so she could see his semen cream reposing in my mouth's cradle. I burbled his semen on my lips; then licked my lips, slowly. I returned the semen to the inside my mouth and swallowed it. I ingested her hopes for a life with her husband. I left her imagination with no hope; only a sense of irretrievable loss.

"I kissed the tip of my index finger, as if it was her husband's cock. I lovingly licked my finger the same way I lovingly lick a cock's underside after it has ejaculated into my mouth. I had perfected this act for my porn films, long before this night. It was second nature for me. But it was a rude shock to her sensibilities. It conveyed that I was a shameless cum guzzler, the sort of degenerate woman that she and her country club friends denigrate at their parties. She was spellbound.

"Her eyes searched wistfully in mine, trying to discover in them some way to accept my licentious behavior; and bind her lusting feelings to me. Our imaginations united. Perversely, they appreciated

my macabre ravishing of her marriage. My shameless whoring had raped her reason for living; savaged it in her mind's eye.

"She savored her vicarious experience. She felt the taste of my lust in the jowls of her cheeks. She imagined the feel of her husband's balls in my hands as I massaged them; fondled them; softly squeezed them. She laid her imagination in the palms of my hands as their paired, sliding strokes stiffened Carl's cock to ready hardness. She visualized my lips sucking cream from the head of Carl's penis; and her imagination joined my tongue while it caressed his balls. She felt my joy of accomplishment when I again aroused Carl to erotic bliss; and while I sucked him off a second time.

"Opening my jaw wide, I extended my semen-drenched tongue and moved it from side to side, much like a snake does while tasting the air. I achieved my desired effect. Her eyes followed my tongue, wishing her visual arms could hold me; desiring that her closed mouth could open and affix her lips to mine, while her tongue kissed mine. She sat mesmerized like a cornered rabbit, paralyzed in its death trance by a viper, measuring it for a meal.

"She now appreciated that her husband adored watching me savor his semen, before I swallowed it. She saw his life essence slide easily down my welcoming throat. She visualized her marriage sliding down my gullet, much like a predator gull ingests a hapless chick. On her primal limbic level, she was awed by what she saw. She intuitively knew I had ingested her life's purpose; and she loved it. On the same level, she knew what was happening to her was real and transformative. Now, she welcomed it. Her eyes returned to my vagina amulet. It was her sanctuary, now; her respite for mental peace.

"She imagined Carl lying under me repeatedly thrusting his tongue into me, lovingly caressing my clitoris. She visualized Carl's determination to pleasure me; patiently bringing me to my second orgasm. This was our moment of truth and intensity; much like

the meeting of minds between the Aztec priest and his victim. It was that precious fleeting moment between the conqueror and the conquered, the living and the dead, when the victim's soul departs its earthly body. She understood this truth: that I and her husband experimented with all sorts of erotic pleasuring. She was so deflated, David. It was like air and life were let out of her. She knew her marriage was dead; destroyed beyond salvation; no way to recover its ruins. I felt the same inner nirvana that the Aztec priest felt. I was glorious in my conquest, proud and unashamed. I knew I had severed her soul from her marriage.

"Now feeling violated and despondent, she sought mercy. She knew her physical life was all she had left. She may have sensed that I might rip that away. Her marriage was what had always defined her as a woman. That had slipped away. She looked at me with that same pleading expression the Aztec's sacrificial man had. Her doleful eyes met mine again. This time they spoke to me with a beseeching, hopeless look. They begged me for mercy; to return Carl's semen to him; to restore her marriage, while realizing the impossibility. Nothing could return to before.

"As if on cue, Gloria's refrains sounded again. We felt something large happen. The Spirit came; told us it was futile to resist fate. We couldn't turn back time or relive our pasts. We needed to proceed with our deadly game; each fated to play her part."

"Her mind begged:

'Please be kind. Have mercy. Forgive me.'

"I seized the moment. Feeling no mercy, I smiled into her eyes. I heard her mind cry out in helplessness. A muffled laugh escaped me. My heart grew colder. I knew I would be cruel. I had to be. I would work her mind until it was incapable of having its own thoughts. It would only think my thoughts and want my wants. I felt empowered by otherworldly forces. I was a goddess woman of lives and worlds. Her life and her world were entrusted to my mercy. But I had none.

I laughed a silent, inward laugh, an evil-loving laugh that mocked her distress. I disguised my heartless intentions.

"I returned her pleading look with the same dispassionate stare that the Aztec Priest gave to the man whose heart he had taken. That priest and I were one. I smiled down at my pitiful victim. In my eyes, she saw the same remorseless stare that the dying victim glimpsed from the priest's face. The priest murdered his victim with his knife and hand. I was murdering her with the powers of my mind and the hypnotic lure of my transformed vagina. It had become her amulet; her obsession quest. My eyes savored their first exalted taste of her impending demise.

"I felt her despair. Her masquerade of bravado was torn away. Her spirit soul stood naked and defenseless before me. The salacious malevolent thoughts, which I'd had moments before, reoccurred. My own self-doubts were dispelled; replaced by confidence. I had the upper hand. Confidence, competence and cunning always triumph over fear, cowardice, and superstition. I told myself:

'I can do this! Her life is in my clutches. I can drive her to such despair that she will kill herself. I only need to keep my hatred in check until she accepts my instructions.'

"I was enthralled at my prospects. I could be rid of her by infesting her mind with my venom of unrepentant wantonness. She was fragile enough to destroy herself. I knew it. I nurtured my deliciously wicked thought. It blossomed into the pernicious driver of my words.

"Her mind was trapped now. Her eyes returned their fixation stare to my vagina, afraid to look elsewhere. They wanted to fly away from her body, taking her soul with them, enter me, partake of my sensuousness and dwell inside me, forever. Her vagina obsession trapped her. Her mind imagined finding eternal comfort inside me; with me. She no longer had any desire to fight me or escape from me. She only sought to dwell inside me, forever. I coiled my

thoughts around her fragile psyche. Then, I squeezed tighter and tighter, crushing her hopes, like a constrictor snake crushes a hapless rabbit. I became, in that merciless moment, a remorseless, predatory murderess; a purpose driven, unrepentant, merciless, vicious whore. I willed that she would die."

David was amazed at hearing Marty's insight into the wife's mind. *"You actually had the premonition that, if you continued taunting her, she would end her life, by herself?"* His question was filled with fascination. *"You have a remarkable ability, Marty. Remind me to work you into life insurance sales. You could have the policy holders name you as beneficiary; then get them to do away with themselves!"* David's mind never stopped working. It visualized a whole new business line.

"Thank you, David. I've had dealings that involved several wives. Experience teaches. I know how vulnerable they feel when I attack their marriages. My strategy for Carl's wife was based on my experience, and my feminine intuition. I had put my mind into hers; taken her denial away and replaced it with reality. But reality was not about to make her do anything. I needed to light a spark under her; move her along; make her act. I needed to play my devilish game. I needed to place hell inside her mind; make her want to escape herself; lead her mind along a path it feared to go. I needed to replace its natural blocking defenses with an attainable goal. Then, send her on her fatal quest to reach it.

"So, here we were. Me standing there. Her sitting before me, staring dumbfounded into my vagina; obviously, deeply distressed, without any plan of action or sense of direction. Her mind was encased in paralysis. The numbing shock of associating her husband's semen with the radical change in her life circumstance had overwhelmed her. She felt helpless, knowing that I had complete control of Carl. She also understood that he wouldn't come out of the cabin to save

her. That engendered an extremely depressing feeling in her, like her husband had abandoned her to be devoured by wolves and jackals. Her heart of hearts suspected that Carl secretly wished she were dead."

"And you kept going?" David asked.

"You bet I did," replied Marty. *"I told you I wanted her out of my life."*

"Well, go on, Marty," implored David. *"This is fascinating."* He appreciated that Marty was revealing these previously unknown depths of her sinister wantonness. He saw that he had an iconic partner, willing to innovate and explore unproven, extreme methods to murder. He liked that about Marty. She was cutting edge; creative. He wondered: what motive drove this? Did her desire to kill arise because Carl's wife interfered with her intimacy? Did her motive arise because she sought to learn whether she could rely on an entirely new method of murdering? Which was it? This plunge into creative lethality was an aspect of herself that Marty had never revealed before. It surprised and intrigued him.

David wondered: *'Where did Marty learn to be so bloodthirsty?'* He tried to remember if Susan had ever displayed that trait; but Susan was always very passive. She always did as Marvin, his father, instructed, or so David remembered. He also dismissed the possibility that the trait came from Marty's legal father, Joseph. That man was not imaginative or devious enough to murder anyone. *'Why have I never noticed that Marty harbored these repressed malicious thoughts? Can I trust trust her, knowing that trait is in her? What is its source? Could the source be Susan? Am I seeing original unlearned behavior?'* Then, he thought that it didn't really matter how Marty came to behave this way. *'Whatever it is, it is rare and directed at a specific antagonist. It's likely coincidental.'* David dismissed his inquiry, altogether. After all, Marty and Susan were women, the fairer sex. Belatedly, years later, David would bemoan that he hadn't more carefully considered the source of Marty's ruthless lethality.

"Gladly" responded a mirthful Marty, unsuspecting that David harbored suspicious thoughts about her, *"I'm pleased you're enjoying this. Tell me, does it excite you enough to make you desire intimacy?"*

"Perhaps; but you know me and how I like to stay focused on the task at hand. Let's forgo our desires for now and see how we feel later, when the sun has gone behind the mountains. Please, continue."

"Okay David. My intuition told me I could destroy her if she realized that, not only had I ruined her marriage; but that I was a constant presence in her husband's mind. I needed to show her there was only room in his thoughts for me and no room in his thoughts for her. I could not spare her any hopeful feelings. I needed her to see my most evil, wicked essence. She needed to know that she could never escape my evil; that my evil would relentlessly haunt her until she died."

"So, wrecking her marriage wasn't enough. Now you set out to destroy her as a person. Am I getting this?"

"Yes. After all, the Aztec priests weren't finished with their victims when they took their hearts out. There was another confirming act that emphatically demonstrated their power. It was their final heinous act. Thus, I approached my task in similar fashion to the way the Aztecs dealt with their enemies. I set out to dismember her self-esteem and demolish it so completely that she could never again reassemble it.

"The Aztec priests sent the clear message that they totally dominated the people. They were ingenious in their brutality. They let the peoples' eyes watch their victims' heads be severed. They tossed those heads down the steps of the temple, followed by the victims' bodies. These heads were then permanently displayed upon stakes to remind the people what could happen to them if they failed to

stay obedient. They fed their victims' bodies to their dogs. The people were trained this way; trained to understand that their individual lives were inconsequential and worthless. The priests knew the importance of constantly reinforcing the vivid memories of the sacrifice. They understood the need to impress upon those who would question their powers that they were ever-present, ruthless, utterly contemptuous, and unfeeling towards their foes. The priests had only disdain for their inferiors."

"But you didn't cut her head off, did you?"

"No, that would make things complicated and messy. I had a better idea that accomplished the same effect. I impressed upon her a permanent reminder, like those Aztec priests did. I made her see that I was first in her husband's life; and that she had no worth whatsoever. She could starve, or be eaten by dogs, for all Carl cared. With that malicious intent, I increased her dosage of psychological horror. I re-entered her mind with my condescending loving voice tone. She sat before me and trembled; eyeing me. She was a terrified rabbit, about to be consumed. Meanwhile, the Credo took its next turn on my music loop."

'Tell her about the photos,' said Miss Iniquity to Marty: 'Make her understand Carl's contempt for her. Tell her about his wedding band. Tell her how he uses her most precious gift to him. Poison her mind. Force her memory to live in the photos.'

"I gave her my first instruction:

'Go to your husband's office and open his lower right-hand drawer,' I continued. 'You'll find a huge envelope containing photos of Carl and me. See the loving tenderness with which he holds my face in his hands. See how happy his heart is; how joy shows in his face as he's immersing his face in my pink valley to perform cunnilingus. Those photos show us making love in every position imaginable. Love like ours can't be faked. You'll see. He loves me. He does not love you. Let me explain how he got the pictures. His camera has

time delay. It took a sequence of us making love. Carl stares at those photos every day; often several times a day. He loves me. He adores my vagina. I'm always on his mind.'

"*Her chest rose and fell to the rising and falling of the Credo's mournful rhythm. She brought her hands to her ears to block me out.*"

'Louder. Make her hear you,' said Miss Iniquity.

'There's one series of shots you must see,' I spoke in a raised voice. 'You'll remember them for the rest of your life. Your husband gives all his love to me. He took them after his hot semen spurt in my vagina.'

'You must be demented and sick,' she wailed. 'I don't know how you two became involved. Why won't you leave him alone? Can't you stop this sickness? You have no idea what married life is like. You have no idea how your behavior affects people.'

Carl's wife had an inkling that Marty would not show her mercy:

'What does she want? She won't forgive my intrusion. I get that. What can I do to make her happy? What can I do to make her forgive me; possibly love me?'

'Catch her here,' Miss Iniquity alerted Marty. 'Don't let her slip away from you. Keep her engaged in her hypnotic state. Correct her misimpression. You know exactly what you've done to her marriage. This is not about letting her make you happy. Make her face reality.'

"*My inner self-esteem was not about to let this bitch tell me what my boundaries should be, David. I laughed a subtle, loving laugh; then I continued:*

'Oh, I think I do know how my behavior affects people,' my eyes smiled knowingly to hers. 'I'm not sick or demented. I'm helping you. I'm your confidential friend. You'll see. Let's talk some more about my behavior and Carl's involvement with me. What I'm telling you is verifiable. You can see the photos. Carl encourages my behavior.

When you see those photos, you'll understand that he craves my wantonness and rewards it. You'll understand why I have the furs and my new car. You'll see the naughty, erotic things I do with Carl. And remember: he loves me for it.

'He took the photos when we were here last year, up on the mountain, by one of the lakes. It's a time sequence of twelve shots. He posed me at the edge of the lake. I'm naked, of course, except for my pearl necklace. I love making love while wearing pearls. They help me feel sensuous. You wouldn't know about being sensuous, would you? Sorry.

'Carl waded into icy cold water to get this shot. I thought he'd catch pneumonia in that freezing water. I didn't want him getting sick. He responded by saying he'd go anywhere and do anything to capture my explicit, erotic poses. I held my lady lips wide open for his camera.'

"My tape played the Sanctus. It was perfect. She heard its serene, fateful music while I explained how Carl captured my glorious vagina by the lake. I said:

'Carl captured a perfect photograph of my inner vaginal lips while his thick, white cream oozed from my iniquitous lady lips. The glistening sheen from my lubricating fluids makes my lady lips look like deliciously yummy velvet. I'm Carl's juicy, perfectly ripened peach, begging to be eaten; but even softer, juicier, and tastier than a real peach. I'm more beautiful, more fragrant, more alluring, and more enchanting than a jeweled rosette. That photo inspires his tongue to probe my peach blossom and never taste another taste. He angled his camera upward to catch my smile. Notice how I beam. I'm proud and radiant. I peeled my lips back over my perfect upper teeth. There's a hint of my tongue. I'm looking skyward, to heaven. You'll see joy beaming from my face. I knew I was presenting beautifully for the camera. I knew I was pleasing Carl.

'*My taupe eye shadow was perfect,*' *I told her as I flared my eyes.* '*My eyes are bright and beautiful. They're alive with passion. They signal desire and lust. They're not dull, like yours. Carl loves my eyes. He kisses them like he's blessing goddesses.*

'*I tilted my hips forward and spread my legs slightly apart for this first photo. I held myself open so Carl could capture my inner lips and channel, oozing with Carl's voluminous offering. The photo captures the tip of a mountain rising up behind my head. It's highly suggestive.*'

Marty remembered how the words of Miss Shameless entered her mind at that time, seeking revenge: '*Wonderfully done,*' said Miss Shameless. '*Can you feel her despair? Can you see how helpless she feels; how powerless she is? You've unmasked this pitiful hypocrite. But control your hatred. Stay measured. Remember, she is the anathema of freedom and love. She represents repression, control, subjugation, and uppity righteousness. She is your WEX classmates. They made fun of you and hurt your feelings. They tried to conquer your spirit. They never invited you to their homes or parties. They laughed at your pain of loneliness. They drove you to find friendship, love, and warmth with boys. They channeled you toward nymphomania. Nymphomania eased your pain. Use your nymphomania now. Return your years of pain to her.*

'*She's another Mrs. Raybenald, that bitch who bullied poor Maria. This woman bullied too. She bullied Carl. She's the one at fault. She drove him into your arms. You rescued him from her. Don't allow her to play victim. She's not innocent. She's guilty! Don't feel sorry for her. Remember, she despises you. She needs to feel your pain; how you felt when your mother abandoned you. She pretends she's sweet and well socialized. You know her better.*

'*Punish her. Show her how you revel in whoring with Carl. Help her visualize your glee while making love with her husband. Make her understand that committing adultery doesn't trouble your conscience in the slightest. Turn the tables on her. Make her the outcast of your new morality world. Do not let her mind know peace. Torture it. Detest her. Dehumanize her. She's a creepy insect! Make her long for her past life, like you once did. If she raises a flicker of hope, crush it. Step on it. Rub salt in her wounds. Grind your past pains into them. She would do it to you, if she could.'* While Marty continued telling David her story, she recalled how she obeyed Miss Shameless; how her heart turned cold, and how ruthless she became:

"Smiling my most pretentious carefree smile at Carl's wife, I said: 'My opened lady parts displayed from that camera angle helps Carl imagine that I've made love with a gigantic penis, shaped like that mountaintop in the background. He calls these photos his 'Marty does the world' series. They help him imagine that I'm welcoming a huge cock into my wanton, insatiable, penis pleasure palace. He loves them because they remind him that he worships me. He does, you know. Your husband prefers to worship what he can touch and feel and taste. He no longer goes to church with you, does he? Here, see me rubbing my hand over my vagina? That's what your husband worships. He loves kissing it and sliding his penis into it. It's not something imaginary. It's real. My vagina is your husband's true religion. See how his photos capture its majesty? It's his true God. But I think you already knew that, didn't you?

"Please tell me what you think of the photos after you see them. Notice how they capture drops of your husband's semen falling from my vagina, splashing into the lake. Every picture captures a perfect reflection of my ravaging, cock thirsting vaginal lips and my joyous smile. I'm at the center of the droplets' splash rings. I send them rippling outward over the water, reaching Carl; connecting me to him.

'That series captures my shameless wantonness. Imagine, Carl sees them every day. He sees my beckoning, irresistible, invitation; welcoming him to enter me and make passionate love with me; fill me with his semen. He fixates on the serenity and happiness of my face.

My smile assures him that I'm secure in his love. And I am. I know he loves only me. As the camera's timed sequence started, the sun's rays shine on me. They shower me with their warm, angelic halo. I stand in their radiant, shining light. The camera captures my innocent, spiritual look. I am goddess. Those photos mesmerize Carl,'

"I began confiding in her, as if talking to a sister:

'*Seeing his semen drops falling from my opened vagina makes Carl incredibly hard. He tells me that makes his heart pound; beating so hard he fears it will burst from his chest. He feels we must fuck again, soon, to replace the semen I've lost. My cock thirsting vagina has that compelling effect on Carl. That photo always gives him an erection. He feels his cock calls him to duty; commands him to make love with me, again. It demands to be in my vagina again, filling me again and again with its fresh offerings of creamy white semen. Carl becomes obsessed. He feels he must ejaculate more and more of his semen inside me. The photo triggers his obsession. It's his male possession thing. He must have me. He knows while he is having me, no one else is having me. He obsesses over making love with me.*

'*You simply must see those photos for yourself. They'll help you appreciate what a shameless lustful whore I am and how completely committed I am to my whoring. I can't imagine living any other way. I have no reservations about committing adultery with your husband, none! You'll understand how irresistible my penis-craving vagina is to your husband once you've seen the photos. Carl tells me he'd die for my vagina. Is that obsession or what?'*

'*I want to go now. Please, stop.'* "His wife stammered her words as she started to stand up. That's how shaken she was."

Marty remembered what Miss Iniquity said to her at this propitious moment. Iniquity's voice reinforced what Miss Shameless' voice had already told her: '*Don't stop,'* she said. '*Remember how those girls belittled you in boarding school? Remember those many nights when you cried yourself to sleep? Don't stop.'*

CHAPTER SIX

The ruling passion, be it what it will, the ruling passion conquers reason still (Alexander Pope: Moral Essays, to Lord Bathurst)

SHAMELESSLY UNINHIBITED

Marty continued telling her story to David.

'Oh, no, no, no! We're coming to the best part. Sit down!' I commanded. 'Remember: what we're experiencing here together will be very helpful to you.' She obeyed me and, like a timid rabbit, she sat back down.

'There's another set of photos. He mounted his camera on a tripod and set its timer for this series. The sequences capture us making love. You'll see photos from three different series. Each series shows us in different love making positions. Carl is a true romantic. He loves every photo from each sequence. The first sequence shows the two of us playing with his wedding ring. He sits beside me on a big rock, his arm around me. He's kissing my mouth; and one hand cups my left breast. He positions his wedding ring over my nipple. Next, he licks my nipple, taking his ring into his mouth. Then, we kiss again. His wedding ring next appears inside my mouth. I hold out my tongue, displaying his ring on my tongue tip. Then, we kiss a third time. Carl takes the ring into his own mouth again. You gave him that wedding ring, didn't you?'

'Slut!' "She whispered hoarsely. She extended her hand, as if to push me away; but her hand fell short. It was a half-hearted effort.

She returned her hand to her lap. She slowly shook her head."

At this time, the wife's limbic mind told her conscious mind its final truth:

'You're doomed. You know you are doomed. This whore has ruined your life. Why don't you care? Why do you find yourself loving her, now that you know she's intent on destroying you? But that's what real love is, isn't it? Perhaps you've finally found it. Perhaps your true love is Carl's whore.'

Miss Iniquity's voice again stepped in at this moment. She felt she needed to talk to Marty:

'That feeble hand push was her last gasp. It was an involuntary reaction,' said Miss Iniquity. *'She instinctively knows she's coming under your control. She's reacting out of fear; but her voyeur curiosity has been titillated. She doesn't want to break off from you. I can tell. She has a prurient, limbic mind. It bubbles over with lust for you. It yearns to express itself. For now, just give her a little gentle pat. Encourage her to accept your commands. Continue, as if she never tried to leave you. Go on as if nothing happened. Pretend to be her friend.'*

"*I gave her a gentle pat on her head,"* Marty continued talking to David. *"That stopped her from moving. She was weak, exhausted, and disoriented. She trembled. That told me she feared me. She felt ashamed of the gesture she had just made. Her mind returned to its surreal reality. My plan came into focus. My devious thoughts brought a smile to my lips. I planned no end to her horrors. I continued speaking softly and lovingly to her, as if we were sisters; sharing our deepest secrets:*

'You'll love the second timed photo sequence. It was taken after Carl ejaculated inside me. I'm lying on my back. My vagina is high in the air. My hands hold my feet up, beside my head. Carl lowered his head over me. He lovingly placed his hands on my derriere, supporting me. Then, he cupped his mouth to my cum-filled vagina.

Using his tongue, he deposited his wedding ring inside my vagina. It was that same wedding ring that you gave to him when you promised him you would love him all the days of your life. I don't mean to belabor this, but isn't it ironic that he'd rather see the symbol of your love inside my whoring honey pot than on his finger? That should tell you he doesn't much care for your love, don't you think? Anyway, the next photo captures his wedding ring in the perfect setting. Its floating, all alone. It appears forlorn, unwanted, unloved, and helpless inside my vagina. It floats there, atop my iniquitous, shamelessly immoral lake; brim filled with Carl's creamy white semen. It appears to be a tiny gold life ring. It floats aimlessly, directionless, on my whoring, white, cream filled lake. It appears to be trapped; surrounded by my majestically beautiful vagina's slippery pink sides. It can't escape me! That's like your marriage, isn't it? Trapped inside my vagina; unable to escape?'

"Coincidently, the Gloria began playing again on my music loop while I continued explaining this second photo series to her:

'I then held my cream filled peach widely open with both my hands. I performed my magic trick. The next photos show Carl's wedding ring disappearing into my bottomless, semen filled lake into the depths of my insatiably craven, whoring, semen loving vagina. That's right! I make Carl's wedding ring disappear. It's a symbolic photo. It shows that your marriage being swallowed up by my fun loving, carefree wanton lust. We used Carl's wedding ring that day to symbolically illustrate how my delicious, fuck happy, immoral vagina made a mockery of your marriage.

'Then, in the next few photos, I squeeze my vaginal lips closed. Your husband's wedding ring magically reappears. It popped up from the depths of my vagina's cum pool, all drenched in Carl's semen. It is half submerged and barely floating. It appears to be helpless and drowning. It's your floundering marriage. My vagina has a talent for creating imagery. Closely observe those photos. You'll understand

how vulnerable you are. You'll know that I and my wanton, whoring vagina can end your marriage whenever I choose to end it.

'You've never considered that a whore could have that much power over you, did you? Consider: I can decide whether you have a husband or not; or even whether you can see him. How do you feel knowing that? Have you noticed? Carl isn't coming out from the cabin to rescue you. I've told him not to come out. Do you still believe I don't understand what my behavior does to people? You were arrogant and insulting to say that. You should think before you say things like that.'

"David, she just sat there, staring into my vagina with voided eyes. She was in no condition to reply to my questions or comment; so, I continued in a softer voice:

'In the next few photos of this second series, I put Carl's semen in my mouth along with his wedding ring. I then roll his ring on my tongue. I purse my ruby lips as if I'm sucking the tip of Carl's penis; then my tongue peeks through my lips with his wedding ring around my tongue tip. Finally, I open my mouth to show my sen-suous, semen-covered tongue with his wedding ring floating on it. Then, I embrace and kiss your husband, putting my tongue into his mouth. That's how I gave Carl's ring back to him. It's a wonderful photo sequence. It's symbolic. I first washed his ring in his semen cream. That washed away any guilt Carl may have felt about loving me. Those photos express a truth. Intimacy is stronger than guilt.'

"I smiled while describing those photo sequences, David. I expressed enthusiasm for all the different ways that I made love with her husband. I was condescending. But that no longer mattered. She no longer had any fight in her. She no longer looked look up to my face. She continued staring into my vagina. I resumed my taunts. I felt defiant and in complete control:

'In this third series of photos, we filmed me with my legs spread widely open, in my perfect Chinese split. I'm naked, of course. Carl

positioned me on three pillows that he brought along to capture these sensational, explicit photos. I'm between two rocks; my juicy, cock thirsty honey pot is suspended wide open in the cool mountain air. I'm feeling a delightfully soft breeze. In these first photos, I'm beaming a smile and lusting anxiously for Carl to lick me.

'Carl then put his wedding ring on his tongue tip. He lay beneath me with his head upon a pillow. He fully extended his tongue into my anxiously awaiting love channel. He arranged those rocks perfectly. Everything was delightful. I always insist that Carl makes things perfect while he pleasures me with oral sex. It makes me feel like I'm a divine goddess. I dominate him in that way. I told him to continue licking my clitoris while giving me a long, sweet orgasm; or else he'd disappoint me. When I was completely relaxed with my vagina perfectly suspended over Carl's face, I told him that I was ready. His tongue entered me. I told him to use his wedding ring to stimulate me. Sex is a mental thing, you know.

'When Carl uses his wedding ring as a prop, it always ensures that I have a majorly satisfying orgasm. It's also Carl's way of admitting that he's happily dominated by me. He welcomes my domination of your marriage, too. He obeyed me. He always obeys me. He is so thoughtful. He licked my vagina; explored it lovingly. He performed beautiful, loving cunnilingus; sweetly and gently; while stroking my clitoris with his wedding ring. The ring rubbing against my clitoris creates sensational sexual stimulation. It brings out intense erotic passion on both the physical and psychological level. It symbolizes sacrifice and slavery. It's Carl sacrificing your marriage to please me. And it's Carl being a willing slave to my ribald, carnal pleasure. I love that dominance feeling. It's victory. It's adulation. It's both those sensations. I beautifully express them in my spectacular orgasms. It seemed like we did this for hours. It was beyond titillating. I believe Carl could lick Gloria forever. He loves performing oral sex with me.

'*But, tell me; how do you feel, now knowing that Carl uses his wedding ring to help me come? The lake is not the only place we do this. I often tie him to bed posts and make him use his ring that same way while he licks me. I love coming while he does that. It helps me feel in control. My feelings are more important to him than you or your marriage. How do you feel knowing that? And, how do you feel knowing that stimulation from his wedding ring is my favorite way to get off?*'

"*She didn't respond to my questions, David. She just stared at my vagina and sat there like a stump. She visualized my domination scenes. The images I pressed into her mind were tearing her guts out. So, I continued:*

'*Carl's tongue escorts his wedding ring along the underside of my grateful clitoris. He does that so beautifully. He's skillful. He's married his tongue to my clitoris and his soul to mine. In that third photo series, you'll notice that my entire body first contracts. Then, see how I convulse in my wild rhapsody. I had a beautiful orgasm. It was the climax of my conquest. I had the full measure of Carl's devotion. My mouth is opened widely. I screamed with ecstatic joy. I ran my hands through my hair and smiled with delight. Carl said that photo confirms how much I love oral sex. It's that; but it's also that I know all his love is mine. Oh, do you hear the Gloria playing on the cabin stereo? I love hearing its refrains while making love. I imagined hearing it that day at the lake, while Carl performed oral sex. Listen. Hear it? Isn't it romantic?*

'*I became serene in the next few photos. I imagined religious music resonating inside my soul. My pride swelled. I appreciated that wonderful, spiritual orgasm. Some orgasms, like that one, are significant milestones in a romantic relationship. I'll always remember what happened when we were at the high mountain lake. I ran my fingers through my hair all during that sequence. I wonder if the animals heard me? I screamed YES, YES! I could not contain the wild lust I felt. It was a beautiful moment. I wanted it to continue forever. I was ecstatic! It's not every day that a man pledges a woman his eternal love and loyalty, like Carl did to me that day. You probably think I'm orgasm obsessed. Well, that is true. I admit it. I am. But what is there in life that's better? I can't think of anything. Can you?*

'Carl often uses his wedding ring to titillate my clitoris, I have my longest lasting orgasms when he does me that way. It's a psychological thing. I relive that special day at our secret lake. A warm feeling comes over me. Knowing your husband is willing to sacrifice your marriage to enhance my carnal pleasures; that's thrilling! He's told me when he uses his ring to caress my clitoris, all his thoughts of you completely disappear. You cease to exist. You can't control him with that wedding ring; don't you know? That's a fantasy. When I tell Carl to divorce you, I'll ask him for his ring. I'll wear it on a special neckless, as my honor token; my gift from him. I'll even wear it while I perform in my porn films. That's will show Carl how proud I am; that I whored splendidly enough to earn his ring.'

"Are you almost at the part where you murdered her?" David was anxious to hear Marty reveal her murder method.

"Yes David. Soon. I next placed my hand upon her shoulder to steady her before I resumed. I needed to tell her the rest of what happened at our secret lake. She swallowed hard. She sat there, stoic and dismayed, staring fixated at my vagina. I continued:

'Our last sequence was climactic; spectacular. We were at our special, intimate quiet place. It's where the upper lake spills over a beaver dam and begins a tumbling stream. I love having sex by that stream. It's mirthful sounds relax me. Lily pads with bright yellow and white flowers bloom near the dam breast. Well, there I was with my legs widely spread. Carl loves me that way. There's something

irresistibly naughty about me when I do that. I think my butterfly tattoo signals that I'm free and promiscuous.

'That day, something magical happened. As Carl lifted my wide-spread legs from my position on the rocks, and eased my insatiable vagina onto the head of his penis, a kaleidoscope of little white butterflies appeared. They fluttered about, joyfully visiting the lily flowers. We watched them drinking the flowers' nectar. Everything was heavenly. The happy butterfly battalion carried our joy on its wings. My vagina was directly over Carl's cock. I was anxious to make love. The butterflies knew it. They understand us, you know. That day, they cheered for me.

'I mounted Carl while facing him. That's his favorite position for making love with me. He placed his hands on my breasts and massaged me. His fingers tenderly squeezed and tugged my nipples with loving, erotic pinches. They became so hard, I trembled. My vagina became hot again. I felt new moisture. My vagina was swollen as I slid onto his cock. My lady lips began squeezing tightly. I love feeling our unity during intimacy. I repeatedly contracted and released my Kegel squeezes on Carl's swollen cock, while kneading his balls with my hands. I love your husband's balls in my hands. I anticipated his eruption flow. I was so eager to feel his hot cum that my vagina began throbbing. He stroked me slowly. He slows his thrusts when he's about to come. His slowed strokes teased me into an erotic frenzy. Meanwhile, those little butterflies circled my head. 'Come inside me. Now,' I whispered.

'That was our moment. Carl's body trembled. His cock strained mightily. It pushed into my deepest wells; touching my cervix. Time was suspended. Magic was happening! I seized the moment. I squeezed his testicles. His explosive burst flooded me with hot, wonderful, thick cream. It streamed over my clitoris, filling me. One photo captures this moment. It's our best. Carl had it blown up to a two-foot-by-three-foot print. It's on his office wall, hidden

behind his landscape scene. He often steals a look at it. It holds him spellbound.

'Our intimacy was on fire that day. I was in my state of oral sex euphoria, smiling widely. It was the most memorable day of my life. My vagina pulsed with wanton rapture. I still felt sensations from Carl's cunnilingus when he ejaculated. When his hot semen coursed over my throbbing, swollen clitoris, it coaxed her to reciprocate. I released my most explosive orgasm of that afternoon.

'Tingles raced through my body. That photo captured my face as thousands of little fingers touched the inside of my vagina. My blood flared hot. I ran my hands over my sides, and up to my breasts. I cupped myself. Maybe I did that unconsciously for the camera. I don't know. I just felt so alive and sexy. Rapture thrills danced on every inch of my skin; everywhere over my body. I came alive with rhapsodic love.

'That was the moment captured in that special photo. Carl calls it our 'spectacular' moment. He thrust his still hard penis deeply into me. Everything happened simultaneously. While in the throes of releasing my explosive orgasm, I gushed a stream of Carl's semen. It flooded over his penis. He stayed rock hard; and he came again! He's amazing! While we had our fantastic, shared orgasm, a Monarch butterfly landed on my wispy strand of red hair. See it?'

"I pointed to it. She glanced up briefly; but then returned her stare to my vagina." 'That streak comes out of my birthmark, where my hairline meets my face. At that exact instant, the sun's rays burst out from behind a cloud. It was as if nature joined our miracle moment.

'The photo captured the butterfly with her wings spread upon my head. The sun's golden reflection highlights her yellow wings. They imitate my outspread legs. The butterfly's body beneath its wings resembles your husband's body attached to my vagina by his penis. Carl's shaft appears golden cream-colored in the sun's rays.

My face is beaming. I'm angelic and radiant. I experienced divine ecstasy. The camera caught my expression.

'The shutter caught the exact instant when my body convulsed with spasms of joyous lust. I screamed: 'Yes! Yes! Yes! I was delirious with delight. Fulfillment was in my eyes and my smile. My eyes looked up, into the heavens. I imagined a hundred handsome men voicing approval of my love making. Each man had a rock-hard erection. They all salivated, waiting their turn to hold me; and make love with me. I don't expect you to understand how I felt. But that's how my nymphomania plays with my mind.

'I imagined hearing the Sanctus, as we hear it now. I experienced complete, inner, holy peace. I imagined making love with every one of those men. My nymphomania overcame me. I don't expect you to understand why I felt this way; but just for one moment, imagine yourself feeling the same way that I felt. Imagine you want to make love, and you can never stop making love because you love lovemaking so much. That feeling enabled me to appear as I did in that amazing, unforgettable photo, when Carl's camera captured my passion-frenzied nymph feeling. I appreciate Carl and his magnificent cock so much! You have no idea! He uniquely understands how to release the shameless lust that seethes within me.

'Carl and I agreed. That photo is our best. It represents the triumph of a sex obsessed, nymphomania afflicted whore over a possessive self-absorbed, snobbish wife. It's the essential embodiment of freedom's glorious conquest over righteous moral rigidity. It captures my rapture state; savors my victory. It's a tribute to my insatiable, lusting vagina, joyously conquering you; your world; and everything you represent.'

Carl's wife shook her head slowly. Her mind registered defeat:

'Yes, you have conquered me. Do with me as you wish. I can no longer think for myself. I'll listen until the end of this.'

Marty continued:

'The butterfly with its widespread wings was nature's standing ovation for the beautiful experience we had. The sunlight on her delicate wings represented God's approval of our lust. That moment was profound. Even now, a year later, my vagina still throbs. I become creamy wet when I think back to it. You must go to your husband's office and see that photo. I insist. It's magnificent art. It's unforgettable. It will release you from the bondage of your ridiculous marriage.

'You need to appreciate that Carl is never truly away from me. I have a hold on him. Whenever he feels lonely, he looks at those lake photos; then he calls. He can't live without me. He's not himself until we meet in a hotel room. We love each other. We understand each other. Whenever he needs me, I go to him. So, please don't tell me that I don't know what my behavior does to your marriage. That's insulting. I know what it does. I know exactly what I'm doing to your marriage; and, I don't care. Look at what your bullying did to your marriage. Before you hurl criticism at me, look in a mirror.'

"Did she go to see the photos?" David's curiosity was peaked. "*I don't understand. Why did you tell her to go see the photos if you were going to murder her? The photos were in his office in Plaintown. Where did you think you going to kill her? Were you going to follow her, after she left the lake?*" David was impatient for answers.

"*Yes David. I followed her all right. I stayed in her mind. She couldn't get rid of me. I lived in her head. Please be patient, you'll see,*" Marty encouraged David to listen while she continued the telling of her story.

"*By now, Carl's wife was sitting on the second step with her hands over her ears, just shaking her head; crying. She was appalled. Her chest heaved in grief. She didn't want to hear another word. She was a typical bully. She refused to see her own behavior or accept her own role in this. There was no way to redeem her. And, I didn't want to. She was never going to change. She wanted me to stop; but I needed to persist. I needed to be cruel; but in a lovingly, devious sort of way, I needed to gain her trust.*

"I collapsed the personal space between us by stepping in front of her face. I showed her no respect; only contempt. I boldly rubbed the crown of my vagina's outer lips against her nose. Yes, I crushed her personal space that much. By touching my vagina's hood to her nose like I did, I focused her attention and fueled her obsession. Then I stepped back a few inches so her eyes could focus where I wanted them focused. I held my vagina's lips widely apart, taunting and inviting her.

"Her mouth opened. She flowed saliva. That awakened my voice of inner wickedness. It lifted from its chrysalis and fanned its deadly wings over my emotions. Miss Wicked's triumphant thoughts embraced my mind. Together we danced and marveled at the wife's fateful tell. Wicked's melodious voice sang sweetly in my mind. She awakened my soul's compulsion to murder:

'She wants you,' my trusted bloodthirsty guide affirmed. 'She'll give up her soul to you. Your patience is about to be rewarded. Savor this moment. Feel glorious and triumphant. Toy with her a while, like a cat torments a mouse, before it bites the head off. Do have fun torturing her mind, before you finish this pathetic wretch.'

"Clearly, David, Carl's wife wanted me. Her true feelings were out in the open. I saw her saliva tell. She was stripped of all pretenses about position, status, and dignity. Her mind was in my clutches. My evil hands clasped her soul; my evil arms embraced it. I could play now. I held her mind and soul in my grasp. I could amuse myself as I pleased. She looked intently into my vagina with her dogged fixed stare. An eerie silence hung between us. I didn't say a word. I let her mind fixate. She stared a long time. She was obviously self-absorbed; leaving her old world; transiting to her new world. There was no turning back. Her thoughts embraced their fascination. She considered her new, permissive sexual world. She began liking it.

She was convincing herself that she belonged. I saw her spirit rise in hope. Much like a mythical unicorn, she was; ready to prance from her dour world into my playful one. I needed to monitor her spirit carefully.

"Her gaze stayed riveted upon my opened vaginal lips, more intently focused now than before. Carl's pasty white cream slowly oozed out of me. She became hypnotic, entranced now by intimacy's wonders. My sex amulet was luring her mind away from consciousness to a new, mysterious, ether place. Looking beyond the flowing white from my whoring's proud reward, her mind now fluttered like a migrating female Monarch seeking desperately to mate; then craving peaceful solace sleep within my inner darkness spirit world.

"She wanted to kiss my mouth; run her hands through my hair; kiss me along my neck and over my entire body. I knew her impulses were true. I could read her sexual thoughts. They presented themselves like pages of an opened book. She wanted to kiss my sex from behind me; savor every inch of me with her deeply probing tongue. She yearned to rub my legs with her hands, while kissing my body everywhere. She wanted to stimulate me with her fingers; and rest my sex upon her face; so that her tongue could probe me; excite me; caress my clitoris while she held my ass tightly in her hands, savoring my orgasm flow.

"She was smitten and hypnotic. Her thoughts fluttered forward; spinning and twirling faster and faster, like a butterfly's mad dash-flight to mate. Her lust crazed senses raced blindly, like a blissful unicorn's, willfully leaping into my unknown mysterious darkness. She wanted to be compliant. Her desire to please me overwhelmed her cautions. Her limbic mind had raised the white flag of surrender. It was now in my control. It yearned to dwell with me, forever, in my darkness; abandon all thoughts of ever leaving there. Now, I could implement the final phase of my plan. I was ready. I would make her desire to do everything that I asked. Her limbic mind needed

to believe that, by obeying me, her deeds would please my amulet vagina.

'Now you know how things are,' I said. 'This was never about you or me. It's about love. My vagina cares about you. Please her. Accept her. Obey her and love her. Then, you'll become complete. Inhale deeply. Take in her delightful fragrances. She's iniquitous. She's semen-filled. She's a whore's heaven-place. You know you want her. You know you adore her. That pleases her. She always gets what she wants. You will do as she tells you. Remember: you must please her. Breathe deeply. Inhale her scents. Love her.'

"She sat there, continuing her frozen stare. From the forward stretch of her neck I knew she was entranced. Her new dark world awed her. The thought of oral sex with me sorely tempted her. She desperately wanted to hold my ass, softly kiss my stomach; slowly lower her head until her face became consumed within my nether place. She desired to leave her miserable life and surrender her soul to me; to let her mind drift dreamily into her transformative chrysalis; and enter her new, wonderful darkness. Her whole being came alive with sensations. She imagined touching her hands all over my body. She desired to become my love slave.

"My stomach and vagina were mere inches from her face. They flooded her field of vision. Hearing me explain the photo sequences had crushed her will power and ended all resistance. I moved my hips slowly back and forth before her face. Her eyes followed my brazen amulet-wonder. She wanted me more than she had ever wanted anything.

"She gazed into my inner lips, flooding her vision with my vagina. A steady stream of Carl's white semen continued oozing freely from me, holding her fascination. She began associating her amulet-vision with the glory of immorality. That cemented her wonderment to her new life. Her old life no longer mattered. My invasion of her limbic senses was complete. I knew that she would never forget this *moment. My dark battalions' forces had enveloped her mind and devoured her consciousness.*

"She now slid, mercifully, into a deeply hypnotic state. Her ability to think of anything other than my unrepentant, marriage-wrecking vagina was successfully blocked. My dark forces had run their swords through her sensibilities of goodness. Those forces lay murdered on the battlefield of souls. Lurid thoughts were now her only thoughts. She loved her new, blissfully dark place. Her semi-consciousness wanted to dwell within my whoring vagina forever. But her soul was not yet quite ready to join her mind. I would command that, too. But first I needed to do more.

"My cream pool and its stream of white awed her; kept her conscious senses arrested. Lust's impulses reverberated through her soul. She stared like a cornered mouse; wonder-paralyzed by its serpent predator. She quivered fearfully from her premonition. Like the mouse knew the snake's maw was its destiny, she also intuited that her soul's lusting spirit would drown in my pool of sin. Her breath quickened. She gasped. She was enraptured by lust, frozen in awe. Her soul glimpsed its first premonition of death. Yet she stared into the medium of her future demise; helpless to resist.

"I smiled down at her; not warmly and into her eyes as a friend would smile; but coldly, my eyes now fixed upon the top of her head, as a snake sizing up the mouse it would soon devour. My revenge feelings came out of hiding. I felt emboldened. My innermost contempt, in its sinister way, visited its pent-up bitterness upon her. Mother's rejection and my boarding school classmates shunning's by would soon be avenged! A transference of years of pent- up vengeance flowed from my thoughts. Certainly, I wanted her dead.

"Sometimes, David, I find myself disliking a certain woman. But this was more than dislike. This was hatred. I had to restrain myself from choking her. I realized I didn't need to choke her. Once I sensed her lust was unwavering; and her shocked sensibilities could

not oppose my darkness, I knew she would obey me. I had the power to end her life. And murder her in a way that no one would suspect.

"I spoke lovingly to her. I used guile, like a snake drawing stealthily closer to its prey. My voice assured her that I always acted in her best interest. I was aided by my soft background music. The Sanctus played again. In Latin, it implied that my vagina was her Lord of Hosts; her salvation opened before her; offered to her in glory. And, she should praise it. I don't know whether she understood Latin; but she seemed overcome with peace in that moment. I encouraged her to think she would become my lover. I knew that her limbic senses would love that outcome to her tormented day.

'My vagina wants to be your love goddess,' I said to her. 'This is the angelic vagina that reflected beauty from the lake into the heavens. Carl has already left your marriage. He has turned his back to you. Now, every time he makes love with me, he walks further away from you. He's made his choice. Now, you can make yours.

'Carl's penis worships my vagina. It enters me and communes with my vagina in a special holy intimacy. His ejaculations repeatedly sacrifice your marriage to me and my sins. LOOK! Look CLOSELY into her. Look DEEPLY into her. She IS your new world. She's ALL you have left. Imagine YOURSELF entering HER. You CAN be with HER. Your husband was here with her, before you arrived. He was honoring her when you came here. You CAN ATONE for your intrusion. You MUST place your trust in her. She is a forgiving, loving, welcoming goddess.'

"I urged her to lick me," said Marty. "I do some women. I enjoy doing them and I'm always willing to try a new partner. I doubted she'd go for my invitation, but I thought I'd control her by making my offer. She could know, with certainty, how amoral I am. So, I presented her with a choice. She could become one of my lovers, or she could reject me. I calculated that she'd reject me. And, I needed her to reject me. That would force her soul to reveal itself and step out *into the open. Then I could plant my seeds of destruction that would eviscerate her soul. I needed her to leave me, while still hypnotized; while despairing that she had made the wrong choice; and feeling inadequate and dispirited. If she was that fragile, I believed she'd obey my order to take her own life."*

"You're deliciously evil, Marty. I love you for that," said David. "Just listening to how your mind works makes me desire you myself, but please continue," David insisted.

CHAPTER SEVEN

"After all," as a pretty girl once said to me, "women are a sex by themselves, so to speak." (Sir Max Beerbohm: The pervasion of rouge)
Variety is the soul of pleasure (Aphra Behn: The rover)

NYMPHOMANIA CALLS

Marty laughed. Her immediate needs compelled her to interrupt the story. *"So, David, I've gone from getting fired to possibly making love with you! David, you surprise me. You know I'm engaged to Bob. I'll soon be a married woman, but I am highly flattered by your thought. Would you like me to stop talking? We could pause my story; enjoy ourselves; perhaps share our intimacy? I'd like that very much, David. It would complete us. You know it would make us both very happy. Consider it. It's a delicious thought."*

"Tempting, Marty, but I think we should wait until you tell the rest of your story about that pesky wife." David's eyes met Marty's but they offered no encouragement. They were emotionless, vacant, disinterested. They may as well have been watching dust particles settling downward within a lifeless room.

"Oh, that's okay, David. I won't lose my train of thought, I promise," Marty assured him; now pushed him. Desire flashed in her eyes, *"I'm ready, David. I'd love to make love with you. It would bring us so much closer together. Please don't feel shy. I'd enjoy it, especially here in the open air. Let's."*

"Ha, thank you Marty, but I'm so interested in the story now, I'd like to hear the rest of it, first." David's head shake affirmed his disinterest.

"But, David, honestly, I'm feeling it really badly. I'm not pretending. I need it." Marty persisted now. She was aroused from the telling of her story. Her erotic passions were stirred. Murder always had that effect on her. Retelling the events of that day made her mind race. She felt like an abandoned child again. Without a penis inside her; and not being cuddled and kissed, she became a delicate psychic organism; deprived of its most important need: that of being loved. With a penis thrusting inside her, with loving hands caressing her body and an eager mouth joined to her own, she could possess the intimacy she especially craved in moments like these. Love making was the only antidote that counteracted her abandoned feeling. Then, she could feel her sex partners' emotive needs while searching for, and discovering her own. Her nymphomaniac urges desperately needed such a sexual partner now.

"What? You can't be that way, now!" David voice tone had a touch of humor in it. But it was blended with an order. Plainly, he wanted Marty to stop talking this way.

"Yes. I am. It's there, David. I can't control it. It's real." She resisted. She didn't want to stop. Her voice sounded like the pleadings of a little girl who wanted her cookie.

"But we have no victim here!" Now David sounded incredulous. He jokingly mocked her. *"We don't even have blood for you. It's not the same, Marty. We've only been talking about a murder."* David tried to dodge her needs and sidetrack her thoughts. He didn't dare comply with her request, no matter how desperate her plea. He knew too many things that she could not know. He would keep his secrets from her until everything was perfect and ready; but not one moment before.

David's words challenged Marty's innermost craven thought. It had to come forward now. The real reason she decided to visit him today had broken containment from its dark hidden place, a forbidden place she had long secreted, even from her own consciousness. Her inner psyche came alive. Hot coals of passion lust suddenly raged. Her psyche's voices sang their favorite hymn of seduction's lust. The strains of *Ave Maria* sounded and echoed in her memory. Stronger and stronger, she felt the powers of the hymn until, through her eyes, it pleaded with David to slake her lust and satisfy her. The abandoned little girl inside her desperately wanted him to comfort her, to love her; and, yes, to ravage her crazily; and finally become an intimate partner with her. Her eyes bared her inner soul to David, pleading with him to take her. *Take me, and fuck me,* they begged.

"I know it, David, but my feeling has come," Marty's confession poured out of her. *"It's the same feeling I have after every time we murder. It's come to me from just talking about killing her. It has swept over me and I'm helpless when I'm in its power like this. I must, David, I really have to make love, David. It's overwhelming me. I can't think of anything else. You know how insanely out of control I become.*

"Remember that man who suddenly realized what I was doing? Remember how he tried to get away from me? Remember how my assistants had to tackle him and hold him down while I retrieved my knife? Remember how loudly he cried and screamed; how he pleaded that he had a family and all that; and how he said: 'No, oh please, God no' over and over, begging me to stop, while I repeatedly stabbed him over thirty times? Remember how covered with blood he was, David? His blood made such a mess I had to stop after every two or three stabs and wipe the blood away from his chest and stomach so I could see a clean patch of skin where I could stab him again. I was so furious with him. I tried to put my

knife into every organ he had. I even rolled him onto his sides so I could stab his kidneys.

"Remember how I laughed crazily every time he writhed and tried to squirm away from the assistants? That triggered me. I went momentarily insane. In my madness, I realized he thought he could get away. He was a fool to think he could prevent me from my ultimate pleasure. I became furious. That's why I kept stabbing him. I stopped thinking of him as a person. He became a problem. He needed to learn a lesson. He was arrogant to think he could get away. I understood then, in those moments, why you wanted him murdered.

"His screaming got me so crazy excited. My nymphomania went wild. I even laughed while I was stabbing him, remember? Every scream told me I was closer to having great sex. Every stab, every scream made me more euphoric. I was so turned on, David! I had to stab him until he didn't scream anymore. I had to kill him! When I was certain I'd killed him, I told you to leave his body lying there, remember? That's because I couldn't wait another minute. I even made you wait to take away his body while I made love with our assistants, remember? Remember how wildly sex crazed I was that night? I was a wildcat! That's how strong my urge becomes whenever I murder, David. It just erupts. I can't hold it back."

"Yes, I remember. How could I forget? That was unreal. I was afraid he was going to get away. I couldn't have murdered him that way. I couldn't have done what you did. I don't even think the assistants could have done what you did. I saw how manic you were while you stabbed him. You stabbed him enough to kill him five times over."

"Yes, that's what nymphomania does to my hormones. When it triggers, nothing stops me. I was furious. He refused to die cleanly, like the others. He wasted my time. My body was screaming with

lust. That's what caused my rage state. I had to get a cock inside me. When I'm like that, I have no other feelings.

"Well, David, that's how I feel now. I have those same desires, because we've been talking about murder. I can't stop my feelings when my addiction takes control of me like this. I can't help myself, David. David, I'm begging you to take me. Please, David, I can't do anything else when I feel this way. Please, it's SO strong inside me. I MUST let it out before I burst. PLEASE David. Please, I NEED you to. I MUST have sex."

David took a deep breath and stared. His eyes met Marty's eyes, but they did not see inside her feelings. Looking into hers, they saw something beyond her needs. He stared as if peering into a deep void, even seeing beyond the bottom of it. His mind was somewhere else, in a time and place long ago and far away. His look was nothing like the warm approving looks of approval he gave her after their murders.

Marty noticed his different, vacuous look. A strange twinge of foreboding crossed her thoughts. She saw and felt something. She had never seen or felt that oddity before; and, she couldn't process it. Her blood chilled. Her mind raced wildly. Her emotions were unsteady. She didn't know what to feel. She knew how to respond to a man's ardor; his hatred or his anger; but this stare that David held contained none of those. It was a nothing stare, a blank slate with the lifeless gaze of a reptilian's eyes looking out from it. It was cold and uncaring.

'*Has he found me repulsive, perhaps too forward? Has my overture disgusted him?*' she wondered.

She willed her lust to chill until she understood what had happened. Her urge to make love receded some. She rationalized:

'*Maybe David's mind is on an important business matter. After all, he is always the strange and impossible to understand David.*

That doesn't need to stop me from reliving the great feelings I had that fateful day when I got rid of Carl's wife. Maybe David will want sex with me later.' Marty waited for David's answer.

"Marty, I'm terribly sorry. It's just the two of us," he said. "Our assistants aren't here. We'll have to wait until after you've finish telling me about Carl's wife and your other exploits. I'll surprise you then. Hold off just a little while longer, I know you can get through this. Take a few deep breaths. Relax a moment. You'll be fine. I insist that we wait. You'll see, just calm down. We'll make love later. Your experience will be that much better. I promise you."

'*I'm feeling something very weird here,*' Miss Iniquity confided to Marty. '*Ninety-nine men out of a hundred would drop everything after you gave them an opening like that. They'd take you in their arms and hold you. They wouldn't care that you're a murderess. They'd understand your feelings after the way you laid them out there like that on a silver platter. They'd embrace you, adore you; and they would make love with you. They'd be kissing your mouth and touching you everywhere. Any normal man would already be kissing your juicy peach, shedding his pants, and touching his penis against your outer lips. He'd be starting to penetrate you. He'd soon be making love with you, like he was lust crazed out of his mind; but not David. What's holding him back? You need to be cautious. You should have taken me out of the closet last night; and listened to me, instead of Miss Promiscuity. You two are trouble! Now, here you are, alone with David in his barn and naked on some hay bales. David may have a hidden agenda. Why must you always listen to Miss Promiscuity? She never thinks of risks. Her mind is always on sex. Just keep your wits about you.*'

"All right, David, I'll continue," Marty steeled herself to continue her recounting of the murder. She forced her cravings back into their dark hiding place. "But I'll gladly stop if you change your mind."

CHAPTER EIGHT

This wild abyss, this womb of nature and perhaps her grave (John Milton: Paradise Lost)

LOVING DARKNESS

Marty's eyes gave an inviting smile to David. He returned her hopeful smile with a wan smile of his own. It was smile enough to reassure her that, despite his rejection of her offer of sex, he was still her trusted partner in murder. Her lips tightened ever so slightly as she doused the glowing lust coals that burned within her bosom. She picked up the story:

"I continued speaking to Carl's wife:

'I'm inviting you to make love with me. I'm offering my vagina to you,'

'You may love her like your husband does. It's all right. It will be our secret. I won't tell Carl that you've made love with me,'

"I promised her in my most confiding, girl to girl conspiratorial voice:

'It will be our girl's-only secret. Go ahead,'

"I encouraged her: 'Surrender your feelings. Kiss your hang ups goodbye. You'll discover the truth about yourself. I'll help you. You can become an immoral whore, like me. Oh, come on, don't hold back. Being a whore is wonderful. You'll see. You'll love it.

'Please kiss me there. Let me feel your tongue inside me. Wouldn't you like to taste me? There's no reason not to,' I said in my most reassuring voice.

'My vagina has already wrecked your marriage. That's gone. But so, what? You haven't really lost anything. You weren't happy anyway. You know that's true. You can admit it to me. I understood the truth about your marriage the very first time Carl and I made love. We both knew your marriage was a joke. You may as well acknowledge it, too. Go ahead,' I said encouragingly, 'Let yourself go. Start slowly by kissing my vagina on her crown; then lick me there; then tell me that you love my lady lips. Being honest will help you accept your own desires. We both know you want to kiss me there. Go ahead. It's a beautiful thing to do. You know you'll enjoy it. You'll wish you'd done it long before now.

'We can be happy. We'll get along beautifully. It's up to you. If you'll ask my forgiveness for interrupting my pleasures; if you'll promise to respect, honor, and love the things that I and my vagina do with Carl, I'll forgive you. I will; promise. I'm a loving person. I'll forget your vile thoughts and your nasty words as if you never thought or spoke them. But if you won't kiss my vagina; and if you won't admit that you honestly love her and the salacious whoring she does; and if you refuse to apologize for intruding here; then you'll insult me.'

"Then, I spoke in a matter-of-fact tone, like a mother would to an adult daughter:

'That would disappoint me.'

"I'm amazed that you made that offer to her. It seems counterintuitive and crazy. It was contrary to your goal of getting rid of her." David frowned with a puzzled look.

"I had my reasons, David. You'll see. I was proving to her that I could be her trusted friend, David." Marty shrugged her shoulders. She smiled her sincere, innocent smile to David. *"She needed to*

believe in me if she was going to obey what I was about to tell her to do.

"Visualize her, David. She sat there, stoically, like a stump. She stared a misty, wistful stare into my vagina. Her conscious mind was gone. Her limbic mind was all she had. And it was following her dreamy stare into her guiding amulet, my vagina; and bringing her soul along into its new dark world. But she made no move to lick me! That was key. Her soul kept her frozen in place! She could not lick me. Her soul's religious training had her body paralyzed. She was behaving much like a butterfly that had entered chrysalis. I knew that I had one last bit of work to do."

'*If only you knew how conflicted I am.*' The wife's thoughts sought Marty's mind; seeking her new friend's compassion; and wrestling with her inner turmoil. The wife knew that this was her key, pivotal moment. Her psyche was on a high dive platform, needing to jump into her new life; but afraid:

'*I want to come to you; but I can't. Can't you see I've fallen in love with you? Please end my hell. Send me away. Be finished with me. Let me die, if that's what pleases you. Only please don't torture my mind any longer. I must know peace. I beg you to stop.*'

'*You are making a decision,*' I spoke to her frozen mind. *After watching her indecision, I warned her that I was about to foreclose on her choice:*

'*Realize that if you don't surrender your moral soul to my incorrigible vagina, I will destroy you. You understand, don't you, that your husband would like you to die? You can see from his semen that was pooled inside me that he wants freedom from you. He's already fluttered away from you. His soul lives in my immoral world now. I'd also like you to die. But I'm willing to forgive you, if you choose to become one of my lovers.*'

"I was gracious when I made that offer, David. I, too, once had rigidities. But the changes that have transformed me pleased my

voices and my spirits, especially Satan's spirit, my inner devil. I knew that many sanctimonious religious types are easily tempted. They harbor secret closets in their hearts, where lust resides. They covet lust but pretend they don't. She was a rigid moralist. I believed that she deserved this chance to open herself to sin; to confess her innermost desires to me; and revel in lust with me. I also perceived that her soul was not ready to convert. It needed more time.

"She continued her transfixed stare while the Sanctus played softly. She didn't move. She didn't act upon my offer. Her core behavior was hopelessly caged by her social and religious indoctrinations. Her brain was imprisoned in the male structured order. I pitied her soul. It was trapped; caged. But I also felt relieved that she didn't accept my offer. That told me her soul wanted to find its own way to perdition.

"Understand, David. I never actually wanted her friendship. If she had licked me, I'd have become obligated to embrace her and help her become a passable whore. There would have been much work involved. I would have reoriented her moral compass; reprogramed her mind and liberated her. I could have helped her earn a decent living. There's a huge market for prostitution. Lots of men enjoy a quick tumble. But most men have little money and big dreams. They're easy to spot. They hit on me constantly with promises of a dinner and a good time. They have corny pick-up lines and they reek of cheap cologne. Some even wag their tongues at me, thinking that might make me cream in my panties.

"Those types are dangerous to women of my profession. They paw women with their grimy hands and slobber on us with their bad breath. Then they expect to use us to vent their frustrations with their parents, wives, and employers. They believe a whore substitutes for a lost childhood or a missed promotion. Some have precious little money to offer. Some become violent when they realize the relationship is *only about money. Those are not my type. I scrupulously avoid them. I study my clients first and then I make the approach; and only after I'm satisfied that my prospect is the real deal.*

"*I thought Carl's wife might be perfectly suited to service the brutish males. I would have given her pointers, even advanced her some cash to get some beauty work done. I even considered, for a few minutes, that she might become my hobby project. That thought intrigued me. She would challenge my management skills. Could I proselytize as well as the religions, with their flashy ceremonies and elaborate rituals? Could I raise money on an organizational scale, like the televangelists; but by using legions of whores instead of television and door to door missionaries? Could I be as successful as the bible thumpers with their TV shows and stagecraft? Could I rake in more money than the Pope?*

"*But my thoughts became muted. Obviously, she wasn't willing to go the prostitute route. The offer of my vagina wasn't going anywhere. She didn't want to become friends. She just sat there, immobilized. Her body seemed frozen and her mind numbed. She behaved like a butterfly that had entered transformative chrysalis. My whimsical fleeting idea about helping her was still-borne. I gave up on it. Her stare was fixated on something more compelling and far beyond the creamy whiteness pooled inside me. She saw the endless misery of continuing her life with Carl and with me as Carl's true love. She sensed that her transformation lay ahead.*"

'*Force her choice, now,*' Miss Iniquity urged Marty during this moment while Carl's wife sat transfixed on my vagina. '*She won't accept you. If she stays frozen like this, you'll know she's been successfully hypnotized. Then you can give her your commands.*'

"*I sensed it was time, David. It was time for me to push her soul into darkness where it could unite with her prurient limbic thoughts. I spoke ever so softly, encouraging her:*

'You need to understand your choice,' I said, all the while know-ing she was already too far gone into her transformation to accept my offer:

'My erotic, cream-filled vagina waits for you. You'll love her taste. You must submit. Kiss her. Love her if you wish to live. Do you understand?'

"She had reached her hypnotic state?"

"Yes, David, she was there."

"And you did this by seducing her voyeur mind with your vagina; by holding yourself open; swaying back and forth in front of her; talking with her; coaxing her imagination to enter some magical ethereal world, where her troubles would fall away? That's incredible."

"Yes, David, where she could find peace of mind and happiness. At this point she could only stare her hypnotic stare. She nodded slightly. She heard me, but nothing I could say or do now would break her concentration. She was fixated on thoughts of leaving her world behind; entering my wonderful, peaceful darkness. She imagined that a magical ethereal place existed somewhere within my vagina. I sensed that she awaited my instructions. She wanted me to tell her how to enter her imaginary dark, peaceful world. I felt certain she was now captive to my wishes and commands. But I needed to test this belief; see if I could touch or push her. And still see her remain in her trance state. I raised my voice slightly, but firmly, to issue my commands:

'Look at her!' I commanded:

'Stare into my beautiful whoring vagina. You're looking at the vagina that owns your husband. It destroyed your marriage. My vagina did you a favor. She has freed you. Your marriage was mis-erable. It needed to be destroyed. My vagina is your best friend. She's right before your face. She wants you. She's touching herself to your nose and lips now. Go ahead. Let yourself go. Put your tongue inside *me. I am life! Taste me. Taste your husband's semen. He told me you've never tasted it. He told me you are wretched in bed. Change that. Show him.'*

"I spoke confidentially. She didn't budge an inch. She stayed fixated to my darkness."

"She was totally hypnotized, right?"

"Yes, David. She was in her hypnotic state. I could program her mind to do as I wished. So, in my softest voice as one woman confiding to another, I said:

'You really should know how your husband's semen tastes, after it has blended with fluids from my orgasm. It will help you shed your inhibitions and become completely uninhibited. You'll be happy. You'll be glad you did it. You'll never forget it, I promise.'

"I set out to open the final door her mind needed to pass through. I sought to show her that she could leave her moral world behind; and walk hand in hand with her soul, into my eternal darkness. I gave her my hypnotic instructions:

'Imagine you have become a miniature version of yourself. You are now deep inside my delicious cream pool. You're holding my clitoris, Gloria, in your hands. You love Gloria. You're licking her. You love licking her. You love the taste of my juices. Carl's cock is above your head. My vagina is squeezing Kegels tightly around his cock. Huge globs of creamy white semen are spurting from Carl's cock. These globs flood over your head. You are now swimming in my creamy juices. For the first time in your life, you love how you feel about yourself. You beg Carl and me to give you more. I squeeze. Carl's cock spurts, again. You open your mouth and swallow Carl's semen. You are finally complete and content.'

"Carl's wife's mind finally discovered hope. She whisper-spoke, tremulously:"

'Yes; I do want to dwell inside your cream pool. I'd love feeling your joys while you orgasm and flow. Help me get there, inside you.

I'm ready. I want to leave everything. Help me leave myself. Help me leave who I am; help me leave my soul; everything that I am. Help me go into you. Speed me there. I want to be inside you.'

"I needed to let her know that her husband's bond to me would never break; and that it gave me strength; that this bond would not be undone. I spoke to her as a friend would speak:

'You first owe it to yourself to know why your husband loves me. This shameless woman you call a whore stands before you. I offered you friendship; and to taste me and kiss me. You didn't expect to shame me or make me run away, did you?'

"Her lips quivered, her head and body trembled a little. She was deeply conflicted. In her trance state she finally understood everything. She desperately wanted to lick me, but she was prevented by her years of male religious indoctrination. Her world, that world that she could once control, now spun out of control. I could feel her psychic energy. She desperately wanted to grab my ass and bury her mouth in my vagina, but she held herself back. Then, she flicked her tongue out for an instant and let it touch the semen that ran down my leg. Then she pulled her tongue back just as quickly; and her head, also. That brief, timid tongue flick confirmed her limbic senses had progressed all the way into darkness. But her soul still couldn't overcome her male ordered taboos. She wanted to do so much more, but she couldn't force herself to come any further. Ingrained rigidity still clung to her. I needed to pry it loose.

"I took some semen. I rubbed it on her lips and under her nose to confirm my dominance; and insult her programmed existence. It was my way of replicating the same disdain for my victim that the Aztec priests showed for theirs, when they tossing their decapitated bodies down the temple steps. I wanted her to feel unworthy of living, because of her programmed life. The mousey coward just sat there. She stared fixated at my vagina; softly sobbing. She was grief-stricken, devastated; yet in a state of beholden wonderment

and in my vagina's amulet trance. Her marriage had been her whole world. My rapaciously lust-craven honey pot had devoured it. Her chest heaved. On some level both her limbic desires, and now, finally, her conscious mind as well, wanted the life I offered, instead of her misery life. But she couldn't quite make her rigid soul take its first step. Perhaps, I thought, that would come later, when she was by herself.

"I was certain my dark forces now controlled both her conscious and subconscious thoughts, but years of religious indoctrination made one last deep recess of her soul difficult to reach. It was hard wired. The choice I had put before her core sensibility had caused her such consternation that she had difficulty breathing. And, the Sanctus continued playing.

"I had achieved my desired effect. I had given her every opportunity to ask forgiveness for interfering with my intimacy. I had given her the opportunity to accept me. There was nothing more to do. She knew that Carl and I came here often. She knew Carl's mind caressed me with thoughts of erotic, romantic love, each day. She knew he obsessed over me. She knew where she could see the photos of our love making. She could no longer pretend I didn't control him. Now, she sat on my cabin's steps, softly sobbing outside the cabin door. Her soul was shaken to its core. From that tortured soul's frayed hard-wired circuitry, her crackled voice spoke. She mouthed a broken, barely audible whisper:

'Carl. Carl, please come to me.'

"That final utterance was spoken more as a reflexive farewell to her past life than an honest plea for help. She was ready to leave the cabin; leave Carl; leave everything, even leave her life; except she could not leave the vivid images I had etched into her mind. Those would cling to her.

"Her half-hearted plea was the voice of hope lost. Carl was not going to mount some white steed and come riding to her

rescue. He would not return her to her past world. He would not enable her to stay in my world, either. She now, finally, understood that she needed to leave my world; the world she never wanted; the one her soul rejected; the world she didn't want to join. The world she wanted was her gracious genteel world. It was where people ate carefully crafted cakes of honor, respect, morality, and high ethics. And where people licked pretentious icings from snobbery's cake. But that was her yesterday world. It was gone now. It no longer existed. My whoring had soiled it; trampled it into the mud; ruined it for her. She needed a husband to navigate the waters of genteel world; but she no longer had a husband. Honest immorality; disrespect for pretense; expressive wanton lust and carnal shamelessness; those were the staples of my world. They had replaced her world and taken her husband to my world.

"Didn't she see my world coming and colliding with hers? Perhaps she did. But she did nothing about it until it was too late. Perhaps she believed I'd stop and leave Carl alone if she ignored me. That might have worked if I didn't have my nympho urges and my incredibly strong need for Carl. Then too, maybe deep within herself, she wanted her marriage trap to end. Maybe she secretly hoped I'd ultimately release her from her confining life. Maybe she intuited that I was the catalyst that would end her housewife hell. I'll never know what thoughts bedeviled her frazzled mind.

"It's hard to be someone when you don't know who you are or who you want to be. Maybe she never thought about such things. Regardless, she did not accept my invasion of her marriage gracefully. That opportunity had now passed her by. But, devious me, I knew she was fated to accept my invasion; perhaps in a fit of ungainly screams; perhaps in some maladroit, harmful way; or perhaps, I hoped, by willfully killing herself and accepting me in death. So, here she sat. Her worthless life was reduced to sitting on my cabin

steps. She whimpered pathetically, locked into her trance-state. She mumbled incoherent mouth sounds.

"Carl didn't hear her. I held myself back from laughing at her. Her life was such a pathetic joke. Tear drops of dying hope streamed from her eyes. They were dissembled emotions from her frayed mental circuitry, nothing more. Her whimpers fell on my deaf ears. I didn't feel sorry for her. I never once felt sorry for her. Her fears and inadequacies were no match for my confidence and cunning. A funny feeling swept me. I sensed it was a blessing to grow up getting kicked around, emotionally. It makes a person tougher if they can come through it. It makes one more circumspect of others and their motives. It tends to sharpen one's wits.

"My thoughts turned back to her. I wanted her to leave. I was half-crazed by this bother she had caused. I was dying to get back inside the cabin and resume love making. I knew I had defeated her. That caused my ego to soar and my hormones to surge. I felt an overwhelming desire to make love again. Lust flames for Carl's body were flaring within me. It was becoming hard to stay patient with her."

'You need to end to this, now,' said Miss Iniquity to Marty at that important moment:

'You're not going to make her any more hypnotized or bereft than she already is. You have the result you want. Be careful not to leave anything of yours or this cabin with her when she departs. You have no idea what she might do.'

"It was the decisive moment. I needed her to leave us and die. It was time to end her pathetic life. I spoke softly, but matter of factly.:

'You've made your choice; We are finished here. You must leave now. You are not welcome here. Your husband doesn't want anything to do with you. You must do as I tell you. You must leave here and die. By dying, you will discover peace. You will awaken to a new life. It will be filled with love and happiness. You have

something important to do now. Do as I instruct you. Do you understand me?'

"She nodded her head. She was ready to follow instructions.

'Very good. Now, look into my amulet vagina.'

"Her stare returned to my vagina. Her eyes fixated firmly on it.

'Very good. Now, remember my eyes. Imagine that you can also see my eyes. My eyes are behind the wings of my vagina's butterfly. Can you see them?'

"She nodded again."

'When you look into my amulet, you can see my eyes behind the wings of my butterfly. Are you seeing them?'

"Again, she nodded."

'Very good. My eyes are there for you. They are waiting to receive your soul. Remember my eyes. When you die, your soul will go through my eyes and into my soul; and, when your soul is inside my soul, you will discover your new life. Do you understand?'

"Another nod confirmed that she was following my directions.

'You are doing very well. You have nothing to fear. Remember, when you die, everything will become wonderful. All your pains and hurts will leave you. By going through my amulet and into my eyes you will discover peace and love in your new life. You will become free to flutter like the butterflies do. Do you understand?'

'Yes,'

"Her spoken voice sounded as if it came from a far away place. My hypnotic trance was working beautifully."

'Now, listen carefully. I'm commanding you to leave here and die. From this moment on, think only of my amulet vagina and my eyes, think how badly you want to kiss my vagina and come inside her and how you must go into my eyes. Think how badly you needed to make love with me. Remember how you wanted to lick me everywhere. You wanted to lick my clitoris. But your old life rejected me. Now, you must punish your old life by dying; and you must take on *your new life. You will find happiness when you die. Think only of my amulet vagina and my eyes. Think of nothing else until you die. You are going away. You are going away to do a good thing. You are going to leave now; and you are going to die. Remember, you are going to die. Always remember, you need to die.'*

"*I softly repeated my commands several times to be sure she would stay under my hypnotic spell. I was confident that I had finally convinced her soul to enter my darkness. Getting her to obey my death command would confirm that my method worked.*"

'Tell me: will you obey me and do as I have instructed you?'

"*Carl's wife's mind understood. She answered me:*

'Yes, I will do as you say, anything to please you, anything to let you know how deeply I love you, and how I burn inside with desire for you. I will obey you.' She nodded while holding her stare.

Miss Shameless voiced her enthusiastic approval:

'*Well done,'*

The naughty voice of Miss Iniquity spoke:

'Go back inside. Be with Carl. Do not feel one smidgeon of guilt over what you have done to her. Remember, she's a bitch. Think of her as a lowly, cockroach pest that you have crushed under your foot. Be glad that you're finally rid of her.

'Go inside. Be the magnificent, irresistible whore that you are. Play your lace nightgown lightly across Carl's face and body. Fill him with desire. Arouse him. Lie on him. Smother him with your passion kisses. Fondle his cock while you whisper loving words to him. He's completely yours now. Make love with him until he forgets his wife ever existed. Go to him. Tie his hands and feet to the bedposts. Lick his balls; take off his wedding ring; place it on the tip of his tongue. Tell him you'd like oral sex as your reward for getting rid of her. Suck his cock while you settle your loving lady lips onto his face.

'Tell him you'd like to experience the greatest orgasm you've ever had. Tell him you want to hear him confess his love to you. Make

him promise you that he'll never regret leaving his wife for you. Suck him until he's hard. Tease him crazy with your oral sex. Slide his fabulous cock inside you and enjoy this precious time. Appreciate your freedom. You are free of her! Have the delightful, uninterrupted orgasm you've been craving to have. You've earned it. You deserve it. Feel proud of yourself! You've crushed her. Feel happy for Carl, too. You've set him free! The way you dismantled her mind was brilliant. You were glorious, wonderful! Go to him. Be proud of what you've done to her. Feel glorious while you make love with him!'

CHAPTER NINE

When I consider life, 'tis all a cheat; yet fooled with hope, men favor the deceit (John Dryden: Aureng- Zebe)

LOVE ME

"I left her sitting there," Marty continued, *"I was confident she would faithfully obey my commands. Her tongue would never live to speak a word of my treachery. The waves that lapped upon the lake shore; the moon, the pines and the birch trees were the only witnesses to my wickedness that night. My words were carried away on the soft summer breeze, never to be heard again.*

"I imagined that the consoling which she so badly craved was my need, not hers. By putting my mind into her place, I summoned up all the hurt feelings I needed to convince Carl that she was the bad actress that night; not me.

'Yes,' I thought. 'I won't stop with stealing her husband. I'll also steal her feelings. I'll use them to take her husband's soul from her. He'll never know the truth. She'll die and never tell him what happened between us. I'll purloin her hurts and make Carl believe those are my hurts. He'll pity my wounded dignity. He'll comfort my injured pride. He'll assuage my feigned abuse from his stubborn, insensitive wife. And, above all, he will love me even more. I'll ply him with sex while I shove her out of his mind.'

"I went back into the cabin, closed and locked the door behind me." His wife's last faint sobs and sniffles were barely audible. She

had given up all hope. She was in her trance. She accepted that she'd lost the confrontation and her husband. Now she steeled herself for the task before her. Her final whimpers died away. A long silence followed. I felt deliciously heartless and wanton, knowing that she was still outside my cabin, sitting on the steps; and I was inside; already kissing her husband. Asserting myself, I placed my hand on his cock. I ignored her and stroked his cock with my fingers. I wanted to make love with Carl more than I've ever wanted to make love with anyone. I could imagine his excited swollen cock touching my yearning outer lips, opening me with its gentle pressure. I wanted my hands on his ass, pulling his cock gently inside me. I imagined my hips cradling him, moving his marvelous cock deeper and deeper inside me. I felt wicked, glorious, and supremely confident in my sexuality.

"Smiling at Carl, I imagined his wife had gone 'poof' and disappeared. I forced all thoughts of her from my mind and willed myself to believe she had taken my advice. I pretended she was already dead. And there we were, the two of us, making love; and with her gone, forever.

"My grin widened. I shook my head playfully, slowly from side to side, holding myself back from an outburst of roaring laughter. Carl and I often communicate silently like that. Our smiles are our secret language. My smile told Carl he owed me for his mistake of marrying her in the first place; and that he owed me double for disposing of her. My eyes told him that I understood that he regretted marrying her; and that I knew he'd be much happier with me as the only woman in his life.

"His eyes returned their understanding to mine. He knew he didn't want any part of marriage or family life; that his wife was the result of his mistaken thinking; and that he was grateful I corrected it for him. His soft, brown eyes told me he understood that I expected him to give me the greatest sexual performance of his life,

in appreciation of what I did for both of us; but, even more than that, his eyes told me how much he deeply loved me and all my incorrigible, whoring ways. He loved me more than any love he'd ever known before, or any love he would ever have in his future. His eyes were telling me they understood that this was his moment of freedom. We rubbed our noses and naked bellies together, smiling to each other. We knew we were about to have delicious fun.

"I teased his naked body by touching him playfully with my silk nightgown. When his face returned my winsome, teasing smile, I slipped into the bed and lied next to him. We were naked. Our hands began touching our bodies, exploring the wonder of our new freedoms. As he lay there, he placed his hands behind his head, lifting it some. He smiled. His eyes were curious."

'She's leaving, isn't she? You stood your ground and she gave up, didn't she?'

'Yes baby. She won't bother us anymore,' "I purred while I caressed Carl's massive chest.

"I felt wildly romantic. I was free to be my shameless sexy self. I could seduce Carl all over again. I wanted to love him so lovingly that night that I'd make him forget his wife ever existed. I'd help him see that she was just wrong headed to meddle in our love making. I applied reverse psychology to make my point. I lifted my head and smiled while I squinted my eyes:

'That bitch really upset me, Carl. She tried to break us up. She was horrible to me.'

"I pursed my lips as if to keep myself from breaking out in tears. I wanted to cleave Carl's sympathies to me for what she had put me through and to cement his love and loyalty to me. I made her out to be the wicked one. I tied Carl's hands to the bed posts. Then I lifted myself up onto his magnificent body, pressed my naked self gently against him, helping him feel how much I needed him; and

how badly I wanted him to make love with me. I kissed him full on his mouth, playfully teasing his tongue with mine, while at the same time rubbing his forehead, temples, and eyelids softly with my fingers. The Credo began playing as I whispered to Carl:

'She came here thinking she could boss you around, Carl. Now she knows she can't. She accepts that we love each other and she'll never change that. She'll leave us alone now. We can make love without feeling any guilt.'

"As I massaged his face, I heard her faintly whisper:
'Goodbye Carl.'

"I heard her car door close. She started the engine and drove away. I closed my eyes and prayed to Misses Promiscuity, Shameless, and Iniquity that my hypnotic spell would hold, and that she would finally be out of my life."

Marty harkened back to Miss Promiscuity's words:

'She's gone. Enjoy him. Be your sexiest self. Flood his senses with lust. Love him. Tell him you need him. Make him feel important. Make love until you both collapse from exhaustion.'

"The Credo's amplitude rose while I whispered softly:

'I'm here, my love. I'll always be here for you. Please help me get my mind off her filthy mouth. Help me forget the horrible, traumatic experience she just put me through. She hurt my feelings. She called me nasty names and insulted me for being in love with you,' Marty pouted and whimpered for sympathy:

'Make sweet love with me. Show me how much you love me. I need to make love, Carl,' I demanded. *'I must get her out of my mind. Her behavior was so terribly vile and disgusting,'* I shook my body to emphasize my revulsion for his wife.

'Please hold me close darling. And love me.'

I pursed my lips into an irresistible sexy pout. Then I whined and begged to make love:

'Make me forget she even exists,'

"I made my command imperative that Carl make love. My eyes told him I was calling upon his manliness to love me and drive all thoughts of his wife from my mind.

"This is important to understand, David. Romance and love take place in the mind. A woman can have a fantastic body and beautiful face, which I have, of course; but the body and face is not the key to making the other person fall in love. The real key is to make them perceive that only one person in the world truly appreciates them. Their egos must be stroked. That's why, during my conversion of Carl, and later when I explain to you the different methods that I used while I seduced Darren; my geometry teacher; the four J's; Fred; Big Ed; George and Bertie; Gwenn and Dominic; you'll notice that I'm praising their minds, empathizing with their feelings, and telling them how special they are while I seduce them. That's why my porn films are wildly successful. Millions of my fans look to those films. They are windows into my mind; and my mind set is that I feel my fans' needs and accept them. I love them, every one of them.

"While I was taking Carl from his wife, I challenged his huge masculine ego. I made him feel like he was the only man on the planet that could get me over the horrible pain that his wife had inflicted on me, by calling me names. All the while I was seducing Carl, I knew it was me who had crushed his wife's spirit; not the other way around. I imagined how terrible she must have felt and projected those feelings to Carl as if they were my feelings; not his wife's. I directly appealed to his pride as a fabulous lover, which he is.

'Make love to me, Carl,' I half pleaded and half demanded. 'I need you to love me more intensely than you've ever loved me before. Oh, PLEASE, Carl,' I begged him, 'I want you so much! I want your beautiful cock inside me. I want us to be lovers for the rest of our lives. I want this night to be so special, we'll remember it forever. Please Carl, I must make love. I need to make love all night long.' Marty's eyes invited Carl to leave his past behind and love only

her. Her seduction performance was brilliant. She saw sympathy register in Carl's eyes. It was her cue to get bolder:

'Carl, my dearest love, I desperately need you to start by making my vagina go crazy to fuck you. Will you do that for me? Will you please use your wedding ring the way you use it so beautifully while you lick my sweet Gloria; pretty please?'

"I took the ring from his finger and placed it on the tip of his tongue. I pouted my lips and wiggled my ass to let him know I was craving cunnilingus to start our lovemaking, while I continued to toy with his sympathies:

'Miss vagina loves you so much,' I said nodding my head and smiling, 'and she wants you to show her that you love her too, and that you accept her. Sweet vaginas have feelings too, you know. She's terribly upset from your wife's nasty name-calling,' I said with my softest pining voice to elicit sympathy:

'She didn't deserve that. Miss Vagina only wants to love you and be good to you, Carl. You're the only man that can make her feel the way she needs to feel. Please show sweet Miss Vagina that you're not ashamed to be with me.' I smiled a deliciously wicked smile. My eyes implored him to obey me.

"'Please Carl,' I purred. 'Thrust your tongue deeply inside me. Please lick my clitoris. Won't you do that for me, please?' I pouted my poor me, seductive pout once again. My eyes begged for my treat of oral sex; and my hips twerked and twisted slowly, boldly communicating my hot desire to feel Carl's tongue caressing my clitoris.

'Please kiss Miss Gloria like only you know how, Carl. Make her go crazy with lust like you do,' I smiled my most deliciously naughty smile and nodded my head, reassuring him that everything was going to be all right.

"'I need you to do that, Carl. I need to forget her and think about us. I need to feel by the way your tongue licks me that you love only me and that you don't want anything to do with her anymore. Please

lick me lovingly like only you know how to do. Help our Miss Gloria understand that you're completely in love with her.' I puckered my lips and mouthed a kiss to him. My eyes flashed encouragement and my expectations that he would give me fabulous sex.

'Make me go out of my mind and scream like only you know how to do. I need that, Carl. I need that to feel like a total woman.' I closed my eyes while my body trembled with anticipation.

'Oh, baby, I need you to do that,…… soooo much,' I whined and cooed. 'Let's make love. Let's not wait another second.'

"I then lifted myself and straddled Carl's face, lowering my vagina to his lips while I touched his face with my hands. He held my ass cheeks as his mouth married my vagina and his tongue lovingly caressed my clitoris with his wedding ring. My butterfly thighs cradled his head. My lust smothered his face. I felt glorious. He was honoring me; driving his wife far from both of our thoughts. His love flowed from his tongue through his ring, to my clitoris; warming the erogenous zones of my body and the limbic recesses of my mind. He flooded me with desire. Carl freely gave me the most intimate of his pleasures, knowing we were willfully defiling his wife and marriage. He defiled her to heighten my pleasure. I knew then, that I had won the decisive contest for his love and his money. I knew if I lavished him with unforgettable sex that night, I'd cement an eternal bond between us, and push all thoughts of his wife from his mind, forever.

'Yes, my love. Oh YES, you're making me feel so wonderful,' I whispered erotically while he pleasured my clitoris with his tongue. I pushed my vagina deeply against his mouth and squeezed his head between my thighs, signaling how much I loved what he was doing with my clitoris; and letting him know that I craved more, so much more, of it.

"I knew my pheromones would overwhelm him, making his serotonin levels and endorphins surge. I was certain that he'd soon forget he ever knew his wife. I intended to conquer his marriage,

his mind; and his body and soul for all time. Some sexual episodes are like that, David. They're indelible moments that the mind will always cherish and never erase. This was that kind of moment. It was my moment of victory. I felt the same sensations that a matador feels when he drives his blade through the heart of his exhausted, defeated bull. My blade was my sensuality. It was at the ready and sharp. I drove it swiftly, and mercilessly through the heart of all Carl's memories of his wife. I twisted it, sliced, ripped, and murdered all thoughts or cares he ever had about her. When I sensed his past feelings about her were dying, I spoke to him in a louder, more authoritative voice, with a tone of praise and encouragement. I had him now. He was mine. I only needed to reinforce in his mind that my immoral lust was a good and wonderful blessing; his personal, unholy gift from me.

'That's it, my love,' I encouraged him to feel that I desperately needed his love. 'I'm the woman who needs you. I'm the woman who loves you. I need you, Carl. I need your love. I need you now more than ever. Please be extra good to me, darling. Kiss Miss Gloria right there, Carl, like you've never kissed her before. Oh, wow, yes! That's so good! OH, YES! YES! THAT'S SOOOO GOOOD! OH, YOU ARE A WONDERFUL LOVER! I'M ALMOST THERE! YES, I'M COMING, CARL! HERE IT IS! YES! I'M GUSHING. OH WOW! AHHH, I FEEL SOOOO GOOOD! I LOVE YOU CARL! I LOVE YOU!'

"I had one hand behind me, fondling his testicles and lovingly stroking his penis. When I felt his life-blood throbbing in his penis, I turned and mounted him in the sixty-nine position. My pheromones didn't fail me. He quickly reached a very hard, full erection. We were ready to enjoy our intense intimacy again! I was thrilled by how eagerly he had responded.

"I felt Carl's chest heaving and heard his breathing quicken. He moaned a soft, anxious moan. I knew I was on his mind. His moan

told me he yearned to hold me in his arms. He wanted to touch me; feel me; appreciate me as a complete, uninhibited woman; wanted to give me pleasures that no other man knew how to give me. We were both ready to enjoy each other; ready to create our intimate 'our' time. I turned my body, straddled his chest, and faced him. I placed one hand on his massive chest. His heart was pounding. Somehow, I knew that he understood things would be different between us from now on. Somehow, we had this empathy moment. Without saying a word his body told me that he knew his wife was out of our lives now; and he was grateful to me for making that happen; more than grateful. Actually, his body silently communicated that he adored me for what I had done. Even though he didn't know the particulars of what I'd done to his wife, he didn't care. He had no feelings for her or the possible hell she was going through now. He only had feelings for me and for us. We were our own world now. And that was all that mattered to him. I loved him for how he condoned what I'd done, without questioning me; without judging me. He trusted me to do whatever it was I did. He knew I did it for us. And he loved me for that.

"I reached my other hand behind me to squeeze his testicles and fondle his beautiful, amazingly hard penis. He was incredibly hard by then. His penis seemed to understand what had happened between me and his wife. The erection had more meaning in it than any of his previous ones. This one silently told me that it was proud of me and proud to be with me; proud to know me intimately; more so now than ever before. It's phenomenal hardness to my touch told me that it wanted to share my triumph with me. It wanted to do so much more than fuck me. It wanted to adore me; cherish me; honor me; and relive my victory with me. Never in all my relationships and porn scenes have I ever felt a cock so enamored with the essence of my yearnings as a woman. Carl's cock knew I wanted this night with Carl to be our most special night, ever. It wanted, with every ounce

of strength that it had, to do its best to help make that happen. I wrapped my fingers around it. My fingers loved the way it responded to me. It became harder, still. It was so eager to feel my touches. It was already releasing slippery, anticipatory droplets onto my fingers.

"I smiled, knowing that Carl's cock and I shared a beautiful, unholy truth. Carl's cock was all mine now. It knew that, from this night on, I was the only woman it would pleasure. It wanted it that way. I knew that by the way it hardened to my touches. I was not just sex for it. I was its ultimate heaven; a heaven with no room for anyone other than Carl and me. The cock's hardness begged me to begin making love, to open my entry lips to it and usher it into my heaven of slippery warmth. I stroked it ever so lightly, anxious to begin; yet wishing to prolong this beautiful anticipation a few seconds longer. I touched its head to my outer lips and gently rubbed it there before I guided it inside me. I was ultra-sensitive; still gushing from my orgasm, and craving more. I was lust-insane, nympho crazed, from the tingling sensations of hot and slippery wet inside me. I wanted to do more than make love. I wanted to fuck like a crazed wildcat; and help Carl forget everything but me. He pressed his hands against my heart. Carl does that when he knows I'm into the moment; when I'm about to unleash my full animal wildness on his cock. He likes feeling the rising passions within me and my quickened heartbeat. My desires intensified.

'Oh, YES, YES,' I cried. 'That's it. That's what I need. YES! RIGHT THERE! Fuck me hard, Carl. Love me like only you know how. Oh, I love it so much when your cock is deep into me. I feel your cock tapping against my cervix. YES! THAT'S IT. I FEEL YOU'RE RIGHT THERE WITH ME. YOU'RE BEAUTIFUUL, CARL. FUCK ME HARDER: FASTER, AND HARDER. Oh, you're so sweet. I feel you shooting. I feel your hot cum filling me. I love it. I love this feeling! You are such a wonderful man. You are such a fabulous lover. I can't live without you, Carl. I LOVE your fantastic, beautiful cock, Carl.'

"As I sat on Carl's lap with his penis inside me, my music loop returned to the Sanctus. I knew it was time; time to complete Carl's conversion; bind all Carl's love and faith to me. Between my French kisses, I pulled his face into my breasts. I rocked him back and forth when the soprano hit her high notes. I wrapped my arms tightly around him, and hugged him tightly while the chorus sang. The Sanctus did its magic. It made our union holy; accepted and blessed in spiritual wonder. Carl's body responded. He placed his hands on my ass and bounced me to the rhythm of the chorale. When he looked into my eyes, I saw his profound adoration and respect for me. He saw my eyes behind my butterfly. He saw my soul; my unyielding commitment to forever be a free woman; and he loved me for it. Carl loved me for me.

"I intuited, in that moment, that there was a simultaneous happening taking place in the mind of Carl's wife. I had this strong feeling. Call it a woman's sense of knowing. I sensed that she was also seeing my eyes behind my butterfly. She was having a vision. I sensed, telepathically, that her vision was leading her into great danger. I didn't like her. I never liked her. In fact, I hated her. Yet, I felt a strange chill come over me. I feared for her. I intuited that my mind was telepathically connected to hers. But I could only receive her thoughts. I could not communicate mine to her. Then I knew what the chill represented. It was the cold chill of death.

"And then I appreciated what I had done to her. I had replaced her god and Carl's god with my immorality; and I had become their new god; the god of a husband and a wife. I had guided their way away from their god, and taught them to disobey all their god's commandments. They had disavowed their god. They both were replacing their god with me, and my unrepentant, immoral, ravenous vagina. They now worshipped my creation force. My vagina and clitoris Gloria within, had become their new god. My god had replaced their beliefs. I had driven away their imposer god and returned their worship beliefs to those of the Anunnaki and their consorts, twenty thousand years and longer ago; beliefs as they were before the Sumerians, the Druids, Abraham, Isaac, Ishmael, Jacob, Moses, the Christ, and Mohammed. Carl and his wife now accepted adultery as guiltless and natural. And they believed that nothing was wrong with it. They now believed adultery was good.

"Carl was silently complicit in his wife's murder. He blocked whatever I did to her from his mind; and felt no guilt about loving me for my sins. Rather, he now saw his wife's life as a necessary sacrifice to my pleasures. His belief system was now the same as a pagan tribesman, beholden to his temple prostitute goddess. He believed his religious duty was to please me and love me. He believed that those who resisted the glorious destructive and creative powers of the female vagina needed to be destroyed. And I had destroyed his wife, a non-believer.

"Like the early druids eliminated their deplorables, I had destroyed her. I had sent her away, like she was an inferior being, flawed in her beliefs and fated to die beyond our intimate inner circle. After what I did to her, I knew her god could not save her. I had no desire to save her; no desire to reverse what I'd done to her. I could not change the forces I had put in motion. I could not reach the thoughts she was having, even if I tried. She was now in the hands of my evil spirits. Beyond the intimate closed circle of pagan cult believers, no protection was offered for outcasts like her. They were simply abandoned, like they were abandoned twenty thousand years ago. Then, they were left to the mercy of the elements. Their flesh became sustenance for wolves and jackals. Like Carl's wife now, they were were left to the forces of destruction.

"I loved feeling the warm, pulsing gushes of Carl's semen. I felt him giving his life's essence to me. I felt him honoring me by his giving and by the way he moaned while holding me tenderly. His adoration for me that night was unprecedented in our many times *together. He was overcome with obsession. He came again and again. He breathed hard during his latest ejaculation. It was time to capture his feelings. I needed Carl to confess his new faith:*

'Carl,' I said, kissing him while I purred like a kitten, 'tell me that I'm acceptable to you. Tell me that you don't want to be with your wife, ever again. Please tell me that, Carl. Tell me that you love that I'm a naughty girl and that you love your naughty bad girl. Tell me that you don't ever want to be with a good girl. Tell me that you love me for being a shameless whore. Tell me that you love me and wor-ship me because I have no conscience and no morals. I need to hear you tell me that you love me, just as I am; for the totally immoral whore that I truly am; and that you want only me, and that you don't care who knows you love me or who sees you with me.'

'Marty, Marty, my sweet darling,' he answered me with the truth from his heart while holding my body tightly to his and looking his sincere brown eyes into mine, 'Of course I accept you. I love you, Marty; and I want you more than anyone and everything else in the world. I don't want to be with her anymore; not ever. Only you, Marty, even if I can only have you for the times we have together. I love you. I will always love you; and only you. You are a pure, inno-cent, loving, free spirit. I love you just as you are. I love everything about you. Let's not drive ourselves crazy with talk of who we are or what we are. Let's share our love and treasure our times together.'

'I love hearing you tell me you love me,' I whispered, kissing him full on his mouth. 'Let's make wonderful love all night, my love. This feels wonderfully right and good, darling. Love me, darling. YES, love me! When you move your cock inside me it makes my hurt go away. I then stop thinking about all those mean things she said to me. You make me feel so good and so loved. YES! That's it. My hurts are leaving me, Carl! You're making them go away! I don't ever want to think of her again. Oh, yes, right there, that feels SO GOOD! You're hard again! You're hard again, already, aren't you? You're amazing,

Carl. You make me feel like a woman should feel. That feels soooo good, Carl. Don't stop! Oh, HARDER, HARDER. That's it, baby. MORE, MORE, OH YES CARL, FUCK ME. KISS ME AND LOVE ME. I'M COMING AGAIN, CARL! OHHH, I KNOW YOU LOVE ME! YES, YES. OHHH, I CAN FEEL YOU SHOOTING AGAIN! YES, CARL, KEEP SHOOTING, YES! YOU FEEL SO HOT AND WONDERFUL!'

"As Carl came inside me again and again, I whispered softly to him:

'Love me forever, Carl.'

'I will, baby, I always will,' he promised me, while he held me tightly close."

CHAPTER TEN

To be an obsessional is to find oneself in a mechanism, in a trap increasingly demanding and endless (Jacques Lacan: The Language of the Self)

IMAGINE LOVE

While Marty made love with Carl, not known to her were the thoughts racing through the mind of his wife as her car ascended the long incline to Mountaintop Pass.

'I must accept my choice,' Carl's wife whispered to herself, over and over while she drove. Her years of rigidity training commanded her to accept responsibility for her decisions and actions. That rigidity was still hard wired in her damaged mental circuitry. She was determined to honor the consequences of her choice. But she longed to return to the cabin and the insatiable vagina that it harbored. Responsibility for her choice refused to allow her to turn her car around.

Her weary eyes repeatedly momentarily closed, savoring a few stolen seconds of rest, before reopening. She desperately needed sleep. Her mind was fighting frustration and physical exhaustion. It returned again and again to the cabin deck. The sweet alluring sounds of the *Sanctus* reverberated through her tormented thoughts, compelling them to return, again and again, to Marty's inviting vagina and fixate there. Riveting scenes of Marty's amulet vagina flooded her mind's omnipresent mental images, reminding her of the whore's limitless lust. These ribald scenes of carnal wantonness became her permanent thoughts. They refused to be dislodged. They blocked out everything else, allowing no room for any other thoughts. The whore's profligate, shameless vagina danced playfully before her eyes. It taunted and tantalized her. Its butterfly wings opened widely, inviting her to enter its world of freedom. Behind the butterfly's translucent colorful wings, Marty's haunting eyes compelled her soul to travel the mystical passage into Marty's nether world of immoral darkness. The amulet's eyes knew her soul wanted to enter them, surrender itself to them, and join them in perpetual pleasure sin, as her husband already had. The eyes waited beckoned her. They wanted her soul. Their vagina's inviting cream pool proved that the whore's iniquitous ways had already subsumed her husband; drowned him in their lust. She knew that resisting the amulet's allure was futile. Her unavoidable truth superimposed itself upon her vulnerable soul. Trying to not think about the amulet vagina only made her thoughts grow stronger!

She heard music. It was the Sanctus! Yes, it resounded from her memory to her ears as surely as if she were hearing it while sitting in church. The sacred passage instructed her to awaken and glorify her god. Her mind was tormented. Where was her god? She needed her god. She desperately yearned to glorify God. Where? Where? Where was God? There it was! Her addlepated mind glimpsed it. There was God! It was very close to her! She sensed its presence. Where? It disappeared! Where was it? Her bleary eyes blinked to see more clearly. There it was! It reappeared! Finally! She could not allow herself to lose sight of it again, never! It was precious; holy! Now it was there again, for her; right before her. It waivered in the refrains of the Sanctus. It beckoned to her to come closer; to believe in it; to love it with all her heart and soul. It appeared from its faded, wavy image into clear focus. It was the apparition of Marty! Marty's voluptuous body stood before her, in all her glorious whoring nakedness. Her legs were widespread. Flames from a fire of evil licked at her vagina. Marty smiled aa comely smile to her and cupped her breasts. Marty was lovely; glorious. She was beautiful incorrigible sin! The wife felt her anxieties fall away. Everything she ever wanted or needed was here! The Sanctus music; the apparition; her desperate need to have something to believe in, all combined and came together in her mind. Her mind raced into Marty's imaginary embrace. The wife was safely in the arms of her god. Marty had become her god. The wife desperately needed her god; needed to touch her; kiss her; clasp her hands to her ass and cup her face to her glorious, shameless vagina; enter it with her tongue and her love parched soul.

The apparition of the glorious self-assured whore was there before her; clearly visible; floating in midair just beyond the hood of her car. It smiled to her, opened its arms to hold her close. It disappeared and reappeared; leaving her mind and returning into her mind, again and again. The amulet vagina, with its haunting eyes, now took its place. It filled the wife's vision space. It would control the wife from here, on the hood of her car. It would flood her mind with tidal waves of lust; drown all other thoughts and never let them resurface. The amulet controlled the wife now. The wife could see nothing else. The amulet danced before her sight. It beckoned her to kiss it; join her tongue to its lusting clitoris; swim into it; entrust her lusts and love to it; drown her face and her very soul within its wanton, delicious debauchery.

The amulet vagina then arose and went to an imaginary door and opened it, allowing the wife to see inside. It flashed imaginary scenes of its conjunction with Carl's cock. She imagined it fornicating with him in dozens of positions. Every time she briefly blinked closed her bleary eyes, the vagina changed positions on Carl's cock. Marty's voice, sometimes taunting, sometimes soothing and comforting, now echoed and resounded through the awareness deadened recesses of the wife's mind. Her voice memory led her to believe that the whore's cavalier, deliciously immoral honey pot might somehow, possibly still be attainable. *'Yes, it has to be there, waiting for me, just beyond the sounds of Marty's voice,'* the wife hoped. Then the apparition of Marty reappeared. The whore mouthed a kiss to her:

'Enter the amulet,' the apparition instructed. *'Your soul must go into my amulet's eyes and lose itself in them. It's time. Your soul is ready. Your soul must discover its new life.'*

The amulet vagina glistened with the sheen of its scented lubricating oils, slathered over its smoothly waxed heavenly paradise. It danced its scintillating temptations before the wife's eyes, tantalizingly just beyond her reach. It tilted its wings upward while opening itself wider still, displaying its inviting nirvana channel; urging her to perform cunnilingus while dreamily listening to the Sanctus. Her hypnotically programmed brain believed she must follow Marty's commands; and, surely, she would obtain the succulent, mesmerizing vagina; surely, she would, at last, taste its insatiable clitoris. She knew with certainty that her course of conduct was right. Following the whore's commands would lead her to her promised new life. Her delusional mind believed it could realize its ultimate salvation within Marty's amulet sex.

'Surely the whore wanted me,' she thought. *'She is my god now. Surely my god wants to gather me up and have me come to her. Yes, I know now that my god is this whore; and I need my god. Surely, if I follow the whore's commands, she'll have me.'* As the wife's car began its long descent from Mountaintop Pass, the wife became hopelessly disoriented. The hypnotic trance had her held fast in its power. She could no longer separate her imagination from reality. She knew she needed guidance. She believed Marty was guiding her. She blindly followed Marty's commands.

She imagined Marty's glorious wanton vagina had reappeared. Its pink lips and creamy flesh were vividly there, wanting her touches; waiting. It wanted to be with her. It wanted her to love it; and it wanted to love her back. It seemed to be; still, as before, less than an inch from her face, tempting her to press her face to it, plunge her tongue deeply into it; savor and love it; and unite her soul with it.

She remembered how Marty held its pink lips apart for her, giving her that full view of Carl's white semen-creams, oozing provocatively from deeply within her. Carl's life essence had come out to her; reached for her, from deeply within Marty's darkly beautiful, immoral world. The semen was her evidence. It was her living proof that happiness and joyful new life existed within Marty, deep inside the love channel of the whore. Marty's dark immoral world was the good world where her burdens would fall away and where love was omnipresent. She now comprehended that she needed to travel that channel's passage into her new world. The whore had demonstrated that there was no shame in immorality in her world; only lust and beauty. Marty had demonstrated that love's forces are stronger than the moral conventions that constrain people. That's why the whore was free! She harbored no guilt over any of the debauched deeds that she did; or the many illicit liaisons that she had. Rather, she reveled in them and thoroughly enjoyed the lust sensations they gave her. Why, the wife asked herself, couldn't she also be free? She thought about the messaging which the whore's vagina signaled while Marty held herself open:

'What was it about those moments that vexed me so? She reached a feeling within me that I never knew I had. Now, my mind plays tricks on me. I hear the Credo now. It tells me that I must believe. I must tell my new god that I believe in her. I must tell her that, over and over, until she accepts me into her world. I'm in an ether world.

I'm not in control. But I must not panic. Marty will guide me. I can trust her. I'll be safe with her. She's opened a door for me to see. She's taking my mind into a museum room. I'm surrounded by murals of her open vagina. It's beautiful erotic art. It fascinates and mesmerizes me. It is copulating in many different positions. It's so glorious, so stimulating; and so explicit! It pulses with life. Her vagina is life! It is gorgeous, lovely. I adore it. I want to possess it. I want to look at it forever. Its butterfly wings invite me to go to it and kiss it. Its lips invite me to enter inside it.

'My mind tells me I should leave this room. I know it's an immoral place. It's the tabernacle of Marty's immoral soul. But I don't want to leave. The credo tells me to believe. And I do believe. My new god is showing me her beautiful powers of creation. And I love her. My love for her is growing stronger; deeper. I cannot leave. I must stay with her beautiful love flower. Now my mind runs from wall to wall. It tries to escape because it has been trained to resist all of this. But I am finding no passageway out. The Credo tells me that I must stay; must not try to leave my belief; my love; my new god. Finally, my mind feels settled. I'm okay with staying and loving my new god. I no longer need my old god. I'm okay with all of this. My mind doesn't care that it is trapped here in its new belief and with its new god. It no longer wants to escape. It only thought it should try to escape, like it had some duty to leave; but it prefers to stay.

'Now, finally, my mind understands that it has no duty to escape. It only has the duty to be happy. It loves being here, with its new god and her glorious vagina and her incorrigible, whoring, immoral soul. My mind loves being with Marty's soul, here inside her holy chamber, because it is unapologetic about the whoring it does. Yes, that's why! That's what freedom is. It's freedom from the burdens of guilt. My mind now knows that it should have felt that same freedom from the beginning, when Marty first revealed her naked self. I should have felt that same way about my own life; long ago. But I do

feel that way now. I believe in freedom and in being free. My god has set me free! Finally! I love feeling free!'

A calmness flowed over Carl's wife. The rightness of acceptance entered her mind. An irresistible longing awakened deep within her breast. It was the same limbic longing she felt when Marty first invited her to kiss her sex. Now the feeling returned with overwhelming force. It displaced her feelings of worthlessness and rejection. The darkness of the secret blackness in her mind had consumed all her mind's proper daylight. Marty's dark forces had full reign of her mind now. Her conscious daylight mind had lost all will to resist. Marty's darkness had purged light from her mind. Chased away forever were the evil forces of misogyny, religious rules of do's and don'ts, and all the practices in testosterone's ordered world which ordered that women are inferior to men. Creation's greater truth had prevailed. Where, in darkness, in the female womb, all life is conceived and nurtured, the wife now yearned to go. She sought repose in the truth of this welcoming darkness; not in a church pew or confessional booth, but in the honest miracle of real life; not in faith to a male invention's fictious life. The amulet vagina and its 'Eyes behind the Butterfly™' had freed the oppressed wife to seek her truth and her new life. Her imagination embraced the mystical serenity of creation's rebirthed eternal darkness. It shed all its learned, old beliefs and cloaked itself in its new belief. Now, darkness was all it believed; darkness was all it wanted. It's indecisive turmoil ceased. It discovered the peace of certainty. It knew it needed to attain the darkness:

'I desperately need to return to the cabin. I want to thrust my tongue into her honey pot and love her with wild abandon. I want her to know that I absolutely love her. Oh, how badly I want to clasp my hands to her ass and hold my face against her. Why didn't I?'

She had recoiled at the thought of doing such a thing then, and had turned away; but now she imagined accepting Marty's offer:

'*What would it be like to be her lover? How would I feel, hearing the Credo as I hear it now, while I positioned her love channel above my face and lowered it onto my mouth? Would she share my joy with me, when my tongue discovers her clitoris for our first time? Would my tongue's caresses feel loving enough to her? Would she like feeling my tongue searching inside her, touching her everywhere? I'm imagining her butterfly tattooed upper thighs pressing gently against my face while my tongue revels in her endless orgasmic juices. It seems so real! I sense her ungodly hot sultry lust consuming my body and soul. I feel it happening; and I love it! I never imagined I could feel intense romantic love for another woman; but I do. I'm told I'm not supposed to feel this way; but I do. Oh, yes; I do.*'

Carl also came and went in his wife's imagination; but only as an afterthought. He was with the two women, kissing Marty's mouth and fondling her beautiful breasts. But the wife's imaginative mind was doing something much more important. It was escaping its reality. It was discovering euphoric love for Marty's delicious, uninhibited lust flower; and embracing the primal, immoral freedom that it offered. The whore's wanton lust summoned the wife's imagination to explore these new, wondrous feelings in her imaginary new world:

'*I'm feeling a complete release from my drudgery of homemaking and the male hierarchical structures that have ruled my life. I'm finding freedom from the expectations heaped upon me by my husband and society. When I close my eyes and imagine my tongue exploring her vagina, I feel inner peace and love, for the first time in my life.*'

In her delirious hallucinating mind, the wife had escaped from being Carl's captive housemaid. But now her dream state ended and she regained her senses. But she had warm feelins about her dream; it was such a beautiful dream! She no longer hated Marty. Now, she loved her! She wanted to go back to her and pound on her cabin door; and beg to be allowed inside. She desperately wanted to turn the car around and go back:

'Could I throw myself upon her mercy? She's a shameless whore. If I told her I didn't care that she ruined my marriage, would she allow me to cup my mouth to her ravenous vulva? What would she say if I told her I wanted her more than I've ever wanted anything before? I could tell her I don't care about my husband anymore. It's the truth. She's welcome to him. I don't care. He's made his choice. He wants her; not me. But what can I give her? Carl gives her money. I have nothing to offer her; except my love. But my love brings no money with it. After all, she is a whore. Why would she let me become her lover when she has Carl, and many others?'

The wife became distraught. She realized she had already made her choice while back at the cabin. She had rejected Marty. Marty and she had then gone their separate ways. What was done was done. She couldn't now go back and tell Marty that she'd reconsidered her offer. And she couldn't turn back time and replay events that had taken place. While she drove onward, another, more profound, transition took place in her addlepated mind. Her transition to peace, understanding and acceptance began. The *Sanctus* melody returned to her mind and haunted her thoughts. She now believed that Marty had offered her something even better than a carnal liaison. The whore had showed her a pathway to a new, special way of life; an eternal holiness of passions and lusts:

'She did offer me that one brief chance. She showed me that she could be unselfish and forgiving. But I was too caught up in my anger to understand. I was too blind to see what my true choice was. All I could see was her beautiful pink lady lips illuminated by the glowing background flames from her cabin's fireplace. All my mind would hear were her taunts from those moments before she offered herself. There, by the lakeshore, with the light breezes rustling in the pines, I felt like my god was judging me and I dared not fail him.

But that was my old god. I was rigid, headstrong, unwilling to feel the needs of another woman. I was unwilling to believe in my new god. In that moment, when Marty tried to be kind and forbearing, I rejected her. I couldn't accept the honest whore for who she was. That was too much for me to ask of myself; the person that I was then. Now, belatedly, I know that I love her, and I adore and cherish all her shameless immoral ways. Seeing her naked honesty has freed me. I see things now in a way I could never see them before. I see them as they really are.

Tears streamed down her face and blurred her vision.

'I don't want to live anymore. Life without loving Marty is no life at all.'

The wife sobbed. Her chest heaved with anxious breaths. She drove faster. There was a hollow emptiness in her stomach. It was not hunger from want of food. It was a hunger for love; a need to be with her new god. Her heart smoldered in tormented anguish. She knew she had lost her husband to another woman. She realized, belatedly, that she had rejected the awakened honest love which she now so desperately craved: *'What I had with Carl was never love. What I might have had with Marty was what she knew now was the honest love that I really need. Now there is no love in my life at all.'*

Her mind returned again and again to that scene where she discovered the raw truth about herself. She relived every thought she had then, every slight movement of Marty's vagina, and every word that the whore spoke. She became angry with herself. She tortured her own mind. She blamed her rigid self and relived her act of rejection, over and over. She caused herself unbearable anguish. She closed her eyes momentarily, seeking peace. But peace would not dispel her torment, nor erase her mind's images of the beautifully bodied, delicious whore; and her profligate, voraciously inviting peach.

'I love reliving those precious moments while she stood naked before me. I can't stop reliving them. And I won't. She was joyful. She flaunted her sexuality freely. She laughingly proclaimed the revelry she felt while whoring with Carl. She gleefully described every erotic feeling she experienced while they made love. She described every one of those photo scenes in vivid detail; and she was immensely proud of her shameless naughtiness. It was only right for her to capture Carl. He's her love slave now. I wish I had made the other choice. If only I'd have kissed her. I could have let her captivate me as well. What a fool I was! What have I done?'

Every time she closed her eyes to escape her reality, her vision of Marty became closer; more defined; more real. She could not escape her thoughts. She knew that was hopeless. Her mind had transformed Marty's vagina into the poignant amulet image of Marty's eyes behind the butterfly. That evocative image with its alluring eyes now danced before her mind. Those eyes lured her forward, faster, ever faster; racing her soul into Marty's love flower; coaxing her to come closer; taunting her imagination.

The image that had first haunted her now consumed her. Her resistance to Marty was an ice cube tossed into a lake of hot lava. Resistance disappeared. Marty and her glorious vagina flooded every thought in her conscious mind, and played the devil temptress with her imagination. She began playing a pretend game with herself. She told herself that, by closing her eyes, her lusting tongue would taste and enter the amulet's love channel. Her mind loved this pretend game. It flited wildly, repeatedly imagining its first tastes upon entering the amulet's wonderment. It replayed the explicit picture images which Marty had vividly described; all the while seeing the amulet's image towering behind the picture images as ever-present background. The picture images had first tormented her; now they enthralled her. Her imagination observed her husband cavorting freely with his shameless she-devil whore.

The wife's anguished fantasies intensified as she drove. She knew Carl was having Marty at this very moment; and that she would never have her:

'Are his lips kissing her vulva's lips? Is his tongue inside her now, at this very moment?' Her jealousy sickened her. Her mind railed at her dilemma:

'I hate myself. Even when I bite my lips, I can't rid myself of thoughts of her. I'm obsessed. I now know I love her. Now, I love everything she stands for. I want her more than I want my own life. She grows ever larger. She floods my mind. I see nothing else. I don't want anything else. Oh, my new God, I love you so much!'

The amulet vision flooded over the wife's mind. It washed away all other thoughts. She found herself immersed within it. She continued hearing the *Sanctus* in her mind:

'Is she straddling Carl's lap now? Is she guiding his penis inside her? Are his arms holding her? Is his body pressing close to hers, with his face squeezed between her luscious breasts? Are the two of them swaying their bodies to the rhythms of this harmonic chorale? And is she bouncing her iniquitous honey pot; twerking it; joyously sliding its deliciously hot, juicy, slippery sleeve over his fuck-crazed cock? Are her wonder lips squeezing his cock; spurring it on to greater hardness? Is she tantalizing it with her unimaginable pleasures? Yes, yes, and yes to all of it! I know it's true! Of course, she is doing all those things. Right this moment, she is celebrating her victory over me. She rejoices in my demise! She truly is a divine whore. She's finally rid of me! She's getting what she's always wanted. I know it's all true! Good for her! What could possibly pleasure her more? How might I please her even more?' Insanity and hypnotism worked their deadly magic.

Like a silhouetted statue of Venus, dripping her husband's semen from its vagina, the image of Marty appeared, disappeared, and reappeared repeatedly; taunting the wife. Its naughty welcoming smile invited her to experience its ravenous sex. Now, the apparition laughed mockingly. It smiled at her while it smeared Carl's semen on its breasts. It blew kisses to her and rubbed its amulet honey pot in a circular motion, while it swayed its hips invitingly. It laughed its playful laugh. It squealed joyous pleasure squeals at its own lust. It invited her to come closer to it and kiss it. The whore's hips danced seductively in her mind. They expressed a temptress's bumping motion, inviting her to come to her vagina; play and enjoy; then it withdrew and mocked her for being hesitant; then beckoned her again to join it in delirious freedom. This experience tipped the wife's mind into madness.

Insanity gripped Carl's wife. It took charge of her. Leading her by her hand, it ushered her way forward. The amulet image now became mind numbingly close; yet barely beyond her reach. It smiled to her. The amulet eyes' windows into Marty's soul reached out to the wife's own soul. They beckoning the wife's soul to lift away from her and come into them. The wife desperately wanted to enter the imaginary amulet. She, her imagination, and her soul decided that they would all enter it, together! Yes! They would! They would embrace it and love it. They would kiss it; discover its clitoris and lick its clitoris with loving caresses. They would will the amulet to consume them. They would follow their enchanted amulet wherever it led them!

A brief, rational thought appeared in the wife's labored mind:

'That whore amused herself by destroying my marriage. It was all a game to her, like a sport. But Carl allowed it to happen. He did nothing to stop her. He loved her, even though he knows he means nothing to her. She has many other lovers. She told me so! But Carl loved, even worshipped, what she was doing to our lives. He welcomed our destruction. He encouraged it!'

In that fleeting lucid moment, the wife finally understood her husband. He was right to cavort with Marty. Their marriage had been a phantom illusion, a sham that deserved to be shattered. She comprehended that now. She loved Marty for revealing that to her; and she felt her spirit lift when she recognized that the one deserving of her love was no longer Carl. It was Marty.

She knew her mind would never be free of Marty. She knew she would never have a happy home. That was gone. Thoughts of the things Marty did with her husband, of what she was undoubtedly doing with him now, plied her imaginings:

'She's making love with Carl. I'm certain she is. I can see her creamy Venetian Goddess flesh pressed against his naked body. Her husky, velvety smooth voice is whispering how much she loves fucking him. I'm sure of that, too. She's laughing and giggling while he plies her vagina with his tongue and gives her orgasm after orgasm. And she's sighing her ooohhhhs and aaaahhhhs, as she takes his cock deeply inside her. Of course, they are fucking at this very moment. She wouldn't waste one second after I left. Well, good for her. She excels at being naughty. She loves being thoroughly immoral. She has no problem with it. She has devoured my marriage with her insatiable vagina; and that's what Carl wants. In truth, I want that, too. She is my god, now. I want her, too. I have every right to be with my god. Fuck you, Carl!'

The wife winced and whimpered as she raced down the mountainside. Carl had Marty. She had denied Marty. She had exiled herself to a life without ever once experiencing Marty's welcoming lady lips. She now assessed herself as an inhibited, neurotic fool. With every breath she took, she remembered the delicious smells that wafted from Marty: the whiffs of Chanel No. 5, gardenia, lavender, sandalwood, vanilla, and rosemary oils; all deliciously mingled with Carl's semen.

Every blink of her weary eyes flashed visions of the butterfly, brazenly tattooed on Marty's uppermost thighs. Why was she so shocked when she first saw that Monarch tattoo? What sort of woman did that? What woman advertises her wantonness so openly? What manner of woman flaunts her immorality and her carnal lust so shamelessly; so boldly? What sort of woman defies shame and embraces lust, like this wanton woman who had captured her husband?

'It's all so clear now. She is alive and happy. She is free and filled with carnal joy. She's not in bondage to the male dominated world. I'll never live the freedoms she enjoys. I'll never know how good that feels. My body will never know the ecstasies that her body knows. But I can still be free! There is a way! Yes, there is still one way to be free. Marty told me the way. She instructed me how to get there. Marty told me I must die! Yes, death will bring me my freedom. I can dream of Marty while I die, until I reach the moment of my death. I can hear the Credo! It lives in my memory. The music tells me to believe. That's all I need now; to believe in Marty, my true god. I feel honored to know her now; honored to learn that what I once believed was evil is actually truth. She is the honest love of life; the one true god. Yes, death will bring me freedom. I must obey her.'

She remembered seeing the butterfly's wings opening majestically when Marty first shocked her. Those same opened wings had invited Carl's penis to enter, feel loved and remain captivated forever. Carl adored Marty's butterfly. He had chosen to immerse his life in it. It often held Carl's penis and his tongue in its grasp. And he loved it! Its erotic shamelessness controlled his life now. It consumed his heart and mind and did unimaginably erotic things with him. It did things with him that the wife had always refused to do. Marty's butterfly was Carl's god now. It was her god, too. But she could not touch it or know it; not just yet.

And Marty's laughing, smiling mouth held Carl's mouth and tongue to it and in it. It lovingly sucked his penis and joyfully swallowed his sperm. Her beautiful whoring mouth had played debauched mocking games with Carl's mouth. Their two mouths mocked the wedding ring that the wife had so lovingly placed on his finger. She remembered her wedding: *'I promise to love, honor, and obey, until death do us part. What a fool I was!'* As painful and abhorrent as their mock ritual was, she now appreciated what it meant to Carl and Marty. It was the joining of Marty's mind and Carl's. The two of them were of one mind. That singular mind transcended the rigid conventional notions of love and marriage. The wife had not accepted their desecration act; resisted and rejected it. She knew she had given Carl his wedding ring in good faith. But all that was gone now. Their desecration deed confirmed that. The two of them believed that using the wedding ring for oral sex, somehow made their experience more intimate and beautiful. The wife's mind wrestled with that thought; then it found a way to cope with their sacrilege:

'Oh, my poor, dear Carl, how tortured your life with me must have been! Everything was my fault. I imprisoned you in a chamber until Marty came and set you free. I had no right to imprison you as I did. I know you are making love with her at this very moment; and I hope you are happy.'

Her chest heaved with grief. She wanted to hold her head in her hands and scream. Her mind was torturing itself. She felt an inner happiness for Carl and his beautiful shameless whore. She accepted that the two of them didn't care what happened to her; and that she could never join them; never attain Marty's living vagina; never touch it; never kiss it, not after the nasty things she'd said to Marty. Her own mind mocked her:

'You're such a fool. You've been a fool all your life. You'll always be a fool,' her mind told her over and over. She knew it was true. She finally understood herself. She wept.

Carl's wife drove on that night, blinded by her tears. Her inner sadness knew that she'd never experience the happiness that Marty and Carl had discovered for each other. Her mind was by inner demons possessed, constantly reminding her that she was a fool. Her heart ached as if she'd been punched in the chest. She drove on. She still had her imaginary amulet. And she took some solace in that.

'Heart, tear away from me and leave me! Oh, look! How beautiful! The road has become an endless river of semen from the penises of many men. It's a river of semen cream. It is being swallowed beneath the hood of my onrushing car. It seeks to enter the amulet that now rides inside the car with me! Semen cream rushes in an endless stream into Marty's insatiable amulet vagina. The river of a thousand men's semen flows towards her. It seeks her lusts and love. The river of life believes in her. She is its god. It's rushes into her open passage like a raging torrent crashing through a canyon, spraying its walls; churning against its bottom channels; and plunging deeper and faster with mighty determination. The river of life must have its god and become one with it. The semen river craves its god's immorality. It rushes toward her honey pot like water seeks the sea. It wants to repose itself inside her; and be welcomed into her bottomless destiny pool of lust. There, it knows, lies understanding.'

Marty's taunting uninhibited laughter blocked out everything, including the wife's attention to the road. The wife wished the whore eternal happiness. She closed her eyes briefly, imagining she had finally kissed the amulet's love lips. The road moved speedily under the car, making her dizzy. Her thoughts turned again to the music of the *Credo*.

She imagined she was swimming, splashing, and tumbling awash in the endless love-seeking semen stream that flowed into Marty's insatiable vulva. The semen river lifted her and dumped her back into her imaginary museum room. It rapidly filled with semen. With each refrain of the Credo's chorale, she swam from one living mural of Marty's semen-filled vagina to another. She reached one of the imaginary honey pots and kissed its outer lips.

Next, she softly, reverently kissed and licked the love flower's inner lips. She savored its tasty fragrances. In the breathless amazement of her imagination, a large, soft object swelled up from the museum floor. It rose above the semen pool and glistened before her face. It was Marty's clitoris! It lovingly rubbed against her face. It begged her to lick it. She welcomed and embraced the clitoris as her truest long-lost friend. As she lavished her licks upon the clitoris, it swelled ever larger. It bathed her in its deliciously fragrant fluids. She clung tightly to it and hugged it. She loved it. It united her to her own glorious womanhood.

She imagined caressing the clitoris softly and tenderly with the velvety underside of her tongue. The floodgates of her salivary glands opened and mingled her saliva with its flowing juices. She extended the underside of her tongue to its maximum, bathing her velvety love over the clitoris's entire length. Vaginal fluids warmed her; flooding all around her. She felt wonderful and enchanted. She was immersed in the vagina's erotic pheromones. She imagined her love offerings of licks and kisses were now accepted by the whore; her rejection was finally forgiven. She imagined unity with Marty's love for the rest of her days. Her hypnotic state steeled her mind from all other thoughts.

Now she imagined a round opening in the ceiling's mural. Through it protruded a gigantic penis. It was Carl's cock! She recognized it. It appeared fuller and firmer than it was on their wedding night. It had swollen to twice its largest size. It pulsed hard and fast; then it strained mightily and erupted. It rained down an explosive shower of semen cream upon her. It drenched her head and face; then the cream flooded over the gigantic clitoris.

The clitoris strained to meet the shower. It rose, now stronger and firmer than before, as if it could somehow swallow Carl's semen flow. The cock pulsed mightily, spurting again and again. It shot out thick, pasty globs of white semen-cream, flooding her head and the clitoris. The clitoris quivered in its ecstasy. Juices flooded the chamber walls. The wife's imagination knew euphoria.

Her imaginary body hugged the imaginary clitoris. She licked its sides, eager to sustain its pleasures. Then she dove down, seeking the depths of Marty's incorrigible wanton vagina. She peered into its deepest recesses, searching beneath hidden repositories of semen-creams from Marty's thousand lovers. She submersed herself and reveled in the depths of the whore's sin pool. Her tongue found her mental figment's clitoral base. She rapidly vibrated her tongue against it, determined to give the whore the greatest pleasures that she could possibly give her. She continued her love fest until the pleasure-paired tongue and clitoris organs resonated in loving harmony.

The inner lip sheaths that shrouded the clitoris now swelled and gushed explosively. Floods of Marty's orgasmic fluids flowed continuously, filling the wife's imaginary mouth. Her mind filled with the sounds of the Credo's finale as the vagina's explosive orgasm continued. She caressed the clitoris with her tongue, while it spurted its endless fountain-showers of fluids; then she held it in her hands; hugged it and kissed it lovingly from its base to its tip. When she found Marty's clitoral head, she placed her lips upon it and held it in a long, adoring kiss, as if confirming her blessings upon the whore's promiscuity. Her mind called out to her:

'I imagine Marty gently placing her hands upon my head and pulling me lovingly into her honey pot. I'm delighted to oblige her. I'll be her willing love slave. I'm obediently holding my mouth against her wonderful, unquenchable, sex-thirsting vagina. I'm reverently licking her clitoris now. I adore it. I adore all the whoring that it does. It's the sweetest taste I've ever known. It's the taste of our intimate human connection. It's the taste of true freedom. She's thrusting her hips upward, pushing her vaginal lips harder over my mouth. Ohhh, how wonderful we are. Marty is coming in my mouth! She's having

her first orgasm with me. My god is accepting me! She's writhing in delight. I feel so blessed. I'm pleasing her!'

Carl's wife felt gratitude, believing that her love overtures were pleasing to the whore. She sealed these moments into her hypnotized imagination. Her heart beat arrhythmically faster now. She felt a deep pressure in her chest. She could have been a devoted love slave to the whore; but, like the priest's victim who could not have his heart returned to him, she also could not reverse the fateful choice she had made. She could not return to the cabin and retract her rejection. But she could at least savor her vicarious union with the honey pot that she had so hastily spurned.

She reveled in her mental love fest. She took one hand off the steering wheel, opened her dungarees and quietly stimulated herself. The finale chorus of the Credo sounded in her mind. It urged her into frenzied stimulation. She was eager to release. She masturbated. Her own juices flowed. Her fingers and panties became wet, something that hadn't happened for years with Carl. She intuited that she might not make it down the mountain alive. But that didn't matter anymore. Nothing mattered to her mind's pleasure thoughts, except reveling in her new nirvana:

'I don't care what lies on the other side of life. I only know my own feelings. I'm like a butterfly, myself, now. I'm straining to come out of chrysalis and set myself free of confinement. I'm ready to leave the life that bound me. I will spread my own wings, like Marty did. I will fly away and live my new love. I will leave my old life behind. I hear the Gloria now! The music assures me that I am entering my glory; my new world; my new life. I will go into my new world; that world which lives within Marty's beautiful juicy peach; and I will discover the endless possibilities of heavenly wonderment. I'm ready.'

She remembered when her eyes last stared into Marty's vagina. The hypnotic vision was branded into her psyche. Her mind raced faster. She was furious with herself. She had foreclosed on her chances of enjoying a future life with Marty. She didn't want her previous life with Carl. Did she even want a life at all? She wasn't sure. Marty told her that she must die. She knew that she needed to obey Marty. After all, the whore was her true love. Now, she desperately sought to please Marty, even if only within her twisted imagination. She hoped that her whore goddess, her new love, would think well of her after she was gone.

She silently began praying to little Miss Gloria, Marty's clitoris, invoking her blessings and thanks for Marty's willful naughtiness and for these brief final moments of her happiness. She felt more alive now than she had ever felt before. She vicariously removed her marriage tag. Only her imagined intimate closeness to the lovely clitoris, Miss Gloria, mattered now. She believed she had become an adolescent girl again, brimming with sexuality.

She was happy. She imagined that she was hugging the clitoris, while mouthing gulps of semen cream from the vagina's semen pool, savoring each taste and swallowing. Everything was suddenly wonderful. Her attitude toward Marty's sinful ways had completely changed, from disdain to adoration:

'I've found a new, dark, and peaceful place. I will dwell there. No light can enter. Every ribald thought I have is now accepted; and I am never judged. I'm inside Marty's vagina now. I hear the music of the Gloria. I know I am home. I'm with the marvelous sensual sensation clitoris that Marty calls Miss Gloria. I'm not coming out again. I'm staying inside here forever. I will lick beautiful Gloria until I die in here. Then I will go into eternity with Gloria; loving her; loving Marty, my true god. I will drown in here; with Gloria and my glory. It's my free will choice!'

Her weary soul visualized Marty's eyes. She beheld them there, peering at her from behind the translucent wings of her Monarch Butterfly tattoo. These were the beautiful, inviting windows into Marty's immoral soul. They were the eternal universal living force behind the amulet. They beckoned her soul to join Marty's soul. They called out to her soul to enter the amulet and pass through it into the dark, sinful forbidden world of Marty's soul. They commanded her soul to follow her imaginary body into the pool of eternal sin.

The wife's soul obeyed the eyes behind the amulet. It unbuttoned its cloak of false pretenses and cast it aside. Now it was eager to surrender itself and pass into the embodiment of all that it had previously opposed. It desperately sought to splay itself upon the altar of Marty's immorality. It dove deeply into the sin pool to join its imaginary body in hopes that the whore would unyoke it from all inhibition and ravage it. Submerged in the pool, it capitulated to Gloria's irresistible allure and sensuous vaginal fluids. The wife obediently drowned her soul's past religious learning's and rigid morality in Marty's debauchery. The soul's will was powerless against the amulet's hypnotic trance. The allure of immoral darkness now pervaded the wife's limbic senses. The wife cast away her old, dead soul. Its beliefs no longer served any purpose in Marty's immoral world. She dutifully donned her new, sinful soul. It was free and vibrant with life and lust. Marty's victory over the wife's morality was complete.

The wife was enraptured with her thoughts of sinful bliss:

'I love my new soul's threads. There's no such thing as guilt. There's only flesh, sex, and sin, all deliciously woven together. This garment fits me well. I hear the Sanctus and the Credo. I believe in Marty's clitoris; my fountain of pleasure. And I believe in Marty, my new god. I love them; and I embrace them. They are my new soul threads. I'll wear them proudly. They fit me and feel good on me. They are the new me; the real me. They make me comfortable in the world where I belong.'

The car driven by Carl's wife sped down Mountaintop Pass that moonlit night. Marty's ribald, mirthful laughter haunted the distraught woman's thoughts; played in her mind and reverber-ated in her ears. The combination of thoughts and voices shoved the wife into the welcoming arms of insanity. She raced into the imaginary amulet's outstretched arms. She embraced its haunting, inviting eyes; and its lusting, willing mouth. She had convinced herself that the amulet wanted her; wanted to love her for all eter-nity. She felt herself entering it and escaping her wifely world of Carl. She was leaving that world which had always demanded too much of her. She and her soul were together now; passing into the amulet. They no longer wanted the stressful world that had trapped and enslaved them. They wanted only Marty's world; that world of carefree freedom they had been invited to join. They understood that they needed to obey Marty's command to enter this world. They had heard Marty's terms. They remembered well what she commanded of them. They knew they needed to die.

In her trance, the wife imagined herself swimming inside the delicious aromatic vagina, experiencing its latest orgasm. She imagined feeling fresh fluids coming from the reservoir of the vagina's juices. She imagined immersing her face in a fresh spurt of semen-cream from Carl's cock.

Nothing could return her to reality now. Insanity had become her new reality. It held her firmly in its grasp. She opened her dungarees and stimulated herself. Her excitement about her new life was palpable. The wetness she experienced was perspiration flooding from her own skin. It poured over her face and eyes. The bathing warmth she felt came from her own orgasmic fluids. Her mind heard only the *Gloria*. She entered her rapture state. Noth-ing else mattered.

Her heart pounded furiously against her chest. It wanted to go faster than her car could take her. It sensed that Marty was out there, barely beyond reach, waiting for her. It raced its blood pressure dangerously high. It, too, sought to offer its love lust to the whore's beckoning vagina. Her blood heard her heart's call, signaling that it was time to escape her body. Her heart would not be denied or slowed. It knocked down the corral rails that guarded its moral, proper conduct. Its world was suddenly larger; free to roam; free to chase lust and sin. It bolted from her body, as if reacting from a lightning strike. It surged blindly forward; free of reins and halter. It became a furious, lust-crazed stallion, galloping unrestrained; running riot wild in its quest to drink at the carnal well-spring of Marty's life-giving freedom well.

Heart, blood, and mind all visualized the delicious image of the all-conquering immoral vagina. The three travelers imagined Marty holding herself open for them, inviting imagination, heart, and blood to come into her, savor her; and live shamelessly in their new eternal home. They urged their driver-wife to speed the car faster to their destiny; faster; much faster. They cast all their cautions aside. They had to reach the loving amulet and enter it. Nothing else mattered. Only by passing through the amulet could they enter Marty's world of shameless sin. Lust's sweet calling was the only voice they heard.

'We want her. We love her. We need her. Take us to her! Take us tour new god! Now! Go faster!' they shouted in chorus.

Heart, blood, and mind strained like mighty race horses to reach their new world. They sped forward, chasing their amulet trance. They surrendered reason. Once they passed through the amulet and reached Marty's mystical love channel, they imagined they would become transformed into delicate butterflies; fluttering, wafting in the deliriously inviting scents of an Elysium field. There they would gorge themselves on whore-lust's delicious nectar.

'Faster! Go faster! We want her. We must thrust our tongues inside her. We love her! We must have our god! You're going too slow. She's right there, in front of us. Take us to her. Now! Hurry!'

Her voices urged the wife forward. Like a mating-crazed stallion, her mind wildly churned. It imagined soft earth; muscles rippling, hooves flying onward towards their passion quest; oblivious to everything, except Marty's open heaven. The wife imagined her lips tasting that heaven now. She believed she had gone through the amulet passage. She was home. Her lips pressed lovingly to Marty's vagina. Her cheeks felt the soft, loving press of Marty's thighs wrapping her face with their waxed flesh-portals of bliss. Her tongue tasted its passion. Its flavors and salts made her deliriously happy.

Her nostrils drank in the wafting fragrances. Her olfactory senses returned her to those fleeting delicious seconds when Marty brought her notorious party magnet against her nose. Her nostrils sensed that heaven now, as she had before. If she had been a gladiator she would surrender now. She would cast off her breast plate, lie prostrate, and welcome Marty to run her sword through her heart! Yes, she would do that. She would gladly advance Marty's cause; surrender her life to experience the blissful tastings of the whore's wanton lusts. She desperately wanted to obey the whore's final command. The fateful words, '*you must die*,' reverberated through her mind. She would obey; surrender to Marty's command now; feel no humiliation, no pride; and no regret.

Her ears resounded with the deafening echoes of her voices' cries. She heeded their commands to go faster. She jammed the car's accelerator pedal to the metal, hard against the floor. Insanity was driving the car:

'If I go faster, I can catch her apparition. I can wrap my arms around the beautiful laughing ghost that dances before me. I will enter and pass through the amulet. I can join my soul to my god. Yes, she is in my arms now! I have her! I can hold her ass cheeks firmly; bring her sex pot close against my face. I'll never let go of her. I'm

there now. Yes, she's holding my head in her hands. She pushes her sex into my mouth. She's allowing me to love her!'

The wife flicked her tongue against her lower gums, giving herself the illusion that she was caressing Marty's clitoris:

'I can taste her essence now. Yes, I can savor her iniquitous uninhibited sins. Her taste and scents flood into me. I am as a butterfly. I embrace my mate and enter. My tongue probes inside her sweet flower. Her soft flower petals caress my cheeks. I am welcome. Like a butterfly's proboscis, my tongue now touches and licks. I reach her innermost delicious flower. I can taste erotic wonders. I am there, enjoying all of her! She is magnificent, delicious; a glorious, godless whore! My life has come alive again. Oh, how I love her!

'We are like two mating butterflies now. My tongue touches her mind through her clitoris and communicates with it, joining our minds together as one. We are inseparable. Our thoughts embrace. We accept each other for the unashamed lovers that we are. My arms hold her feelings close to me. And her arms hold my feelings close to hers. Together we dance and flutter above the flowers. We kiss and cavort together. We rub each other's' bodies everywhere; and we know we will love each other forever. I have surrendered my soul to hers. I wanted to and I did! I am a freed butterfly! I know nirvana!'

The ordered world the wife once knew was now thoroughly ravished by Marty's temptations. A wild buffalo stampede burst through the wife's thoughts. They ran pell-mell in their raging charge, rushing toward an unseen precipice. Those thoughts were followed by another vision, a plunging stream from a high waterfall; then, in her speeding blur of thoughts a downpour of rain and hail from a dark brooding thunderhead opened and soaked her from the heavens. Everything seemed real. Carl's wife was experiencing the only orgasm she'd ever had. Never before had these sorts of images raced through her mind; and never before had she felt so unburdened from care. She instinctively knew she was leaving the male ordered world behind, never to return. She was entering spirit ordered nature, where she would be loved as an equal partner; and respected as a worthy person. Was it the spirit world or the afterlife? She didn't question or care. She was eager to embrace it, run toward it and love it.

'Good riddance,' she thought. *I can't escape from my righteous hell fast enough!*

A guard boulder on the edge of the road failed to stop her car. She sensed a jolt followed by a convulsive shudder as the car's under-carriage separated from its body. The thunderclap she heard was not lightning from a storm. It was the steel wire that joined the guard posts. It snapped, unable to hold the four-thousand-pound car that hurtled through it. Car and driver, both severed from their moor-ings, plunged into freedom's expansive abyss. When she opened her eyes, it was too late. Her imaginary onrushing stream of semen-cream had only been the road. And the road had become air:

'My body is trembling. My soul is leaving my body. It rushes forward to embrace the beckoning amulet. The amulet calls for my soul to enter it and join with it. My soul is kissing and worship-ing the amulet and entering it. The Gloria is sounding its refrain. I hear it! I am going into my god! My soul is passing through the amulet now and disappearing into Marty's soul; becoming one with her soul. My soul has married hers. My new soul is free! Her soul has absorbed mine. Hers has become stronger, more con-fident, and even more glorious by swallowing my soul. My soul will reside within hers forever, fueling its confidence; nurturing its strength and purpose.

As her car tumbled end over end for thousands of feet down the mountainside, the wife's last thoughts were of Marty's liberat-ing vagina:

'Make love often, my beautiful darling Goddess. Free many others as you have now freed me. And become their god as you have become mine. Be happy and glorious and free.'

Before she succumbed to death, she silently prayed:

'Please forgive my foolish rejection. I finally understand you. You are about all women, aren't you? Whores, sex workers, housewives, professional women, waitresses, pilots, flight attendants, drivers, barista's, clerks, managers of this's and assistants to that's; those are all simply titles that say nothing about us; about who we really are. But now, at the end of my life, I can see for the first time in my life. I now know why my mind kept seeing your eyes behind your butterfly wings. That was how you hypnotized me. That was how you brought me into you, to chase your amulet vision until I have finally captured you. That was how you helped me to see that I, too, could become free of my inhibitions; and that I, too, could become my own person and be free, like you. Those EYES BEHIND THE BUTTERFLY™ announce who you are. EYES BEHIND THE BUTTERFLY™ announce that you are your own person. They say that you decide what is right for your life; and that you make no apologies for that. They say that you are only accountable to yourself and to no one else. EYES BEHIND THE BUTTERFLY™ announce that you have self-esteem; that you depend upon no one else to give that to you. That wonderful mind set makes you a goddess. Thank you for helping me see. I will always love you and adore you for helping me free my own mind from its chains.

'Forget all the bad feelings that I had for you. Imagine that we were always good friends and lovers. Imagine that we laid together in a bed, snuggled together on a cold winter's night, with our window open to the fresh cold air; and that we hugged and kissed and loved each other. That is how I will remember you, my love. Accept me. It was right that you stripped my beliefs from me. I now believe in you; and in us. It was right that you committed adultery with my

husband. You freed him and me. And it is right that you found this imaginative way to end my life. What you've done is okay; honest it is. Don't ever feel guilty about it. I didn't want my old life anymore. I am glad to leave it now. I have regrets about how I lived it; but now, I am finally happy. Allow my soul to live and love as part of yours, forever in your world.'

She imagined hearing the soft music of the Gloria's *Amen* as her broken, bloodied body passed from this life. Then, in the midnight snow-flurried mountain breeze, a shaken ghost arose; departed the wife's corpse, and reached out its hand to touch the welcoming amulet.

'I've searched for you. I seek to join you and strengthen you,' voiced the ghost.

'I'm here. Come into me,' beckoned the spirit amulet through the uninhabited air. The ghost lifted its searching eyes to behold its caller; then reached out its love starved arms. It seized the elusive amulet; brought it close; kissed its inviting intimacy with its lust parched lips, thirsty for the amulet's unbridled immoral passion. Into the amulet's deep dark love channel flew the joyful ghost, freed from its haunted past. The two spirits vanished into eternity.

Back at the cabin, Marty returned to her love making. She had achieved her goal. Her orgasm that night was the most sensational release she'd ever experienced over her lifetime. It started as a deliberate, gradual build; then it rose to a higher orgasm peak than any before it. Strengthened by her conquest, her carnal spirit soared; rising higher and higher on knowledge that she had been freed from her nemesis. Like a songbird newly escaped from its cage, her libido-lust flew skyward. No ceiling limited her high peaks' intensities. Her great orgasmic releases came. Her orgasm surged, becoming like fiery hot lava; endlessly pouring forth from her erupting super volcano. Flow after flow, eruption after eruption, heat following heat; each burst overwhelming the sensations of the heat that escaped before. All miseries caused by the wretched intrusive wife melted away while Marty came and came. Writhing wildly, screaming: *'yes, yes, yes and YES,'* endless minutes of Marty's gushing ecstasy burst forth, again and again; as if her volcano would erupt continuously for thousands of years.

Marty's soul tingled with the joyous vibrations of its new found freedom to make love, unchallenged; feeling miraculously and mysteriously suddenly strengthened somehow; and completely uninhibited. Shock wave after shock wave of indescribable pleasures pulsed within her, fueling every cell in her body with unlimited sexual energy and insatiable inner pleasures. Her feelings of joyous orgasm releases vibrated across the galaxy. She finally had unfettered access to Carl and his wondrous pleasure penis! She could enjoy her orgasms unhurriedly; openly, wildly; and often. Her concerns over intrusions by his wife-pest evaporated like murky morning fog dispelled by confident, glorious sunlight. A carnal radiance glowed brightly within her sex. Her hot murder-impassioned blood carried its glowing victory message to every cell of her body. She held Carl's cock tightly inside her defining pleasure channel; securing his gorgeous body within her thighs and arms. She rocked him slowly, beginning her long descent from orgasm; sweetly, lovingly. Their mouths French kissed in hot thirsts of unquenchable shameless love. Then, their shared mirthful belly laughs rejoiced in lust's passions and joys at their foe's undoing. Sex organs enjoyed their joined feelings of inseparable, naturally married intimacy. Carl's inexhaustible penis repeatedly released hot semen spurts, meeting the exquisitely timed love harmony of Marty's clitoris. Only Carl could provide her with pleasures so divine. She lived an unforgettable night filled with sensational sex.

Carl also passed through a narrow portal that day. By doing nothing while Marty dissembled his marriage, setting his wife upon her journey of death, he became one with his vixen vamp. Now, not only devoted lover; he also became silent co-conspirator in murder. His soul understood that Marty's depraved psyche would destroy his wife. He knew she was the more willful of the two women. By doing nothing, while Marty's psychic sword ravaged his wife and marriage, he tacitly accepted Marty's lascivious ways whole-heartedly; without reservation, equivocation, or question.

Marty held him closely now. His body sweats and breath comingled with hers, fueling his lust-smitten passion fever. His soul knew that this remarkable woman could never be owned or ordered about. She would never be a meek compliant housewife that cooked his dinners or made his bed. At her core of being, Marty was a wild, untamable whore. He didn't care. He wanted her; and what she was. Knowing what his made bargain was, he loved this whore without reservation or hesitation.

Oh yes, he loved her. And with an eternal intensity. Oh yes, he accepted, nay needed, everything unholy, ungodly, and immorally debauched about her. Yes, he would do everything she asked of him. He could not break with his obsession; could not live without her. He drank in her sins and cherished them. His soul lived on the other side of his life's mirror now. But he was unable to see himself; could not reflect a sobering look at his life. The back surface side of that mirror was black. It did not know him; could not identify the love slave that stared vacantly into it. Carl was not his own man anymore. He was Marty's love slave now. His lifetime would work tirelessly and ceaselessly for her; eagerly awaiting her calls; her touches; her love making. Now, Marty was everything Carl lived for. He would throw all his superhuman effort into his work, awaiting Marty's love, like a devoted dog. Her priceless reward of sex compelled him to give her all the monies he earned; every valued possession he had; and all his love; and after that, still more.

Miss Promiscuity voiced her assessment of where matters stood: *'Carl is ours now. Congratulations! Enjoy him. But now we need to focus our attentions on Fred.'*

Marty's emotions experienced sturm and drang effects between her seductions. Immediately after she seduced Carl, her mind brooded and roiled. She anticipated that her next challenge was coming. Miss Promiscuity kept her mind churned with thoughts about entering Fred's heart and stealing his love away from his wife. Anticipation stresses rose higher and higher, requiring the emotional release that only Marty's nymphomania disease could bring her. She readily responded to her overwhelming urge to fornicate again. Her thrusts came faster, harder. Seeking one more orgasm, she pressed her clit harder against Carl's cock. It was difficult to pay attention to Miss Promiscuity at a pleasurable time like this; but she knew she had to:

'Fred thinks you are his next trophy.'

Marty nodded. Miss Promiscuity had taken Marty's mind in her hand. Marty knew she was being led forward to her next conquest, even while still making love with Carl. She subtly reassured herself that she could feel her initial penetration thrills from Carl's cock and his magnificent thrusts and playful pleasures any time she wanted them. But she knew that her truest measure of nympho accomplishment was the seduction of a new lover. Seductions tested her desirability. Miss Promiscuity provided needed guidance. This voice of seductions now directed Marty's thoughts:

'Focus on Fred. He is a much bigger financial prize than Carl. Let him think you are his, but don't get trapped.'

'Any thoughts about his wife, Petunia?' Marty checked with her voice.

'Pretend she doesn't exist. Just go into Fred's life. Push Petunia away from him. Displace her. Throw her aside. Take her money. She

won't fight. She's not a dunce like Carl's wife. She'll simply leave him. She'll try to wait you out. Don't give her that luxury.'

Marty's observations agreed with the intuition Miss Promiscuity was revealing to her:

'Fred's weakness. What do you see?'

'His ego. It's huge. He'll want to show you off; take you to his club. He craves recognition. That's good. Welcome it. He'll open doors for you; show you the pathway to monied players. He'll expand your circles. He'll treat you like his queen.'

'Any jealousies? Will he be hard to control?' Marty was cautious about jealous types. They could play rough. She didn't want that.

'No, none. He's not the type. He's into upmanship. You saw his trophy sheep heads when you had that tryst. That's what he cares about.'

'So, be like a sheep?'

'Something like that; but a very special sheep. But not an actual sheep; not part of that flock of women who have not figured out their lives; who don't know how to handle men or how to be honest with themselves about what they want out of life. Be a femme fatale; a confident; a woman sure of her herself and her attractiveness; a proud, glorious sexpot woman that Fred will want to present to his club members. Make him see you as that elusive, hard-to-get woman that only he is able to conquer. Girl, sell your sizzle!'

'But he already knows I'm a top executive at a major securities and investment firm.'

'That's not enough. That won't cut it. You need him to see you as the world's most exotic trophy girl; that special one whom others want but aren't good enough to have.'

'Like how?'

'I'm thinking porn.'

'Tell him?'

'Yes, I think so. When it's time; after you've sucked him and made love, just reveal. Be honest. Confide in him. Tell him that you love creating pornography; that you feel no guilt or shame in it. Reveal that you've made hundreds of films and plan on making hundreds more. Reveal that you have posed for thousands of porn pictures doing seduction sequences with solo partners and multiple partners. Tell him that you love performing the work; that's it's a pleasure for you, not really work; and that you have a fan base of millions. Let him know your goal is to become the world's most sought-after femme. And that your chosen venue for gaining that notoriety is not traditional film or politics or the corporate ladder; but pornography. Tell him your star is rising fast because your films show your fans that your love making is the most salacious, mouth wateringly delicious pornography in the world. You're tracking to become the number one porn star of the entire world. Let him grasp that fact. His mental wheels will engage. It something is the best the world can offer; he naturally wants it. A woman should be no different. Assure him that fame is what you want for your life; that you trashed your moral compass when you were only a teen at WEX School, and you made your career choice then. Let him know that you'll take great pride in being the world's top porn star, and female aficionados' most sought-after femme. He'll be proud of you for that. He'll respect that competitiveness about you. He understands how hard it is to become the very best. He seeks out superior animal specimens because that puts him on that same superiority level. He won't care one wit about whether porn is moral or immoral. But he will want you for his trophy woman. His ego is driven to capture the most highly prized trophy.'

'That's it, then? Play up the porn angle?'

'You bet. Also, tell him about Rita's orgies. Describe how wonderful and lifestyle affirming they make you feel. He'll admire that immorality about you. Help him appreciate that you are

the very paragon of immoral erotica; the world's most shameless, profligate whore; truly a thoroughly uninhibited, willful woman; focused upon being the hardest to get, most desirable, and most expensive of all trophy women. Make sure to tell him that you seek one superior male partner; only one, who can appreciate you for your uniqueness; a man whom you can trust and love as a partner who fits with your lifestyle. Let him know that you will not settle for some inferior male You will only allow yourself to be displayed at social events as the escort to a highly accomplished, superior male.

'And wear some of the diamonds that your mother gave you. Treat them casually, like you are used to having expensive, luxurious things. Remember to hold your diamond neckless in your mouth, like you often do while you contemplate a thought. Drop subtle hints that you expect to swim in diamonds and rubies, like your mother did in her photos for Marvin. Do not ever let him know that the secrets of the jewels are true; not part of some fictional story. If he ever figured out that you know where there are ten billion dollars' worth of jewels, he could become a problem for you. He is a hunter, remember? Say nothing to Fred about the jewels. Do not let him scent that trail. Focus. Make him reach for you.'

'You think he'll reach?'

'Yes, he'll reach, all right. I know he will. But always keep yourself just slightly out of reach. Demand that he first proves himself to you. You set the terms of the chase. Remember: You are the trophy. Behave that way. You'll be that much more desirable to him. He'll crave and adore you for that. Remember: He loves the hunt. Once he understands what a prize catch you are, he'll immediately ditch Petunia for you. She will not be your problem. He'll take care of her, for you. You'll see. Once he knows your body; once he knows your pheromones; your intimacy, he'll do whatever you ask; anything; whatever it takes to please you. Trust me.'

'Yes, I understand; but let's not talk any longer. I am loving what Carl's cock is doing inside me. I'm really feeling him. We're both coming so beautifully now. Let me enjoy him, please.'

Meanwhile, as Marty's insatiable clitoris quivered and pleasure-basked in Carl's ejaculations; while her thoughts sharpened on her forthcoming seduction of Fred, on a treacherous mountain road, miles from her cabin love nest, images of her insatiable vagina destroyed another woman's capacity to reason. Marty's ravenous, multitalented vagina was devouring Carl's wife; consuming her body, mind, and soul.

Marty's immoral soul knew no remorse. She was enjoying her orgasms; capturing every semen drop of Carl's love within her iniquitous vagina. Her eyes smiled to Carl. Her pelvic rocking motion urged him to maintain his erection a while longer. She loved making love with Carl. She didn't want to stop.

Marty was perfecting her self-aggrandizing, dual-faceted persona. She could dispatch her enemies with the ruthlessness of a soulless Cleopatra, who brilliantly crafted the murders of her own brother and sister. And, she could simultaneously summon the irresistible promiscuity of a wanton temptress Cleopatra, who seduced Rome's mighty Caesar and ruled the world. Unhindered by a conscience; unconcerned about what was right or wrong, or moral or immoral, Marty measured her successes by results. She was unfazed by the collateral damage caused by her adulteries. This night she rejoiced while celebrating her first major milestone triumph. Carl's cock, his tongue and his money were hers now; hers alone.

More to come.

Marty now understands that she holds incredible power between her butterfly wings. Seduction, hypnosis, manipulation, and her own pleasures all seem to be under her control. Our beautiful nymphomaniac is out of her cocoon. She is about to spread her wings and soar. She is about to discover the delights of the larger world and all it has to offer her. Men are finding her irresistible. Her porn film career and private member prostitution service demands are skyrocketing.

Her voices are adamant that she must soon leave David and move on to greener pastures. She knows a big decision is needed soon. But David still hasn't revealed why he wanted her to rejoin the company. He patiently listens to her tale. Maybe he's trying to understand women better, like he said; or, maybe he needs to get a full understanding of her newly acquired skills to make best use of them; or maybe there's something else on his mind. He seems to understand her addictions and he alone knows how to satisfy her greatest addiction of all: murder.

Maybe David wants to know how Marty's newly discovered powers will affect her. Will she seek to expand her private client business; or perhaps she'll work more toward becoming a movie star in the burgeoning erotic romance and explicit porn genres; or, perhaps she'll throw away all her professional opportunities and choose to become Bob's happy homebody wife? Without really knowing David, it's hard to know how he's assessing all that he's hearing from Marty. But we know from David's questioning that he's keenly interested in everything she's telling him. It can't just be about the sex. But what then, is it? It's said that the best kept secret is the one you keep only to yourself. And David sure is quiet.

Well, dear readers and listeners, this is Melanie Monarch, your narrator once again. Let's flutter onward from A WOMAN'S VOICES© to our next segment, PROMISCUOUS DREAMS©, and discover where Marty's ambitions will take her. Pay close attention to the questions that David asks her. He always has reasons for everything he asks and everything he does.